Dark Descent

Dark Descent

Nyx Fortuna: Book Two

MARLENE PEREZ

www.orbitbooks.net

This book is a work of fiction. Names, characters, places, and incidents are the product of the author's imagination or are used fictitiously. Any resemblance to actual events, locales, or persons, living or dead, is coincidental.

Orbit
Hachette Book Group
237 Park Avenue
New York, NY 10017
www.orbitbooks.net

Originally published as an e-book by Orbit Books
First print on demand edition: December 2013

Orbit is an imprint of Hachette Book Group. The Orbit name and logo are trademarks of Little, Brown Book Group Limited.

The publisher is not responsible for websites (or their content) that are not owned by the publisher.

ISBN: 978-0-316-40412-9

Printed in the United States of America

For my best friend Michelle

Chapter One

If I cannot deflect the will of Heaven, I shall move Hell.
—Virgil

The whispering woke me.

"Nyx, get up. You're in danger." I recognized the speaker as Sawyer Polydoros, but that was impossible. I was on the couch, TV blaring, with a tower of empties on the coffee table beside me, but all I could hear was the sound of Sawyer's panicked voice.

It had to be a dream. How else could I be hearing my dead uncle's voice?

But I was the only son born to a Fate and stranger things had happened.

I inched up into a sitting position and listened. The whispering had stopped.

There was someone in my apartment. Whoever or whatever it was barely drew breath, but a strange odor enveloped the room. Less pungent than a troll, but stinking of death nonetheless. A thin stream of moonlight lit the room enough for me to make out a long shadowy figure.

A wraith. I'd tangled with one a few months ago, managing to hack off its arm. I was guessing it was back for round two.

The thing was blocking the door between me and my bedroom, which is where my athame was. I'd need my knife if I had any hope of making it out alive.

There was another shadow by the front door. He'd brought a friend. Fantastic.

Sawyer's warning had given me a few precious seconds. The wraiths didn't know I was awake.

Wraiths used to be human and still retained a certain humanlike appearance, until you got close enough to look into their cold dead eyes and then you realized they weren't human in the least. By then it was too late. The trick was not to let them get too close or they'd rip out your heart and have it for a snack.

I needed to get to my athame. I jumped over the coffee table, but my foot caught on the cans and sent them falling. The noise distracted my guests for a split second while I made a run for the bedroom.

I charged the wraith in my way. As I had suspected, it was the same one who'd attacked me at Hell's Belles. Its arm had been hacked off. I needed to finish the job this time.

Only a necromancer could summon and control a wraith, but Sawyer had been the only necromancer in Minneapolis, and he was dead. It was finally occurring to me that Sawyer might not have been the only necromancer in town, just the only one I knew about.

The wraith saw me coming. I kicked its legs out from under it and ran into the bedroom. I grabbed my athame and pivoted, but the thing was already upon me.

The wraith opened its mouth and the smell of rotting flesh filled the room. I threw a lamp at it, but it kept coming. I choked back vomit and lunged. The knife went in with a wet noise and the wraith fell to the floor, gushing dark, noxious blood all over my floor.

I'd momentarily forgotten about the other wraith. Until it came up behind me and bit me on the back of my neck.

My body went numb immediately. I fought to hold on to the knife as an icy sickness traveled down my spine.

"Nyx Fortuna, you will die this evening," it hissed.

It knew my name, but not that I couldn't die? Interesting.

"I can't die, you rotting piece of filth," I said. Or that's what I wanted to say, but my tongue was swollen.

"Not yet," it replied. "But soon." The wraith clawed at my neck. I thought it was trying to rip out my throat, but it latched onto the thin silver chain around my neck and yanked.

There was no way it was getting the only thing I had left of my mother. I gathered my remaining strength and stabbed it in the eye. It shrieked with pain.

The knife clattered to the floor and I fell next to it before I lost consciousness.

When I woke, Talbot was leaning over me. His eyes shone silver light in the darkness. "Nyx, what happened?"

"My knife," I said. "Where is it?" I started to get up and then swayed as the icy sick feeling hit me again. I put a hand to my neck.

"Don't get up," he ordered. "Tell me what happened."

"Wraith. Bit me," I managed to get out. "My knife. I need it."

"Where did it bite you?" he asked. His voice went from calm to panicked.

I pointed to the back of my neck.

"I'm calling my dad."

"Knife first," I mumbled.

Talbot's hunt for the athame took so long that I was starting to think the slow-moving poison from the wraith's bite would paralyze me before he found it.

To my relief, he came back with the knife in his hand. "Got it."

"Good," I said. "You're not going to like the next part."

He looked at the knife like it was a three-headed snake. "What?"

"Put it in the wound," I said. "You're going to have to draw the poison out." My mind was slowing, thoughts spiraling lazily out of control. "Not much time."

"You want me to stab you?" My best friend sounded horrified.

I managed a nod. "Yeth, now!"

There was a sharp pain when the knife went in and sensation immediately returned. I bit back a scream, but the feeling, even an agonizing stab wound, was welcome. It meant the athame had stopped the poison. It would leave a scar, but what was one more?

I was shaky, but the sickness was passing. I groped around for the silver chain, but my fingers were still numb. "Where's my necklace?"

Talbot couldn't understand me at first, but finally realized what I was asking. "It's around your neck."

I relaxed. I could deal with everything else, but not losing that.

"We've got to get you to a hospital," he said.

"No hospitals," I said. "Just your dad." The swelling in my tongue had disappeared, but my brain was fuzzy with strange images and I couldn't stop shivering.

Ambrose would know what to do. At least I hoped to god he would. Talbot made the call.

"He's on his way," he said. "He's across town, though."

"Help me to the couch," I said. There was no way I was going to lie in bed like an invalid.

"You can barely walk," he protested. But he slung an arm around me and dragged me to my feet. Moving sent my muscles screaming in agony, but I made it.

While we waited, the shivering intensified. Talbot piled blankets from the bedroom on me, but I couldn't stop shaking.

"Can I get you anything?"

"Tea," I said through chattering teeth. Maybe liquids would help flush out whatever was still in my system. "Top shelf."

By the time Talbot had put the kettle on, I was sweating profusely. When he handed me the tea, I was shaking so much that most of it spilled onto the floor. He took it from me and gave it to me a spoonful at a time.

Ambrose, Talbot's dad, burst through the apartment door a few minutes later. My vision was blurring.

He didn't bother to ask what happened, but shoved his son aside to examine the bite mark.

"It hasn't turned black," he said. The relief in his voice was obvious. "Talbot, run back to our place and get some slippery elm and thyme."

"I already gave him tea," he replied. "I managed to get about half a cup down him."

"He's not going to be drinking it," he said. "I need to make a poultice to get the rest of the poison out."

By the time Talbot came back, my vision was almost gone and I'd heaved out whatever was in my stomach. Would I live forever, but without my sight?

Ambrose mixed up a concoction and then rubbed it over the wound. He pressed a steaming hot towel over my neck.

I instinctively reached up to remove it, but he slapped my hand away. "Leave it."

"He's burning up," Talbot said right before I passed out.

When I woke up, I was in my bed. The room was dark, except for the glow of the bedside lamp. My mouth felt furry, but the shivering had disappeared and I was no longer sweating. Whatever Ambrose had given me, it had worked.

"You're awake," Talbot said. He'd been sitting in the shadows and I hadn't even noticed he was there. I was getting soft.

"A little fuzzy-headed," I admitted.

"No wonder," he said. "I saw that impressive pile of cans in your living room. You're drinking too much."

He was right. If it hadn't been for Sawyer's warning, the wraiths would have had the jump on me. My reflexes had been dulled by the gallon of beer I'd consumed.

"So what's new?" I was trying for flippant and failed miserably.

He snorted. Talbot was a good friend. Willow was another. I didn't have many. They had a tendency, thanks to the Fates, to die gruesomely.

My aunts, the three Fates, couldn't kill me because my mother had hidden my thread of Fate. I was sure it was in one of my mother's charms, which had been lost after her death. I was in Minneapolis to locate them, but was sidetracked when the Fates blackmailed me into looking for my missing cousin, Claire.

I trusted Talbot and his dad, and I didn't trust many people. At least not after Elizabeth betrayed me. It had been to save her brother, but the knowledge wasn't any comfort.

"Dad thought you were going to die," Talbot said.

"That'd be quite a trick," I said. "I can't die, remember?"

"Want a cup of tea?"

"I'm not helpless. I spent an hour putting new wards on the apartment." Despite his protests, I staggered to the fridge and grabbed a bottle of absinthe. Tea, my ass. I was going to get good and drunk. I doubted the wraiths would be back, and if they were, they'd have a nasty surprise waiting. I passed out on the couch and, in the morning, woke to noises in my kitchen. Talbot was making himself at home. He stood at the stove making eggs. A steaming cup of coffee was next to him.

"That looks good," I said. "I'm starving."

"That's your breakfast there," he said. He pointed to a bowl of thin gruelish mixture. "Doctor's orders."

"Can I at least have some coffee?" The absinthe had been a bad idea. The smell of the gruel was making me want to hurl.

He shook his head. "Herbal tea with a little honey. No coffee or alcohol for at least a week." His glance was stern.

My alcohol intake had become legendary, at least at the Red Dragon.

"You'd drink, too, with a family like mine." Not the most tactful thing to say, since he was dating my cousin, but it was true. The Wyrd family would win any dysfunctional family contest, hands down.

He carefully avoided my gaze. "I thought you were going to take it easy. Is that why there are so many empty bottles in the living room?" Talbot had gone to bed before I'd finished the first of the bottles.

"Yes," I told him. "And I was betrayed by my girlfriend." Elizabeth's deception had hurt worse than any hangover. "That's *ex*-girlfriend." I corrected myself.

"Nyx, you're not in love with her. You never were. You *want* to be in love with Elizabeth," he replied. "It's not the same thing."

"The only person who ever truly loved me is dead," I said. "Do you blame me for trying to find happiness? After two hundred years of being alone?"

"You're not alone, Nyx," he replied. "But you will be, if you keep it up." He slid a plate of dry toast over to me.

Was Talbot right? Was I clinging to Elizabeth because she looked so much like my lost love, Amalie? Two hundred years was a long time to be lonely, but had it all been an illusion, orchestrated by my aunts? I knew the answer, but it didn't mean I liked it.

"So I remembered something about last night's attack," I told him as I munched on a piece of dry toast. "Apparently, someone thinks they can kill me."

"Thinks they can or just wants to?"

I grinned at him. "The line is long for the people who want to kill me, but apparently, someone thinks they can actually get it done."

"You don't seem worried about it," Talbot replied.

"If my aunts can't find my thread of fate, I don't think some third-rate summoner is going to do the trick."

"It's dangerous to underestimate your enemy," he warned.

"But I have so many of them," I said. "It's exhausting to keep track of everyone."

He laughed in spite of himself, but sobered quickly. "I mean it, Nyx. You need to be more careful. And stop drinking so much."

"I can stop any time I want." God, I sounded like such a cliché. An alcoholic in denial. But I wasn't an alcoholic, only self-destructive. I really could quit, I just didn't want to. Booze alleviated the boredom of my too-long life.

"Prove it," he said. "Maybe you'd have better luck finding Claire with a clear head."

"No drinking tonight," I said. "I promise. And I'll find her. I've got to catch a break soon."

I should have known better to be the slightest bit optimistic. Because the one thing I could be sure of was that if the Fates could mess with me, they would.

Chapter Two

After breakfast, I headed for my job at Parsi. I'd lied my way into a job there when I first arrived in Minneapolis. Killing my aunts and then myself had been the original intent.

It was still on my to-do list, but it had moved way down in priority. The shit had hit the fan once they figured out who I was, but my aunts never fired me. Morta's golden scissors practically had my name engraved on them, but she couldn't do squat until she found my thread of fate. They probably just wanted to keep a close eye on me, which suited me fine. I wanted to do the same to them.

There was no time to sit around wallowing in my misery, not if I wanted to keep Elizabeth safe. Even though I'd never even met my cousin Claire, my aunts had blackmailed me into finding her. Claire had gone somewhere she thought no one, not even the Fates, could follow her. Unfortunately, it was my job not only to find her, but to bring her back. I had to find Claire, but every clue led to a dead end. For once, being the son of Lady Luck hadn't helped me one bit. Maybe my luck had finally run out.

How could someone I'd never even met be such a monumental pain in the ass? Claire was a Fate in training, that's how, and the Fates, my three aunts, gave new meaning to the phrase.

I still showed up there when the spirit moved me. I couldn't be bothered punching a clock, though, and the workers at Parsi never let me forget it. My cousin was no exception.

"Nice of you to show up," Naomi quipped when I walked through the reception area.

Trevor, the receptionist, looked up from his *People* magazine and then quickly looked down again. I didn't blame him. It was out in the open now that I was the son of the lost and forgotten Fate, Lady Fortuna, also known as Lady Luck. That didn't mean anyone from the House of Fates was going to welcome me with open arms.

"Is your mom in yet?" I asked Naomi. Nona would know the name of the new necromancer in town. The Fates had run most of them to ground a long time ago.

I tensed at the thought of the conversation ahead. The wound at the back of my neck throbbed. The sick feeling, worse than any hangover, returned.

"She's here. Why?"

My cousin took one look at my face and followed me down the hall to her mom's office. My feet sank into the thick carpet patterned with the House of Fates symbol, a pair of shears.

I burst in without knocking. "Two wraiths showed up at my place last night," I said. I didn't mention her dead husband had warned me before the attack. Sawyer's death was fresh for both Nona and Naomi.

"Not possible," Nona said flatly. She'd recovered poorly, the steel in her spine slipping away after her husband died. She still looked a little crazed around the eyes.

"Why would Nyx lie, Mom?" Naomi inserted herself into the conversation.

Nona and I turned and glared at her.

"The only necromancer I know would never cross me," Nona finally said.

"Who is he?" I asked.

She gave me a thin smile. "He dated your girlfriend's roommate briefly, I believe, after Gaston," she said. "I'm surprised you don't remember him."

"Danvers? You think that golf-shirt-wearing blowhard had the balls to send wraiths after me?"

"I never said that," she said. "But he is the only necromancer I know of in Minneapolis."

Elizabeth's roommate, Jenny, was drawn to trouble, so it was possible there was more to Danvers than I'd previously suspected.

Nona returned to staring at Sawyer's photo on her desk.

I left her to it. Naomi followed me out into the hallway.

"Who else could have sent the wraiths?"

"My money is on Deci," I said. Nona was too drunk most of the time and Morta wouldn't stoop to sending someone else to do her dirty work. That left Deci, my least favorite aunt.

"Aunt Deci is too busy trying to replicate the ambrosia formula to worry about you," Naomi replied. "And she's not stupid enough to use black magic."

The conviction in her voice almost convinced me. "But she could call a wraith if she wanted to," I persisted.

"Any powerful witch could," she admitted. "But that doesn't mean it was one of the Fates."

I went back to my desk and contemplated my next move.

It was almost quitting time when Deci found me. I was

loitering in the accounting department, flirting with Aspen, a curvy blond wood naiad who worked as some sort of junior number cruncher for my aunts.

"Son of Fortuna, I would like to speak to you. Alone," she said. She still seemed frail, but one glance from her was all it took for the rest of the staff to scatter like frightened deer at the sight of a hunter.

"Aunt Decima," I said. "What a pleasant surprise."

"Is it?" When I'd first arrived, Gaston had been slowly poisoning her. She'd been near death. She was taller than I had previously thought. She'd been in a wheelchair then, but was now walking with the aid of a cane. The fierce look in her eyes was the same.

It wasn't going to be a pleasant conversation. The hatred in her eyes gave it away.

"Now, Auntie Deci," I said. "What can I do for you?"

"Son of Fortuna, you can quit the messing about and find my niece," she spat. "And don't you dare call me auntie."

I smiled. I knew it irritated her.

"Call me Nyx." I didn't like to hear my mother's names on her lips. My mother's sisters had hunted us my entire childhood. When they'd finally found us, Morta had snipped my mother's thread without even pausing to think about it. They were murderous old crones and it was wise for me to remember that.

"I'd prefer to call you the devil's own spawn," she said. Deci's illness had caused the flesh to melt from her bones, but she was as feisty as ever.

I stepped close to her and bent down until we were eye to eye. "Don't you ever talk about my mother like that."

"Who said I was talking about your mother?"

I wanted to ask if she knew who my father was, but I didn't want to give her the satisfaction. She probably wouldn't tell me the truth anyway.

"Anything else?" I was growing tired of our banter.

"You will be betrayed. Again."

"I won't," I said. I didn't tell her that Elizabeth was out of my life for good.

"Maybe, maybe not," Deci replied. Her tone made it clear she thought my denial was utter bullshit. "But I'm going to give you a reminder of what will happen to your mortal should you fail."

"I'm not even seeing her anymore," I said. Whatever Deci had planned for Elizabeth, it wasn't going to be good.

"Doesn't make any difference."

"Is there something you three aren't telling me?" I asked. "Claire seems to have vanished off the face of the earth."

She flinched. I almost missed it. "Do as we've commanded you," she said, "or your pet will pay."

"It's hard to be scared of someone who let Gaston pull the wool over their eyes for so long," I said. "He almost killed you and you didn't even suspect a thing."

"Yes, you killed our Tracker," Deci said. "He could have found Claire."

"He was poisoning you," I replied. "Normally, I'd be all for it, but he was also hurting someone I care about."

Her hand trembled and I realized then just how old and frail she was. I felt like a jerk for bullying a woman.

Until her next words. "You will die, son of Fortuna, if it's the last thing I do."

Chapter Three

The next few days, I skipped out of work at Parsi and stomped all over downtown Minneapolis looking for my missing cousin.

I'd gotten used to the protective anonymity of the occulo spell, which had suppressed the essence of what made me *me* and changed my looks enough that my aunts hadn't recognized me on sight when I first came to town. I felt self-conscious without it, but they knew who I was now. I was also without my treasured leather World War II fighter pilot jacket, since the weather was too warm to wear it without looking shifty or like a crazy person, or both.

I passed a sorcerer from the House of Zeus. The man murmured, "Buona Fortuna," before crossing the street. Without the occulo spell, the magical citizens of Minneapolis were starting to recognize me as Nyx Fortuna, the son of Lady Fortuna, also known as Lady Luck.

I stopped at the coffee shop across from Parsi. I needed caffeine. I ordered a Red Eye and sat at a small table where I could face the door.

The wound from the wraith twinged. I looked around, half expecting to see a wraith charging, but the store was full of mostly mortals. I noticed Aspen, the cute naiad from Parsi, in an intent conversation with a guy whose back was to me. The deep tan and liberal use of cologne identified him as Sean Danvers the necromancer. What was she doing with him?

She gave me a nervous little wave and then returned her attention back to her date. Danvers pivoted in his seat to see who had interrupted their little tête-à-tête, if even only briefly. His eyes gleamed when he saw me. He gave a short nod and a wide smile. The smile faded when I didn't jump all over myself at being the recipient of such largesse. He scraped his chair as he made a show of turning his back to me.

"Feeling's mutual," I muttered. I drained the last of my Red Eye and resumed my search for leads on Claire's disappearance.

But luck was in still in short supply, at least as far as the search for the missing cousin. I finally gave up and headed to Eternity Road, the pawnshop Talbot's dad owned. I worked there most weekends.

One of the benefits of my job at Eternity Road was that magical items sometimes came through the door. Plus, Ambrose had stuff stashed in every nook and cranny and had promised me a generous employee discount if I found anything of my mother's.

"No luck finding Claire?"

"It's like she's vanished off the face of the earth," I said.

Talbot and Naomi were busy making gooey eyes at each other. Naomi was my other cousin and Fate-in-training and the only relative of mine I could stand.

I tugged on her red braid to get her attention. "Did you hear what I said?"

She slapped my hand away. "Honestly, Nyx, you act like you're five sometimes, instead of an immortal."

I didn't tell her I had no intention of staying immortal. My mother had stolen my thread of fate and hidden it from Morta's deadly scissors. When I finally found it, I was going to borrow them, snip my thread, and end my life.

My hand went to where the chain lay hidden under my shirt. A diamond-studded key, an emerald frog, a little coral fish, and a black cat carved from Indian ebony dangled from the chain. I still had to find the rest. I hunted for a miniature book, an ivory wheel of fortune, and a horseshoe made of moonstones.

"We're running out of time," I pointed out. "If I don't find Claire, the aunties have something nasty planned for Elizabeth." And I'd have to live through watching my aunts torture anyone unfortunate enough to get close to me. Again.

Eventually, with or without my help, my aunts would die. Then Naomi and Claire would take over and then after a time, they would die. And I would still be there. Trapped at twenty-three. I had an acute case of arrested development.

Naomi's expression softened. "I know," she said. "I've already checked with all of Claire's friends, but I'll check again."

"It's like she's a fucking ghost," I said.

She paled. "You don't think she's dead, do you?"

It was a remote possibility, but not likely. The Fates would know if one of their own had died. It was Morta's job to show up and cut the thread of fate that held someone tethered to life.

People vanished every day. If I could find out why Claire had vanished, maybe I'd figure out where she'd gone.

Talbot kicked me hard.

"No, I'm sure she's alive," I said. "I'll find her. I promise." She had to be alive or Elizabeth would pay the price. My aunt Morta, Claire's mother, was not someone who tolerated less-than-perfect results.

Talbot stopped staring at my cousin and gave me a wide-eyed look that told me he'd thought of something. "Naomi, were there any changes in your cousin's routine? New friends?"

"She always ate breakfast at Hell's Belles before work," she replied.

"Doesn't seem like her scene," I commented.

"'Scene'?" Naomi choked back laughter. "Nyx, sometimes I forget how old you really are."

I met her eyes. "I don't." I'd been alive a long time, too long really. Every once in a while, some quaint phrase from another time would come out of my mouth. It made other people uneasy, but it was worse for me. It only reminded me how many lonely years had passed.

"I just assumed she had a crush on one of the guys who hung out there, but was too shy to say anything," Naomi replied.

Claire? Shy? An unlikely trait in a Fate-in-training. My expression gave me away.

"She's nothing like Aunt Morta, you know," Naomi said. "You'll never find her if you keep thinking of her like that."

I crossed my arms. "Like what?"

"Like she's the enemy."

I'd never met her, but I knew Claire was the enemy. She was from the House of Fates, after all.

Naomi, despite being a Fate-in-training, had proven her

loyalty to me. Right up until the time she went along with holding my girlfriend hostage to get her cousin back. I'd been pissed at her, still was, but I needed her help. And my best friend was in love with her, so I'd forgive her. Eventually.

"You didn't think it was odd?" I asked. "Her sudden enthusiasm for Hell's Belles?"

"No," Naomi said. "It was just breakfast."

"Let's go," I said.

The café was frequented by mortals, magicians, and demons, which made it hard to snag a booth.

A couple of House of Hades ferrymen sat at a prime location and nursed their sodas. I gave them a look and they grabbed their check and vacated the booth.

Naomi touched one of the horseshoes on the wall for luck. "I'm starving." I'd examined the wall a thousand times, searching for my mother's horseshoe charm, but it wasn't there.

A new server came to take our order, which made me jittery. The last time that had happened, someone had tried to poison me.

"Coffee and the sandwich special," I ordered. Hell's Belles didn't look like much, but the food was incredible.

I waited until Bernie's section emptied out to question her. She was manning the counter, so I left Talbot and Naomi playing footsie under the table and sauntered over.

Bernie was a barrel-chested demon with sad basset hound eyes. I showed her a picture of Claire. "Seen her around?"

She nodded. "She comes in sometimes with the little redhead, but I haven't seen her in a while."

"She's her cousin," I replied.

"Your cousin, too, then," Bernie said.

I didn't exactly advertise that I was related to the Fates, but news had a way of getting around. Bernie knew more than she was letting on. Demons weren't known for being helpful. I gave up and went back to the booth.

I took a bite of my avocado BLT and then sighed with appreciation.

"How old is Claire, anyway?" Talbot asked. The question wasn't random. The Fates, and presumably, Fates-in-training like Claire and Naomi, aged slowly, but they did age.

Naomi ignored him. Interesting. "The aunties already searched her room for clues. And so did the Tracker. And they didn't find anything."

"That you know about, anyway," I replied.

Naomi managed to look hurt and offended all at once. "You make it sound like they don't want to find her."

The thought had occurred to me, but I'd dismissed it. Aunt Morta had a spine of steel, but by the tiny bit of emotion she'd shown, she obviously loved her daughter. Besides, it was in Morta's own best interest to find her daughter. Claire would take her mother's place as Fate one day. What would happen if there were no Fates to meddle in mortal affairs?

"Starling, Claire's best friend, finally called me back," Naomi said.

"And?"

"She said that Claire had been distant lately. She'd met someone, but Starling never met him."

"Did she tell you his name?"

"No," Naomi said. "She said Claire rarely talked about him. But she saw the mystery man and Claire once."

"What did he look like?"

"She said she didn't get a good look at him. Tall, blond, good-looking."

Minnesota was full of people of Scandinavian decent. *Tall, blond, and good-looking* described half the population, including the Fates' recently deceased Tracker.

"Are you sure?"

She nodded. "Starling never lies."

It was another dead end. How would I ever find a nameless, faceless guy in a city the size of Minneapolis? I'd killed the only Tracker I knew. But it had given me an idea.

"Naomi, do you know where the Tracker lived?"

"He had an apartment on Main," she said. "Why?"

"Because it's possible he knew more about Claire's disappearance than he let on," I said. I didn't want to remind her that the Tracker had betrayed the Fates in the worst possible way, poisoning Deci and stabbing Sawyer to death.

"I'll be back," I said.

"We're going with you," Talbot said.

"Someone needs to mind the store," I said. "Your dad will be pissed if nobody shows up for work."

It was safer if I went alone. When he'd died, Sawyer had been tutoring Gaston in the fine art of necromancy. Hades only knew what kind of booby traps were waiting for me at the Tracker's apartment.

The wards around his apartment had been breached. I drew my athame and turned the handle. It was locked. I used a quick spell to unlock it. Someone had taken the time to lock the door afterward.

Gaston's place was a studio apartment sparsely furnished with IKEA furniture. I'd assumed being a Tracker paid better than his apartment suggested. A futon in the corner served as both bed and couch. There was no TV, no stereo, and only one faded poster on the wall for decoration.

Someone had been there before me. The place had been tossed, neatly and carefully, but not carefully enough. The futon's cushion was slightly askew, but other than that, whoever it was had taken the time to tidy up after snooping.

There was little evidence that the Tracker even lived here. Before I'd killed him, he'd spent most of his time hunting and torturing me, so maybe he hadn't had time to decorate.

A search of the kitchen cupboards yielded a couple of chipped mugs and some plastic bowls. I stared at the David Bowie poster hanging above the futon. I was missing something, I could feel it in my gut.

The poster didn't fit Gaston's personality. Besides, I was pretty sure Bowie was a House of Zeus guy, so what was Gaston doing with his poster?

I stood on the futon and carefully lifted the bottom. There was nothing there. I thought for a moment. "*Aperio,*" I said. The Latin for reveal didn't reveal much, at least not at first.

A thin file materialized on the wall behind the poster. I reached for it and then pulled my hand back at the last second. Gaston had made an effort to conceal the contents. He'd probably booby-trapped it, too.

There was a nasty little curse tablet attached to the file. If I had touched it without removing the curse, something very bad would have happened to me. A curse tablet asked the gods to bring harm to another. This one specifically cursed anyone other than the owner who opened the file.

The curse looked like it had been painted in oily black paint, but it was bespelled demon blood. It was old magic and black as my Docs.

"What now?" I asked to no one in particular. I nearly jumped out of my skin when Sawyer's voice replied.

"Carefully trace the shape in reverse, but don't touch it."

I gritted my teeth and did as he ordered. It freaked me out that my dead uncle was talking to me from beyond the grave, but he had been a necromancer. "So is this going to be a regular thing?" I asked him.

"What?"

"You're talking to me like you're still here, but I watched you die after Gaston put a knife in you. Are you going to be hanging around?"

"Don't you enjoy my company?" There was a trace of amusement in his voice.

"It's definitely been useful," I admitted. I returned my attention to the hex and traced the shape in reverse in the air.

"You must do it three times," he instructed. "And then—"

I traced the symbol in the air as ordered. "And then what, Sawyer?"

But he was gone.

I had only a few seconds. I went through everything I knew about magic and came up with a one-word solution. I was gambling it would work.

"*Rememdium,*" I said.

I held my breath and waited, but nothing happened. No boiling oil, no hail of knives, not even a bad case of gout. It worked.

I grasped the folder gingerly. There was a troubling smear of dried blood on the tab, but just under it, I made out "Claire Foley."

I opened the folder and found a brass skeleton key taped to the inside. I put the folder underneath my shirt and left the building. Where or what did the key open? It was related to Claire somehow, but how?

Chapter Four

Back at Eternity Road, Talbot and Naomi were in the exact spot I'd left them. It felt like I'd been gone for days, but the clock told me I'd been gone a little over an hour.

"Why don't you two take off?" I suggested. "Get some fresh air. I'll mind the store."

"Are you sure?" Talbot shot me a grateful look, but my offer wasn't completely altruistic. I needed time alone to think. And maybe snoop through Ambrose's vast collection of books for any mentions of keys.

"Yeah, get out of here," I said gruffly. "All that young love is making me a little queasy."

Naomi blushed, but she grabbed Talbot's hand and they made a quick exit.

I was sitting on the chair behind the pawnshop's register, reading a book on the history of hereditary magic, when Aspen walked in.

"Nyx, I was hoping I would find you here," she said. Her normally flirty smile had been replaced by a serious look.

"How can I help?" I asked. I didn't flatter myself that a

naiad as good-looking as Aspen had to come to the rough side of town for a little action. Men would set themselves on fire for a night with her.

The bell above the door jingled as Elizabeth came into the pawnshop. For a minute, I forgot to be angry that she'd betrayed me, forgot the breakup, forgot to breathe.

She looked so much like Amalie, my dead first love. I was too consumed by memories to remember those pertinent details, let alone that I'd been flirting with the naiad only seconds before.

"You changed your hair again," I said. Elizabeth was a bit of a chameleon—gorgeous, but she had the ability to try on personalities the way other people tried on blue jeans.

She'd been blond when we met, but her hair was currently a shade of pink only found in a digestive aid.

"It's for a role," she said.

My head snapped up. "What kind of a role?" We'd met when my aunts had blackmailed her into breaking my heart. She'd hidden the fact that she was an actor then, but she'd certainly embraced it since.

"Drama class," she said. "What did you think?" She attended a fancy private college, but I wasn't sure if she'd been drawn into another one of my aunts' schemes. I didn't tell her that, though.

Conversing with the ex was difficult and it wasn't just because she was the only ex I'd had who'd actually survived the aunties. So far.

"How's Alex?" I'd rescued her brother, but he had been in bad shape when I'd found him.

"Better," she said. "But he still has screaming nightmares."

"What about you?"

"My acting teacher says I have real promise," she said.

"You're a great actress," I replied. She'd done a bang-up job of fooling me into believing she loved me when, in reality, she'd been working for my aunts.

"That doesn't sound like a compliment the way you say it." She moved away and crossed her arms over her chest.

And I thought I'd been careful to keep my voice neutral. It hadn't been a compliment. More like an accusation.

I thought I'd worked through the betrayal and was ready to see her again. I had loved her, once, after all. Hadn't I? But now, she seemed like someone I could pass in the street and not even recognize.

"Was any of it real?" It took an effort, but my voice was steady.

"I think I should go." Her voice was trembling.

"No, stay," I said. "Tell me the truth, Elizabeth."

"Nyx, I like you," she said. "But I don't..."

"You don't love me," I said flatly, but the anger managed to seep in somehow. "You were just acting, to get me to do want you wanted. What the Fates wanted."

Finally, true emotion flashed on her face. She was angry, but it was something. "You're emotionally constipated," she shouted.

"And you're a liar," I said.

Her throat worked, but she didn't deny it. She sucked in a breath. "Nyx, I never meant to hurt you."

"But you did."

There was no sense arguing about it. Part of me wondered why she'd waited so long to tell me the truth. It was long after I'd rescued Alex. In the end, it didn't matter. She'd finally told me what I'd secretly feared: She didn't love me and never had.

I cleared my throat. "Why did you come here?"

"A play at the college," she said. "And my professor says I have real talent." Elizabeth was pursuing a drama degree at a posh private college. My education was spotty at best. Just another way we weren't suited.

She held up three paper tickets. "These are for you."

I didn't touch them. Why was she offering them to me? She'd made it pretty clear that we were over.

My confusion must have showed on my face. She held them out again. "They're from Alex," she said. "I told him..." She glanced at Aspen and then looked away. "I told him that you probably couldn't make it, but he insisted."

I frowned. Alex was fragile, still out of tune with the real world since his kidnapping. "Is he okay?"

"He wants to talk to you," Elizabeth said in a low voice. "But he doesn't want you to come to the house." Her tone made it clear that she wasn't keen on the idea either.

What did Alex want to talk to me about? There was only one way to find out. I took the tickets. "I'll bring Talbot."

"You can bring whoever you want."

"I know," I said.

"So you're in this play?" I asked Elizabeth. We didn't have anything else to talk about, but I hoped we might be friends. Eventually.

Her smile brightened. "I have a lead role," she said. "And the professor is in it, too."

"You like this professor?" I asked. I tried to keep my voice neutral, but Elizabeth was no fool.

"You're jealous," she accused.

"I'm not jealous," I said. "I'm cautious."

Aspen shifted on her feet and I realized I'd forgotten her the second Elizabeth had entered the premises.

"I'm sorry I didn't introduce you two," I said. "This is Aspen."

"How did you two meet?" Elizabeth had a tone in her voice.

"Aspen is a friend, Elizabeth," I replied.

"How nice for you both." Definitely a tone, one verging on jealous.

"We work together at Parsi," I clarified.

"Parsi?" Elizabeth asked. She gave Aspen a genuine smile. "Did you know my brother, Alex?"

"Of course," Aspen said. "Your brother is a genius. We miss him."

There was an awkward silence. "Aspen, you wanted to talk to me about something?" I prompted.

"No, it's okay," she said. "I'll leave you two alone. See you on Monday."

"What was that all about?" Elizabeth asked, after Aspen left.

"I have no idea," I said.

Elizabeth made an excuse and left soon after Aspen. What had Aspen wanted to talk to me about?

I didn't realize that it would be the last time I saw Aspen alive.

Chapter Five

The mood was somber when I arrived to Parsi on Monday. The human resources manager didn't even bother with her usual pointed glance at the clock when I walked in a couple of hours late. I checked the time for her and noticed it was almost noon, which was pushing it even for me.

Employees were talking in hushed tones and a few even held balled-up tissues to their eyes.

My aunt Nona hadn't checked in yet, which was becoming more and more common since her husband's murder. Lately, she'd spent more time drinking away her sorrows than I did.

Naomi was in her mom's office, head cradling the phone while she talked and tapped on an adding machine at the same time. Her eyes were puffy and she seemed preoccupied, but she held up a finger to signal for me to wait.

"What's going on?" I asked her when she finally hung up.

"Didn't you hear? Aspen was murdered last night."

"Murdered?"

She nodded. "Everyone is freaking out."

"She came by the store this weekend. I liked Aspen," I said.

A thought occurred to me, which must have shown on my face.

"Nyx, her death had nothing to do with you." My cousin wasn't a mind reader, but she *was* a Fate-in-training.

I gave her a sharp look. "What do you know, little witch?"

"There have been others," she said.

"Other murders? Why haven't I read about it in the paper?"

She put her chin on her hand. "All of the murders have been females from the House of Poseidon," she told me. "The Houses have managed to keep it quiet, at least in the mortal world."

The door opened and Talbot stuck his head in. "Ready for lunch, babe?"

He looked at our faces. "Am I interrupting something?"

"One of our employees was murdered," Naomi explained.

"Where is she?" I asked. I wanted to see the body.

Naomi frowned, but she scribbled an address on a piece of paper and handed it to me. "You can head to the morgue tonight. Ask for Baxter, House of Hades. He works the night shift," she clarified.

"Thank you," I said.

"Don't thank me yet," she said. "You're not going to like him."

"He's a flesh eater," Talbot explained. "And he's tricky." I didn't know he knew anyone tricky. I knew plenty of tricky individuals, but Talbot was a straight arrow.

"He eats people?"

"Just the dead ones," Naomi replied.

"Oh, that makes it so much better," I said.

"Do you want information or not?" she said. She gave me a severe look. "Just to make sure you're on your best behavior, Talbot will go with you."

They headed for lunch and I spent the rest of the day brooding.

Around midnight, I knocked on Talbot's apartment door. "You ready?"

"Are you sure you're up for this?" he asked. "I know you and Aspen were friends."

"Let's just get it over with," I said. "I'll drive."

We headed to the medical examiner's office downtown.

"How does he manage to eat flesh and not get caught?" I asked.

"He only eats from the bodies that are scheduled to be cremated," Talbot said. "And he's very careful."

The morgue was in the basement behind a door with only a number on it. The room was only remarkable because of the bad lighting. It smelled terrible, which was only minimally masked by strong antiseptic.

I'd expected a slug of a man with breath like a corpse, but I was wrong.

"Nyx, this is Baxter Lamos," Talbot said. Talbot's acquaintance was tall and broad-shouldered with dark hair and eyes.

My cousin was right. I didn't like Baxter. Talbot had warned me that he was a flesh eater, but I didn't expect to see the evidence right in front of me.

There was a pile of limbs on a plate next to him. "I'm on my lunch break," Baxter said. A bit of gristle dangled from the corner of his mouth. "Gotta fuel up. I've got a date later."

I tried not to throw up. He was a bottom-feeder, but we needed him.

"Do you know anything about the naiad deaths?"

He grinned. "I had a bite," he said.

"Listen, you little cockroach," I said. "Tell me what you know. Now!"

"Say *please*." He chortled at my reaction and my fists clenched.

Talbot laid a restraining hand on my shoulder. "Baxter, quit being a pain in the ass and tell us what you know. Please."

"Two of the naiads came in as Jane Does," Baxter said. "I've never seen anything like it."

"What do you mean?" Talbot asked.

"They looked like they'd been split open from the inside out," Baxter replied. "It looked like something inside of them just exploded."

There was a closed expression on his face. He knew more than he was telling us.

"You said you've never seen anything like it?" I asked.

"That's right."

"But you do know something," I pursued.

He remained stubbornly mute until I slammed him up against the wall. "The last victim was a friend of mine. So if you know anything, anything at all, now is the time to spill your guts. Before I do it for you."

"All right, all right," he said. "No need for violence. My theory, and it's only a theory, is that someone or some*thing* was trying to gain possession of the naiads."

"Possession?" Talbot repeated. "The House of Hades banned possession over fifty years ago. Too much bad press," he added for my benefit.

"Nobody's seen Hades in over two hundred years," Baxter said. "His House is crumbling."

Baxter was a scumbag, but he didn't strike me as a *stupid* scumbag. I didn't know much about possession. I had a long night of hitting the books ahead of me.

"What happened to the bodies?" I asked.

He licked his lips. "Still here. Most of 'em, anyway."

"You're disgusting, you know that?" I said.

Baxter laughed again. "Son of Fortuna, you are so holier-than-thou. And so young."

"You're older than I am?"

He met my gaze and something ancient and primal slithered behind his benign brown eyes. "You have no idea."

Talbot cleared his throat. "I hate to interrupt the pissing contest, but what about the newest naiad? She would have been brought in sometime yesterday."

"Her name was Aspen," I said.

Baxter jerked his head toward a white body bag on the slab. "Help yourself."

Talbot unzipped the bag and the stench of dark magic filled the room.

"You forgot to mention the magic," I told Baxter.

He shrugged. "You didn't ask."

"Have you seen magic like this before?" He was going to make me play twenty questions. "And if so, when?"

His smirk disappeared. "I have never in all my years, seen anything like this before. It is the darkest of black magic. Not something for wet-behind-the-ears necromancers to tangle with."

"I'm not a necromancer," I said.

"I never said you were," he replied smoothly. "Nice athame, by the way."

The guy was jerking me around. Talbot took one look at my face and saw that the situation was deteriorating. He slid a business card over to Baxter. "Call us if you get any more."

"And don't eat them," I commanded. "Not even a nibble."

Baxter grunted his assent. "The last one gave me indigestion anyway."

We went back to the Caddy. I started it and then said, "You're right."

"About what?" Talbot asked.

"I didn't like him."

"But he did give us something to go on," Talbot said.

"Not much," I said. "We're going to have to check your dad's library. Maybe there's a mention of something like this in one of his older books."

"It's going to have to be pretty old, if Baxter's never seen it," Talbot said. "He's the oldest House of Hades member I know of."

"We'll keep looking until we find the answer," I said.

"Maybe you can take a peek into the House of Fates book," Talbot said. "That's the oldest book I know of."

"You think the aunties will just hand it over?" I snorted.

That shut him up. But Talbot had a point. I needed to take a peek at the book, but the aunts didn't need to know about it.

Chapter Six

I spent the rest of the night reading, but I didn't come up with any leads. I gave up around three, but my dreams were blood drenched.

In the morning, I drank an entire pot of black coffee and then took the key I'd found at Gaston's to a lock shop to see if they could identify it. I checked PO boxes and safety deposits at banks, but no one could tell me what the key unlocked.

It was dark by the time I made it back to my apartment. *Now what?* I took the key out again and examined it under a magnifying glass. Three symbols were engraved on the thickest part of the bow. It was the Tria Prima, which made me think that Claire had gotten tangled up with Hecate followers somehow.

I finally caught a break in the search for my cousin. I knocked on Talbot's apartment door but wasn't surprised when Naomi answered it.

There was a bottle of wine and a half-finished pizza on the coffee table in front of the couch. Talbot sat up and buttoned his shirt while I looked away.

"Claire's gone to the land of the dead," I said. I held up the brass key. "And this is a key to one of the gates."

"Where did you get that?" Naomi asked.

"Gaston's," I told her. "I knew he was holding out on the Fates. It was probably just in case he got caught. He needed a bargaining chip."

I wasn't sure the information was reliable, but it was the only thing I had to go on.

Naomi said, "You don't know what Hecate will do to her." Hecate: keeper of doorways and crossroads, badass goddess of the underworld, and my aunts' worst enemy.

"How did the Fates manage to imprison Hecate in the first place?" Talbot asked.

"The Fates drained Hecate of her powers," Naomi said, "and then turned the underworld into a permanent prison."

"What did they do with the powers?"

"I don't know," Naomi said. "But, Nyx, you have to rescue Claire."

"Rescue her? How am I going to do that? I don't even know where the gates are yet."

"You are a necromancer," Talbot butted in.

"No," I said. "You assume I'm a necromancer, just because of the knife."

"Athame," Naomi said helpfully. "I didn't know you had one."

I glared at Talbot. "That was the general idea."

He glared back. "Do you have any better ideas? Claire's life is at stake. Elizabeth's, too."

"Even if it *is* a necromancer's knife," I said, "I'm not a trained necromancer. In fact, I don't know the first thing about it."

"I do," Naomi said. "I caught Mom throwing out some of"—she gulped and then bravely continued—"some of Dad's stuff, so I hid it. You can have it all."

Gaston had killed her dad, and then I'd killed Gaston. Or at least tricked him into cutting his own thread of fate, which was the same thing.

"I don't know that I want it," I said.

"You'll need it," Talbot said. "How else are you going to find a way into the underworld?"

"What's the real reason you're hesitating?" Naomi demanded.

Talbot and I exchanged glances. Was it possible she didn't know about the prophecy? *"He, born of Fortune, shall let loose the barking dogs as the Fates fall and Hecate shall rise."*

Her next words disabused me of that notion. "Don't be such a wimp," she said. "Don't tell me you believe that moldy old prophecy?"

"You don't?" Talbot asked her.

"It's probably just wishful thinking on Hecate's part," Naomi said. "Her followers have been spreading that rumor around for ages."

"Why don't you fill us in?" Talbot asked her.

"Mom says it all started when the Fates took the harpies away from Hecate and then imprisoned her in the underworld. It was way before Mom was born," Naomi said.

Being a Fate was a hereditary position, which meant Naomi would take over for her mom one day. The Fates weren't immortal, but they lived a long time. Aunt Nona had dated Shakespeare when she was a teenager, and as anyone who'd read *Macbeth* might be able to figure out, it hadn't ended well.

Hecate, however, was a true goddess, and therefore, an immortal. And like all good goddesses, she knew how to hold a grudge. It wouldn't surprise me if she'd started the prophecy rumor herself.

I thought of something else. "How did the Fates manage to take something away from a goddess?"

"Don't know. It might be written in the Book of Fates somewhere."

"What's the big deal about the Book of Fates?" I asked. "Besides the prophecy, that is?" According to the prophecy, the first male born in the Wyrd line, which would be me, would bring about the fall of the Fates and set Hecate free.

Talbot and Naomi stared at me. "You mean you don't know?" she asked.

"Hello, black sheep here," I snapped. "My mother and I were too busy running for our lives to talk about family traditions."

"Every House has a book," Talbot explained. "You do know about the Houses, right?"

I gave him a dirty look. "I'm getting a whiff of I'm-so-superior House of Zeus right now. Of course I know about the Houses." There were four houses and every magical creature belonged to one of them: The House of Poseidon, the House of Hades, the House of Zeus, and finally, the House of Fates.

Talbot and his father were card-carrying members of House of Zeus, and sometimes a little entitlement showed. The only house that trumped Zeus was the house of Fates, of which I was a very reluctant member. My mother had been Lady Fortuna, the fourth Fate, but her role as a Fate had been all put expunged from modern memory, thanks to her sisters.

Talbot had the grace to look abashed. "Sorry, Nyx," he said. "I forgot you don't believe in all that..."

"Nonsense," I finished his sentence, knowing he was about to say something else entirely.

He cleared his throat. "The house book is where the Custos, the keeper of the book, writes down lineages, any noteworthy events, house secrets, that kind of thing. Anyone who belongs to the house has access to the book in the keeper's presence."

I gave my cousin a questioning glance. "Fates, too?"

She nodded. "Deci keeps the book. She got it back after Gaston died."

My aunt Deci was ill, most likely poisoned by that traitor Gaston when he tried to take over the family business. "Do you think she'd let me see it?"

"I'll ask," Naomi said. "But I'm not making any promises."

"Do the aunts even want me to find Claire?" I asked, frustrated.

"Of course they do," she said. "She's Morta's daughter."

"Since when does blood matter?" I snapped in reply. "How am I supposed to find Claire and save Elizabeth if they won't tell me anything?"

"I'll ask," she said again softly.

I gave in. "Can you bring me your dad's stuff?" I asked. "I might as well get started. The clock's ticking."

She nodded.

Talbot changed the subject. "Seen Willow lately?"

"Why do you ask?" I sensed a lecture coming on and I wasn't disappointed.

"It's not polite to sleep with someone and never call," Talbot said. He was blushing.

"I've never been described as polite," I said bluntly. It was true, but I'd never been so careless about another's feelings before. Deep down, I knew my actions were ungentlemanly at best.

"You're not worried about a pissed-off naiad?" Talbot continued. He had a point. Naiads liked to collect men's teeth and wear them around their neck as pretty trinkets.

"If you haven't noticed, I've had a few other things to worry about," I said angrily. "Such as staying in one piece long enough to figure out who wants me dead."

"This time," Talbot added. I looked at him in inquiry and he clarified. "Who wants you dead *this time*."

I barked out a laugh in spite of myself, then sobered.

Talbot was right. There was no sense in getting the naiads up in arms.

"I'll catch up with you later," I said. "I've got something to do."

"Going to check up on your favorite naiad?" he asked.

"She did save my life," I reminded him. "Alex's, too." Alex was Elizabeth's brother and, through no fault of his own, nearly became Gaston's victim.

I hadn't seen Willow in a few weeks and I didn't want to admit it, but I was worried about her. I was going to make sure she was okay, not sleep with her again. Aspen's death had left me with a lingering sense that something wicked had arrived in Minneapolis.

After I left the Bardoff residence, I headed to the lake. Willow had been a good friend and I owed her an explanation. It was going to be humiliating, embarrassing, and probably physically painful.

I was right. When I found Willow, she was ready to strip the flesh from my bones with her teeth, but not because I never called.

I sat at my favorite bench and said her name. There wasn't even a splash before she was standing next to me, her long hair streaming water and barely covering her interesting bits.

Her skin was pale blue, translucent, and she wore a necklace of river stone. She'd added bits of glass and driftwood since the last time I saw her.

"Tell me what's been going on in your world," I said.

"Death," she said gravely.

"I am sorry, Willow," I said, then remembered the formal words of mourning: *"Non est ad astra mollis e terris via."* Which translated as "There is no easy way from the earth to the stars." The saying was often attributed to Seneca, but I heard it first from a naiad. My mother and I had lived with a colony of naiads for a summer in Capri.

"Sorrow will not bring her back," she said.

"Your human was here," she said. "Crying loudly. Disturbing the birds. Tell her to stop. Go make her happy."

"I can't." It was hard to explain my complicated relationship to a naiad. My words had a ring of truth that I'd been avoiding.

She gently touched the silver chain I wore and set the charms jingling. "What about you? Any luck?"

"Not at all," I replied.

I'd gotten lucky when I arrived in Minneapolis and found several of the charms, but had hit a dry patch recently. Where were my mother's remaining charms?

Lost in thought, I took the path back to the Caddy and sat in the driver's seat. The night was as cold and dark as my thoughts.

Chapter Seven

The night of Elizabeth's performance arrived. I put on my best shirt and tie and bought a bouquet of bright flowers. Talbot and Naomi had taken pity on me and were my dates for the evening.

Elizabeth attended Blake University, a posh private school. The college looked more like a country club than an institution of higher learning.

I parked the Caddy in the parking structure and then opened the door for Naomi. "Let's do this."

Talbot laughed.

I walked ahead of Naomi and Talbot, who were stopping to kiss every few feet.

"Hurry up! We're going to be late," I called out, but they didn't hear me. I walked faster. They'd find me eventually.

Sawyer had been on some fund-raising board for Blake. I looked around for Aunt Nona, but she wasn't in the audience.

The theater was state-of-the-art and the audience well dressed. I tugged on my tie. Someone mistook me for a stagehand, but she was being kind. Even the help was better dressed than I was.

There wasn't any assigned seating, so I wasn't surprised that Jenny had come early to get a good seat. She had been Elizabeth's roommate when we'd first met, but she'd moved out after I killed her on-again, off-his-rocker-again boyfriend Gaston, aka the Fates' Tracker.

Alex, Elizabeth's brother, sat next to her. He was still pale and twitchy, but he'd lost the crazy glazed eyes and gained a few pounds. When I found him, after being left to the Fates and Gaston's tender mercies, he'd been gaunt and raving.

"Nyx, Talbot, over here," Alex said. "We saved seats for you."

Jenny's giant pocketbook took up almost all the space. I was touched that they'd saved us seats, but she soon disabused me of the notion that she'd done so willingly.

"I only saved you the seats because Alex begged me to," she hissed. "Besides, this way I'll have the perfect view. I can't wait to see the expression on your face."

I ignored her and slid into the seat next to Alex. "Looking good, Alex."

"The professor says so, too," he confided.

"The professor?"

"He's Elizabeth's friend," he continued. "He plays Scrabble with me."

"He is?"

"So that's the roommate, huh?" Naomi whispered. She sat between me and Talbot, but I realized that might not be far enough away from the girlfriend of her father's killer. I squirmed, but Jenny and Naomi didn't seem interested in conversing with each other.

I scanned the crowd and noticed a trio of familiar heads. The Fates had arrived. Morta's silver hair stood out in the darkened theater.

"What are they doing here?" I hissed at Naomi. I had a good idea. Their presence at Elizabeth's performance was meant as a warning.

"What?" She craned her head to see. "I have no idea."

Alex shifted uneasily next to me. My aunts' Tracker had terrorized him. I didn't want him to have a full-blown freak-out. I changed the subject before he figured out who Naomi and I were talking about.

"Everyone misses you around Parsi," I said. He jerked at the mention of his former place of employment and I realized I'd stepped in it. When Alex had been kidnapped, he and Sawyer had been working on a secret formula for ambrosia, a new and improved nectar of the gods.

Alex's foot tapped continuously. He was more nervous than he'd first seemed. He didn't answer me. His expression told me he'd checked out.

"Elizabeth said you wanted to talk to me about something?" I prodded, trying to bring him back.

His expression didn't change, but he whispered. "Not here." He was careful not to look in Jenny's direction, but I got the hint. He didn't trust her. I didn't, either.

Before I could say anything else, the lights dimmed and the curtain rose.

It was a modern play, something written in the last fifty years or so, and I was bored. Until Elizabeth walked onstage.

The play was about a couple's search for the fountain of youth. Elizabeth played the woman who drank the water and became young again.

What did Alex think of the subject matter? It was uncomfortably close to his own research at Parsi.

He seemed to understand my unspoken question. "I wish I'd never heard of ambrosia," he said.

I changed the subject. "Elizabeth's really good," I told Alex.

"Yes, she's quite the actress," Jenny said, but it wasn't a compliment. "She fooled you, didn't she?"

I ignored her, but it took an effort.

I glanced over at my aunts. Morta and Nona had their attention on the stage, but Deci was watching me. I looked away, but I could still feel her staring. I was ready to shout at her to stop when heavy smoke filled the theater.

Some dumbass screamed, "Fire!" and jumped out of his seat. Other people followed suit, pushing and shoving anyone in their way, which started a full-on stampede for the exit. I looked over at Alex, who looked like he'd start screaming himself any second.

"Alex, keep it together," I said. "Go with Talbot. Do exactly as he says and you'll be fine."

He took a shaky breath. "Okay."

"Talbot, get them out of here," I said. "I'll find Elizabeth and then try to put out the fire."

He started toward the main exit, but there was no way he'd get through. "Not that way," I said. I pointed to an alternate exit, to the right of the stage. "Go through there."

The smoke was thick. I tried not to breathe, but my lungs filled anyway. "*Extinguere*," I shouted, but it didn't have any effect.

We found the exit and I shoved Naomi through, but Alex balked. "I'm not leaving without my sister," he said.

"Get out of here," I said. "I'll find her. I promise."

Jenny didn't wait for more conversation. She gave him a shove of her own. "Let's go!"

"You, too," I said to Talbot.

He didn't move. "I'm immortal, remember?" I said. "You're not."

He nodded and then exited the building.

I jumped onto the stage, but I didn't see Elizabeth anywhere.

It was chaos backstage. I couldn't see much through the smoke. "*Aqua*," I said. The water quenched the flames in one part of the room, but roared to life in another.

"Elizabeth," I shouted and inhaled a lungful of smoke. There was the unholy smell of scorched flesh in the air, the screams of the dead and dying, and everywhere I turned, flames. It was an inferno, what people quaintly described as a four-alarm fire, and I had no doubt who was behind it.

I tripped over something. Instinctively, I reached down to grab it. A metal lighter, already hot to the touch. Was it evidence of who had started the fire?

I shoved it into my pocket and crawled along the floor, which is how I finally found her. She was unconscious but, thankfully, breathing. When I rolled her over, at first she seemed unharmed, but then I brushed her hair away and saw it: The skin was already black and blistering. Fire had scorched half of her face.

The rest was a blur. I remember I carried her out of the building and into the arms of a firefighter. "Help her, please."

Chapter Eight

I stayed at the hospital, but they wouldn't let me see her. I sat in the waiting room on a hard orange plastic chair. Jenny and Alex sat opposite me. Jenny was stone-faced and silent, but Alex rocked back and forth.

I wondered if it was too much for him. He'd been a mess when I had found him imprisoned in the Driftless, but he'd improved once he'd reunited with his sister. Elizabeth's hospitalization might send him back over the edge.

He started muttering something under his breath.

"Alex, what is it?" I asked. I touched his shoulder, but his gaze was cloudy. He was in another world.

"It's okay. Elizabeth will be okay." He shook his head and then his eyes cleared. "The Fates will find a way," he said.

"What does that mean?" I asked, but he remained silent. I had an awful feeling Alex was trying to tell me my aunts were involved somehow.

My fault, my fault, my fault ran through my head on a continuous loop.

"Talbot, you should go home," I said.

"I don't think I should leave you," he replied. He went outside to call his dad. I barely noticed when he came back. It could have been an hour or a day.

"Nyx, snap out of it," Talbot said.

"I need to see her. They won't let me. I want to see Elizabeth." I was ready to tear the place apart to get my way. Some of that must have been evident in my voice because Talbot grabbed my arm.

"Calm down," he said. "I'll get you in after visiting hours are over."

I finally caught his meaning. We were going to use magic to sneak into Elizabeth's room. Why hadn't I thought of that before?

I gave him a jerky nod. "Understood."

Before we could implement the plan, a nurse came out. "She's awake and asking for her brother."

Alex jumped to his feet. "That's me."

"I'm going with you," Jenny said.

I tried to follow, but the nurse stopped me. "And you are?"

"Her boyfriend," I lied.

"You're Nyx?" she replied. "Then it's *ex*-boyfriend, isn't it? I'm afraid she doesn't want to see you."

I watched, stunned, as she led Alex and Jenny away.

"Talbot, is there any place I can take her? Someone who could speed the healing?"

"You know the Houses don't like to get involved in the affairs of mortals," he said. He avoided my eyes.

"I gave her a bloodstone," I said. "Why wasn't she wearing it?"

"She must have been," he said, "or it would have been much worse for her. The bloodstone probably saved her life."

His words made me feel a tiny bit better. "So you know someone who might be able to help her?"

He hesitated. "Maybe," he said. "He's hard to find. And if he'll do it, it will be expensive."

"I have the money," I said.

He grimaced. "You don't even know how much money we're talking about."

"It doesn't matter," I said. "I'll get it."

"It may take me a few days to find him," Talbot warned.

"I'm not going anywhere," I said. And neither was Elizabeth—not if I could help it.

When they finally allowed visitors, Jenny and Alex went in first. An hour later, Jenny came out. "Go home, Nyx," she said. "She doesn't want to see you."

"Like I'd believe anything you say. I'm not leaving until I see her."

"Of course you won't," she said. "Because you're such a prick you don't care about her feelings. You just care about your own." I'd killed Jenny's boyfriend, Gaston. He was a bastard who had enjoyed hurting women, but that didn't stop Jenny from hating my guts.

"I want to see her," I said. My voice cracked. "That's all. Just to make sure she's okay."

"She's not okay," Jenny said viciously. "And it's your fault."

"My fault? I didn't start the fire."

"You seriously didn't smell the magic in the theater?"

"What are you talking about?" There had been something off about the fire, but I'd been too worried about Elizabeth to pay close attention.

She crossed her arms over her chest but didn't say anything.

"Jenny, if you noticed something, please tell me," I begged, but she remained mum.

The burn unit waiting room emptied out as the night went on. I curled up in one of the chairs but couldn't sleep. Around two, Talbot tapped me on the shoulder. "I found him."

I worked a kink from my neck and the wraith scar twinged. "Where is he?"

"Outside," he replied. "He won't come in until he talks to you first."

I followed Talbot to the parking lot, where a man in an oversized coat, heavy for this time of year, stood smoking a cigarette. The man's jittery movements made his shadow dance.

When the streetlight cast his profile into sharp relief, it revealed the scar marking one side of his face. His right profile was elegant, handsome even, but his left side looked like someone had slammed it into a hot waffle iron.

My footsteps slowed. "I know him," I said to Talbot in a low voice. I held up the emerald frog on the chain around my neck. "He gave me this."

"Why?" Talbot said. "How?"

"I think he knew my mother."

"Don't pester him about it," Talbot replied. "He's skittish enough already."

To prove his point, the man wheeled and walked in the opposite direction.

"Hey, wait up!" I sprinted over to him and grabbed him by the arm. He was still wearing the same mangy fedora and the black trench coat he'd had on when we'd first met.

He put up a hand like he thought I was going to hit him.

"Please," I said as soothingly as possible. "I need your help.

My girlfriend"—I cleared my throat—"my *ex*-girlfriend has been hurt, pretty badly. Please help her."

"Your eyes," he said. "Your mother's eyes."

I desperately wanted to ask him about my mother, about how he knew her, but I knew if I did, he'd run.

"Will you help her?"

He nodded.

"What's your name?" I asked.

His throat worked. "No names," he finally croaked. "Just get me into her room. Can you do that?"

I used a handy little obscura spell on the scarred man and me. Talbot opted to wait in the hallway to play lookout.

Elizabeth had a private room. Everything was cool and dark and still, including the figure in the bed. She was covered in bandages. The only sound in the room was the hum of the machines on one side of the bed. The IV made a plopping noise and the scarred man flinched.

Under her layers of bandages, Elizabeth was still. So still that I panicked. "Is she...?"

"She's sedated. For the pain," he said.

I exhaled shakily.

"Now get rid of the obscura spell," the scarred man said. "It's making me itchy."

I didn't bother to object. I needed to keep him happy so he would heal her. I reversed the spell on him but left mine in place.

He was so nervous that he was practically tap-dancing. The injuries to his face must have occurred in a similar fire.

"Are you okay?" I asked. "If this is too much for you..."

"You are kind," he said.

"You say it like it's a bad thing."

"Sometimes it is," he said. "But I'm fine." He seemed to be telling the truth. His hands were steady as he reached for Elizabeth's limp ones.

"Leave us," he said. "Come back in fifteen minutes. Not a second less."

"You won't hurt her?" I was reluctant to leave, because after all, what did I really know about him?

"I give you my word that no harm will fall upon her while she's under my care," he said.

The pledge reassured me enough that I did as he asked and joined Talbot in the hallway. I tapped him on the shoulder and he jumped, since the obsura spell still rendered me invisible.

"Damn it, Nyx," he whispered. "You scared the hell out of me. Anything yet?"

"He kicked me out," I said. "Are you sure about this guy? He told me to come back in fifteen minutes."

"He's the best healer in Minneapolis," Talbot assured me. "If he can't help her, no one can."

I paced until the clock ran out and then ran back to her room.

"She's awake," I whispered.

"I did my best," the scarred man said, "but there was a lot of damage to her face."

"I don't care," I said. "She's better, right?"

He nodded. "Much."

Elizabeth still hadn't looked at me and I realized my obscura spell was still in place. I broke the spell and approached her bedside. He had removed the bandages. The blackened skin and bubbling blisters were gone, but in their place was a large purple scar that ran from cheekbone to chin.

"Nyx, what happened?" she asked.

"There was a fire," I said. "You're in the hospital."

"Fire?" Her gaze cleared as she remembered. She put a hand up to her cheek. "I want to see."

"I don't think that's a good idea right now," I said. "You need to rest."

"Bring me a mirror or I'll get out of bed and get one myself."

I stomped into the bathroom and yanked the small mirror off the wall. It had been bolted into the drywall and it left a gaping hole.

I carried it to her bed and held it up in front of her.

She looked into it for a long moment. "I've seen enough," she finally said. The spark of mischief in her green eyes was gone, stamped out by fate.

"I don't care what you look like." I meant it, but she took it the wrong way.

"Just go."

"You don't mean that," I said. There was a burgeoning sense of dread in the pit of my stomach, which told me she did mean it.

"But I do. I never want to see you again," she said evenly.

"Elizabeth, please don't do this," I said.

"I don't love you," she continued. "I never loved you. It was all to save Alex."

She was telling me exactly what I'd feared most.

"It doesn't matter," I said. I already knew she didn't love me, but I wanted to help her anyway. I hadn't been able to save Amalie.

"You never once thought the same thing yourself?" she asked. "After everything? I betrayed you to your aunts, lied to you since the moment we met. You don't think it's possible? You're so full of yourself. You think because you're gorgeous, that I couldn't be faking it? Well, I was."

It was the cruelest thing anyone had ever said to me, but her words held an undeniable ring of truth.

"I'll leave you alone," I said dully. "But if you ever need anything…"

"I won't," she replied.

I took the mirror with me and as soon as I was out of her room, threw it against the wall. The sound of shattering glass brought an orderly running.

"Sorry, it slipped," I told him. "This should cover it." I handed him a hundred-dollar bill.

He pocketed the cash and went off to find a broom.

The scarred man put a hand on my shoulder. "She could change her mind."

"She won't."

I dug the rest of the cash out of my pockets and handed it to him. "Thank you."

I didn't wait to see where he went. I made it back to Talbot in a daze. "We've got to get her out of here."

"Out of the hospital?"

"Out of the city," I answered. "Hell, maybe out of the country?"

"What's wrong?" he asked.

"The Fates had a hand in this somehow," I said. "She won't be safe here. She hasn't been safe since she met me."

"What can I do to help?"

"We have to get her out of the city. Tonight."

My plan was a simple one, but there were two very crucial factors that had to work or it would fall apart.

He nodded.

"Let's go find Alex."

He was hunched over in one of the orange chairs. For a minute, I thought he was asleep, but when he heard our footsteps, he sat up and wiped his eyes.

"Any news?" he asked.

"Where's Jenny?" I hedged. Alex was unpredictable, but he was our only hope.

"She went home to get some sleep," he said. "Tell me what's going on with Elizabeth." His voice had taken on a ragged tone.

Talbot and I exchanged glances.

"She's much better," I said. "But we need your help, Alex."

We outlined the plan: Get a car and get Elizabeth out of town. The Abernathys were wealthy, so money wasn't an issue.

"Do you think you can do it?" I asked.

His feet tapped out a jumpy tune on the faded tile.

"Alex, maybe Jenny..."

His gaze sharpened and the tapping stopped. "Not Jenny!" he yelled. Then, in a softer voice, he added, "I can do this, Nyx. We have a place in—"

"Don't tell me," I said. "This is good-bye."

"What about a car?" Talbot asked.

Elizabeth's red Lexus was too conspicuous. So was my purple Caddy. I could buy something, but nothing was open this time of night and my gut told me to get her out of Minneapolis. I was stumped.

"I have a car," Alex said softly. He jumped to his feet, suddenly galvanized. "I'll go get it. I have the keys and everything." He gave me a mischievous grin. "Elizabeth doesn't know I took them."

He started to rush off, but I stopped him. "No, Alex," I

said. “It might raise suspicion if you go. Talbot can get in and out of there without anybody noticing. Right, Talbot?”

“Right,” my friend said.

Alex handed him the keys. “It’s in the garage,” he said. “I bought it right before I”—he gulped and continued—“before Gaston kidnapped me.”

For the next hour, the only sound was Alex’s tap-dancing feet as we waited. Finally, Talbot came back. “It’s parked in patient loading,” he said. He handed Alex the key.

“Take care of her,” I said to Alex. I held out my hand. He grabbed it and then folded me into a tight hug.

“Thanks, Nyx,” he said. He slid something into the pocket of my leather jacket.

“What’s that, Alex?” I asked.

He was already in the corridor leading to his sister’s room. “Just a little thank-you,” he said. “Are you coming to say good-bye?”

I shook my head. “Already been said.”

“I’ll go with him,” Talbot said. “I can manage a cloaking spell, so that the night shift won’t notice them.”

My throat was too tight to speak, so I just nodded.

I stayed in the waiting room, waiting breathlessly for the sound of an alarm, but it was quiet.

Talbot came back into the waiting room. “They’re gone,” he said in a low voice. “Alex said he’d get a message to you when they made it out safely.”

“Thanks for everything. Let’s get out of here,” I said. “Now.” I was barely hanging on. I didn’t want to lose it in public.

Elizabeth hadn’t even said good-bye. I didn’t blame her. I went back to my apartment and wallowed. She had helped to fill up that hungry, hollow feeling inside me, but now she was gone, and I was alone.

Chapter Nine

It had been three long days since Alex and Elizabeth had stolen away like thieves in the night.

"I need a drink," I said to Talbot. Which was convenient, since we were sitting on stools at the Red Dragon.

"Are you sure that's a good idea?" he replied.

"Elizabeth is gone, her face is permanently scarred, and it's all my fault."

"It's not your fault."

"Tell that to Elizabeth," I said. "She never wants to see me again."

"Maybe the time apart will do you both good," Talbot said. "You need to think about things."

"Like what?"

"Your feelings. You said yourself that Elizabeth is the spitting image of Amalie."

My dead ex, killed by the Fates.

"You think what I feel for Elizabeth is *nostalgia*?"

"I think you don't really know how you feel," Talbot said.

"And I don't blame you. It's not like you and Elizabeth have a normal relationship."

"Yeah, thanks to my aunts," I replied. I shifted in my seat and took a chug of my beer. "Deci warned me, but I never thought she'd do something this loathsome."

"Your aunt Deci?" Talbot said. "I thought there was a cease-fire going on."

"Not anymore," I said grimly. "But that goes both ways."

"Naomi isn't involved in any of this," Talbot said.

"I would never hurt Naomi," I said. "But the Fates are up into their necks in it."

Talbot had given up on me after the bartender had cracked the second bottle of absinthe. The last thing I remembered was closing down the Red Dragon.

My first conscious thought was that someone staring at me. I was right. When I opened my eyes, I was lying in a naiad's lair with a naked Willow beside me. She was leaning on one elbow as she watched me.

"This is becoming a habit, son of Fortuna," she said softly.

"What is?" I asked. My mind was still blurry with sleep and alcohol.

"You, using me for sexual comfort when you are drunk and in pain," she said bluntly.

Then I remembered. Elizabeth's singed flesh, her reluctance to look in the mirror, and how she had to flee Minneapolis.

I pushed away the thought and reached for Willow. "I'm sober now."

She avoided my grasp. "But still in pain."

"Yes," I said. "Still in pain. But this helps." I kissed her and she didn't avoid me this time.

A naiad's magic was as heavy and sweet as honey and the taste of her kiss lingered on my lips.

I drew her down until she lay across my body, but I could tell she wasn't into it. "What's wrong?"

She moved away from me. "A naiad was found murdered."

"May she return to Poseidon on gentle waves." I said the traditional words of mourning automatically. It was a naiad equivalent of "I'm sorry for your loss." I was quickly running out of platitudes.

"Thank you."

"You said 'murdered.' Are you sure?"

"She was torn apart from the inside," she replied. "Like a bomb had gone off inside her."

"Like the others," I said.

"Yes, like the others." Willow's voice trembled.

"Talbot said there have been others from the House of Poseidon. We think it might be someone attempting to possess a naiad, but we don't know why."

"Possession?" she repeated. "But that has been outlawed."

"I know," I said. "But that doesn't mean someone isn't breaking the rules. The question is why?"

She threw my clothes at me. "You must go now. I have something I must do."

"But..." It wasn't the first time I'd been shown the door after a night of passion, but I had to admit, this ranked up there with the hastiest.

"We'll talk more later," she replied. "Leave now."

"Promise me you'll be careful," I said.

"I promise!" she said. "Now go."

I threw on my clothes and did the walk of shame with my Docs in hand.

I spent the next few days trying to drink away my feelings. I missed shifts at Eternity Road, argued with Naomi, and took a swing at Talbot. It didn't change anything.

But finally, when I'd puked out the hurt and self-pity, I realized it was time to sober up or spend the rest of my days swimming in a bottle of absinthe. I needed to get the Fates out of my life, which meant finding Claire.

I spent two miserable days purging the alcohol from my system. I finally took a shower and got up the nerve to head to Eternity Road to see if I still had a job. And a best friend.

When I walked in, Ambrose looked up from the cash register. I paused in the doorway, uncertain of the welcome I'd receive, but he walked over, clapped me on the back and said, "What are you waiting for? My office needs dusting."

I had to pass by Talbot several times, but he pretended to ignore me.

I ignored him right back. By lunch, he was giving me sideways glances like someone waiting to be asked to the prom.

"What?" I stopped dusting long enough to stare back.

"You look like shit."

I nodded. "I have a hangover."

He snorted angrily and turned away. He fussed with the fedora on Harvey, the enormous stuffed bear that never seemed to sell.

"You don't get it," I said. "I have a hangover. Which means..." I waited for him to fill in the blanks.

"You stopped drinking?"

"The incredulity in your voice is not reassuring," I told him. "But, yes, I stopped drinking. At least for now."

"What do you want?" he asked. "A parade?" There were equal parts anger and relief in his voice.

"I'm sorry," I said. "I'm a crappy friend."

"Yes, you are," he replied. "But I can count on you. Can't I?"

I nodded.

Talbot tried to get me to talk, to tell him about my feelings, but I was so full of pent-up rage that I was afraid if I said another word, I'd explode.

"There's nothing to talk about," I finally said. "She never wants to see me again. She's gone. Left Minneapolis. Can you blame her?"

"It wasn't your fault," Talbot protested.

"A fire of dark magic that injured my *mortal* ex-girlfriend? Yeah, that doesn't sound like my fault at all."

I tossed the lighter on the table. "Besides, I found this at the theater."

"That doesn't prove anything," he said. "Naomi was there. Her aunt would never—"

"Never put her niece in danger to exact revenge?" I replied. "She's a Fate, Talbot. Get with the program. They killed their own sister."

He stared at the lighter like he'd never seen one before.

Naomi walked into Eternity Road and I quickly pocketed the lighter. She kissed Talbot and then gave me a long measuring look. I met her eyes, but it took effort. Whatever she saw there seemed to satisfy her.

"You don't reek of alcohol," she said. "It's an improvement." Her eyes were shiny with unshed tears and I felt like an ass for making her worry.

Chapter Ten

Talbot, Naomi, and I were holed up in the office at Eternity Road, searching a map of Minneapolis for clues to the location of Hecate's gate to the underworld.

"You can find Hecate's gate at a three-way crossroad," he said.

"Where can I find a three-way crossroad in Minneapolis?" I wasn't a native, but my question stumped my friends, too.

We studied the map.

"I can't tell anything from this tiny map," I said.

Talbot got out a magnifying glass, and we took turns staring at the roads of a miniature city.

"Hell's Belles is near a three-way crossroad," Talbot said. "And we were attacked by a wraith there not that long ago."

"You think Hecate sent a wraith after me?" I asked. "I thought the prophecy was supposed to work in her favor?"

"Do you have any better ideas?" Talbot replied. "She might not have the motive, but she definitely had the opportunity."

He was right. You couldn't walk in the underworld without tripping over a dead person. Or so I'd been told.

"Bernie knows something," I said. "I just don't know what."

"She's a demon," Talbot reminded me needlessly. "She'll never talk."

"We're going to have to find a way to make her talk," I said.

"The location seems too obvious," Naomi said. "Right in plain sight."

"It's not like anyone can stroll into Hecate's domain," I pointed out. "She'll have some nasty surprises for the unwary or uninvited."

"Talbot's not going with you," Naomi said.

His face darkened. "Can I talk to you for a minute?" he said and then he pulled her aside, while I tried to stare at anything besides them. I tried to look busy, but my gaze returned to their angry faces. Talbot's eyes had turned to silverlight, which was never a good sign.

I'd never seen my best friend and my cousin argue, not once, since they'd started dating, but it was clear they were fighting now.

I felt more awkward by the moment, and even worse, I was wasting valuable time. I cleared my throat. "Uh, I'm taking off," I said. "See you later."

I walked away, but Talbot caught up with me down the block. "You were gonna just bail on me?" he asked.

"I recognized that look in Naomi's eyes," I said. "And I didn't have time to watch your lovers' quarrel."

"She's stubborn," he said. "But I'm worse."

"She's a Fate," I said, suddenly serious. "Don't ever forget it."

"Naomi would never do anything to hurt me," he replied. "Or you."

I wished I were as certain of that as he seemed to be. "The supper rush should be over by now," I said. "The restaurant will be emptying out. Maybe Bernie will want to talk."

Talbot snorted, but didn't say anything, We were almost to the café when he put a hand on my arm. "Someone's tailing us," he whispered.

"Are you sure?" I looked back in time to see a shadowy figure dart into a doorway.

He nodded and then increased his pace. "We need to bail on this idea."

"No way," I replied. "What are they going to do? Beat us to death with a pie?"

The figure moved again and a streetlight illuminated his features.

"It's just Doc," Talbot said. "He's harmless."

"You sound disappointed," I said. "My cousin isn't enough excitement for you anymore?"

"None of your business," Talbot replied. There was an odd note in his voice, but my attention was focused on the homeless guy.

"Who's Doc?" I asked.

"The guy who helped us with Elizabeth."

Now I recognized the mutilated face of the guy tailing us. "Hey, wait a minute."

I owed him money and he owed me an explanation. I wanted to know why he'd given me my mother's emerald frog. I wanted to know why he had magical powers, powers that people would pay for, but instead, he was homeless. I wanted to know who he was, really.

He took off running. Fast for an old guy.

"Stop!" I said. I took off after him. "I just want to give you some money. I'm not going to hurt you."

If anything, that made him run faster.

I chased him for three blocks, but he gave me the slip.

"Why are you chasing him?" Talbot asked, panting as he came up behind me. "I told you he was skittish."

"I just wanted to ask him some questions," I said.

"You probably scared him," Talbot said.

"He knows something," I said.

"Freaking him out isn't going to get you answers," he said.

He was probably right. "What do you know about him?"

"He's been coming around the store since I was little. Dad feeds him, tries to get him to stay, but he always slips away."

I was unconvinced. "I need to find him."

"Another time," Talbot urged. "I'll let you know next time he's in the store. We have things to do, remember? Finding the gate? Claire?"

I reluctantly let him point me toward Hell's Belles. We walked for a block or so in silence.

"So what was the argument with Naomi about?" I asked.

He hesitated. "You wouldn't understand."

"Try me."

"Hard to believe, but the aunts don't think I'm good enough for her." Underneath the joking tone, there was a hint of hurt.

"Why do you care?"

"Because I'm in love with her," Talbot said quietly.

"You couldn't have picked a worse future mother-in-law," I said.

"I thought you liked Nona," he objected.

"She's the best of the worst," I admitted. "They probably disapprove of you because we're friends."

"That's what I thought," he said. "But it's more than that."

The restaurant was dark, which was strange, since Hell's Belles was a twenty-four-hour diner.

Talbot checked his watch. "Now what? Hell's Belles is closed."

"This is our only chance," I said.

"We picked the one night Bernie closes," Talbot said.

"Even better," I said. "She won't be there."

When we checked, the main part of the restaurant was dark, but I could still see a light in the kitchen.

The front door, though, was locked.

"Let's check the back," I said.

We went around to the rear of the building. There was a smelly Dumpster and the area by the door was littered with cigarettes.

Talbot put his hand on the knob and turned it slowly. "Door's unlocked," Talbot said.

The back kitchen was in darkness.

"What now?"

"I doubt the gate is out in the open. It's probably somewhere in the kitchen or—"

"The basement," Talbot interrupted. He pointed to an interior door.

From down below, someone was chanting. We followed the sound down stairs lit by rows of lit candles.

We tried to be as quiet as possible, but the stairs squeaked as I reached the bottom.

Talbot and I froze, but the guttural chanting continued.

We hid behind a stack of restaurant supply boxes. Bernie

stood before an elaborate wooden altar carved with Tria Prima symbols.

As we watched, she drew a blade across her hand and spilled drops of blood into a golden goblet.

"Don't breathe it in," I whispered to Talbot. "And whatever you do, don't get any on your skin." Demons' blood wasn't like ours. It scalded the skin, and if it got into the bloodstream, it did much worse.

When I turned back again, Bernie was no longer standing there.

"Did you see where she went?" I asked Talbot.

He ignored the question and moved closer to the altar. "Look familiar?" he asked. He motioned to the wall. Hanging on a hook by a silken thread was a key, twin to the one I'd found at Gaston's.

Talbot went up to the altar, careful to avoid the goblet full of demon blood. "Do you hear that?" he said. "I hear a dog."

He pressed his ear to the wall and stayed like that for a long minute. "Definitely a dog."

There was only one goddess who came to mind when I thought of dogs. Hecate.

We went back to our hiding place. "Now what?" Talbot whispered.

"We wait."

I had almost dozed off when Talbot nudged me. "We've got company."

Hooded figures filled the room.

We watched as the disciples slowly approached the altar one by one, and then, just as Bernie had, each one disappeared until the room was empty except for Talbot and me.

"Should we follow them?"

"We'd be outnumbered," I said. "Let's get out of here."

Back in the Caddy, Talbot turned to me. "Now what?"

"Now I check back with the Fates to see what they say." I wasn't looking forward to telling Morta that her mortal enemy had her daughter.

Chapter Eleven

I wanted to catch Morta alone, so I got to Parsi Enterprises early the next morning. Nona was still in a fog and I loathed Deci, so Morta was my only chance at getting some answers.

Trevor was playing guard dog in front of her closed office door. Or maybe he was eavesdropping.

Even from where I stood, I heard raised voices.

"Heard anything juicy?" I asked.

Trevor stepped away from the door and crossed his arms over his chest. "She's in a meeting."

"Too bad," I replied.

I didn't wait for his response, but pushed my way through.

"You're not going to believe what I found out," I said.

"I'm in a meeting," Morta snapped. My aunt had the same high cheekbones as my mother, but where my mother's hair had been a soft brown, there was nothing soft about Morta, not even her hair. It was the color of burnished steel and was cut at sharp angles.

"So I heard." I smirked at her until I realized who was sitting in her comfortable guest chair. Sean Danvers. The golf-loving necromancer who Jenny had briefly dated to try to get over Gaston.

He wasn't bad-looking, tan and fit, but his skin carried an oily film of evil. Or maybe it was his pungent cologne that left the residue.

"What are you doing here?" My surprise made me ruder than usual.

He stood and smiled pleasantly. "I was just leaving." He picked up a grocery bag the right size to contain a six-pack. I should know. I'd bet money the bag contained what looked like innocuous orange soda but was, in reality, ambrosia.

Then to Morta, he said, "You'll consider my proposal?"

She gave a curt nod. "Now if you'll excuse us?" Her smile was pleasant, but her tone implied *Don't let the door hit your ass on the way out.*

"Good day, Ms. Foley. Mr. Fortuna." His smile was robotic, like he'd programmed it into his hard drive but had no idea what it was supposed to do for him.

It sounded weird to hear him address my aunt as anything other than Fate, but she didn't seem to mind. Why were the Fates giving Danvers a free sample of their ambrosia? The formula was gone, missing since Sawyer's death. What did Danvers have on them that they'd be willing to break into their limited stock?

"I'll walk you to the elevator," my aunt said. "As long as my nephew can manage to stay out of trouble for five minutes."

I gave her a sunny smile. "I'll try." After they left, I took a seat in Morta's chair, knowing it was going to irritate her.

Trevor bustled in with a pot of black coffee and some Tums. The breakfast of champions.

He slammed the tray down with more force than necessary. "You're not supposed to be in here."

I raised an eyebrow. "I have more right to be here than you."

"Quit bullying the help, son of Fortuna," My aunt said.

"I've been called a lot of things before, most of them by you," I said. "But I've never been called a bully before."

"Then don't act like one," she said.

I felt a twinge of shame. I didn't like Trevor, even though I had absolutely no reason. "Sorry," I said to him.

"Apology accepted," he said. "Now I better get back to the phones."

"What did Danvers want?" I asked, once Trevor was out of earshot.

"He wants to invest in Parsi Enterprises," she said carefully. "He's particularly interested in our bottling division."

"I'll bet he is," I replied. The Fates had been trying to manufacture ambrosia, also known as nectar of the gods. Mortals would and had killed to get their hands on a way to stay young forever.

"What did you want, son of Fortuna?" she asked, but I ignored the question for one of my own.

"So what happened to Mr. Foley?"

"He died," she said. "Why do you ask?"

"Seems to be one of the hazards of the job," I said.

She gave me a level stare to let me know she wouldn't be prodded into revealing anything else. "Is there something you wanted?"

"I found Claire," I said. "At least I'm pretty sure I know where she is. But I need your help."

"Where is she?"

"I think Hecate has her." I expected her to freak out or something, but she didn't even blink.

"Then fetch her." Her lips pressed together tightly. She wasn't as calm as she tried to appear.

"That wasn't part of the deal," I objected. "How do you expect me to bring her back from the land of the dead?"

Morta gave me a look that would have chilled the bones of a mortal man. "That is not my problem. I have no power there."

Her lips curled like it hurt to say the words. Maybe it did.

"You're asking a lot of me."

"Your beloved, is she not worth it?" she asked.

"She's not my beloved anymore." I shifted uneasily at the knowing look in her eye, but Morta didn't comment on the pathetic state of my love life. Elizabeth had been the means to an end for her.

"It is settled, then," she said.

"How did the Fates manage to trap Hecate in the underworld?" I asked.

"None of your business," she snapped. "I wouldn't put it past you to free her just for spite."

"She can't be much worse than you three," I muttered, but Morta heard me. She looked at me with more contempt than usual, if that was even possible.

"You have no idea," she said. "Whatever you do, do not set Hecate free and fulfill the prophecy."

"I don't believe in the prophecy," I said. I folded my arms across my chest.

"Then you have nothing to fear, son of Fortuna," she replied, but she didn't seem to believe her own words.

She refused to call me Nyx. It had been her mother's name, my grandmother's, and I'd appropriated it a long time ago. I don't know why I kept using it, except it fit me now. And it pissed Morta off, which was always an added bonus.

Chapter Twelve

On Saturday, the pawnshop was full of window-shoppers who spent hours looking at the knickknacks. Talbot watched them with an eagle eye, but I was bored.

"I'm going back tonight," I said.

"I don't think that's a good idea," Talbot said.

"I don't have a choice," I said. "Deci doesn't let the Book of Fates out of her sight and Morta refuses to help me."

"But Claire's her daughter," Talbot said.

"Doesn't seem to matter right now," I said. "And if I can't get her out of Hecate's clutches on my own, my aunts will hunt Elizabeth down and hurt her. They probably already know where she is."

"Then I'm going with you," he replied.

"Talbot, haven't you noticed? People get hurt around me."

"That's life, Nyx," he said. Then he slapped his hand on his head. "I forgot. I'm supposed to go out with Naomi tonight."

"Then go," I said. I was relieved. I didn't want to have to worry about both of us getting out of there alive.

"No way," he said. "I'll make up an excuse."

The store finally emptied out about an hour before closing and Talbot flipped the sign over and locked the door.

He laughed at my surprised look. "Nepotism pays sometimes."

I parked the Caddy a block from Hell's Belles and we walked the rest of the way. We could have hoofed it, but I liked knowing I had a quick getaway if I needed it. The restaurant's sign was in sight when I realized there was a flaw in our plan.

"How are we going to get in without being noticed?" I asked. "We're walking in right in the middle of the dinner rush."

"We can't use an obscura spell this time," he said. "Too many demons around."

Unlike mortals, demons could see right through an obscura spell, which is why Talbot and I had been hiding last time we were in the basement. They weren't completely immune to magic, but it took dark magic to get a demon to do your bidding. I wasn't interested in trying.

"You're right," I said.

"Which is why I brought this," he said. He took out a map and handed it to me with a flourish. "We'll go this way instead."

There was the sound of running footsteps and then Naomi called out, "Wait up!"

"Did you tell her?" I asked him.

"Of course not," he replied.

I surveyed her. "What are you wearing?"

My cousin wore clothes similar to mine and Talbot's: jeans, sturdy hiking boots, and a heavy jacket. "It's going to be cold down there," she said.

"Down where?" Talbot couldn't pull off the innocent look.

"I know you're up to something," my cousin said. "I saw the map."

"And if we are?" My tone didn't discourage her, although that was the intent.

"I'm coming with you," she said.

Talbot and I exchanged a look, but she caught us. "I'm going and that's all there is to it. Do you think Claire will just leave with you two? She doesn't know either of you."

Naomi had a point. I had the impression that she and Claire were close. Maybe she could coax Claire out of there.

"What makes you think Claire is there willingly?" I asked.

"You don't know her," she said. "No one could stop her if she wanted to leave."

"Why do you say that?" Talbot asked.

"She's a Fate," Naomi said simply.

She had a point. "Fates aren't invincible, Naomi," I said. I regretted it as soon as her face clouded.

"What Nyx means is that we should consider all the possibilities," Talbot said. "Even the remote ones."

We huddled together to study the map.

"I think this is an alternate path to the gate," Talbot said. "This tunnel is right under Hell's Belles."

"An underground tunnel?" Naomi didn't sound thrilled.

"Claustrophobic?"

"A little," she admitted. "But I can handle it. For Claire."

"Did you remember the key?" Talbot asked me.

I snorted. "Of course." I held it up.

"Then let's go," he said.

After some searching, we finally found the entrance to the underground tunnel about a block from Hell's Belles.

Talbot strapped on a helmet with a light attached and Naomi giggled.

The entrance of the tunnel was full of beer cans, used condoms, and a horrifying smell, damp and foul, like an ogre's armpit.

"Humans are disgusting," Naomi sniffed.

"It's going to get worse," I warned her. "At least you're dressed warmly." The tunnels would be cold and damp. And that's if we were lucky. Who knew what had made a home down below or what was guarding the gate.

"There's a warren of utility tunnels all over the city," Talbot said. He led the way as we stumbled over the uneven dirt. We were heading down and it grew darker and darker, except where a dim bulb flickered, meant to show workers the way.

We walked until Talbot's light shone upon what to the average person would look like graffiti, but to those who read the ancient language it was written in, it was meant as a guide. Or as a warning.

"Not far now," Talbot said.

The air smelled stale, full of pungent odors I didn't want to try to identify. I tried to breathe through my mouth, but the air was so foul it coated my tongue. I shut my jaw, deciding that smelling the stench was better than tasting it.

Hecate was a pissed-off virgin or a wrinkled old crone, depending upon who you talked to. Which meant she was probably neither of those things.

I suspected she was a border lord, guarding the gates between this world and the underworld and destroying anyone who got in her way. Why did she have Claire? Besides the fact that she hated my aunts.

Brittle bone crunched under our feet and Naomi whimpered.

I turned on her. "This is why I told you not to come," I whispered. "Go back home where it's safe."

She was trembling, but she shook her head. "I'm coming with you."

Talbot put up a hand, signaling for silence. We listened for a moment. "Did you hear that?"

"I didn't hear anything," I said.

"Baying dogs," he said.

"I expected something to be guarding the gate," I said.

Talbot's light shone into the darkness, revealing the shadow of three canine heads.

"Cerberus," Naomi whispered.

Instead of Cerberus, Hades's three-headed dog, there were three dogs with one enormous head apiece.

"I wish," I said. "Much worse. Hecate's hounds." Her dogs were about five hundred yards away, but approaching fast. Talbot's headgear wouldn't be enough to see to fight the black dogs.

"*Fiat lux*," I said. Translation: "Let there be light." When in doubt, use the Latin.

The tunnel was lit by a bright white light. They weren't ordinary dogs. They stood almost as tall as a grown man and had muscles on their muscles. Their eyes were pale yellow and their long white fangs looked like they'd been sharpening them on the bones scattered at our feet.

The dogs, used to the dimness of the tunnels, slowed down, confused.

"Don't hurt them," Naomi cried.

"Great," I said. "I'll just pet them while they tear me to bits."

Talbot ignored us and worked on a little spell of his own. "Obey me! Heel! Sit!"

To my stunned amazement, the dogs did as he ordered and sat on their haunches. "How did you do that?"

The biggest hound snarled at the sound of my voice and Talbot held up a hand. "Stay!" he said.

He turned to me and grinned. "Command spell combined with a few things I learned from hours of watching *The Dog Whisperer*."

We walked around the dogs, who quivered when I walked by, but didn't move from their position.

The gate looked like an ordinary barricade. There was a heavy chain around a padlock that looked like something you'd pick up at the local hardware store.

I took out my athame and held it to my arm.

"Nyx, don't," Naomi said.

"You know the spirits demand blood," I said. I made a swift cut across my arm. My blood dripped to the ground as I completed the ritual.

I put the key into the lock and we stepped into another world.

Chapter Thirteen

A rough dirt path cut through a forest of ancient trees, their trunks blackened and twisted. A heavy growth of mandrake, belladonna, and dittany told me we were in Hecate's domain.

"Dark lands, under strange moons," Talbot said.

It took me a minute to place his reference. "Will you quit fuckin' quoting Tolkien and haul your ass?" I snapped.

Through the trees, I could make out the outlines of a building in the distance.

"Isn't there a saying about the road to hell and good intentions?" Talbot joked.

"I have plenty of intentions," I replied, "and none of them are good."

"You're bursting with good intentions, Nyx," he replied. "You're a good person, no matter what anyone else says."

I shrugged off his comment, uncomfortable with praise, even the backhanded sort.

"Let's head that way," I said.

But no matter how long we walked toward it, we never got

any closer. The undergrowth grew thicker and the air smelled of acid.

Naomi would stop intermittently and trace a symbol in the air with her finger.

"What are you doing?" Talbot finally asked her.

"Leaving breadcrumbs," Naomi replied. "You two want to get out of here, right?"

"Smart," I told her. "Otherwise, we might have ended up wandering around the underworld for an eternity."

"It could still happen," she replied, which didn't reassure me.

"I need a five-minute break," Talbot finally said. He was careful to check the ground before sitting on a rock, which was shaded by plants taller than our heads.

"I have a feeling someone doesn't want visitors," he said.

Something splashed on the ground near him. I looked up. The plants over our head were bucket-shaped and filled with a noxious liquid. I knew now why I'd detected the smell of acid.

"You should get up very slowly," I told Talbot.

He grinned. "You're a slave driver," he said. His smile faded when he saw my face. "What is it?"

I pointed up. "Pitcher plants full of acid."

"What do you suggest we do?"

"Run!"

Talbot moved right before the pitcher plant dumped acid, but it set off a trigger in the other plants. A splash of acid hit the leg of my jeans and ate its way into my skin.

"Are you okay?" I asked them.

"I'm fine, but there's got to be a key to get there," Naomi said. "Nyx, what about some sort of location spell?"

"It's worth a try," I said. "Why didn't I think of that?"

"I think it worked," Talbot said. "We're actually getting closer."

Naomi tried not to look smug as we walked along.

Hecate's forest made it clear she didn't welcome visitors. The path narrowed again and then forked. The one we chose was laced with enormous, sticky spiderwebs and a treacherous bog before we eventually came to an imposing structure built from shiny stone and the same black and twisted trees we'd seen earlier. It was at least seven stories high and looked like it could withstand Armageddon.

"Black as Hecate's heart," I said.

Heavy wooden doors opened into a room with gleaming white marble floors and dainty white furniture. The hall was illuminated by torchlight.

It looked as if we had interrupted a party. Four demons sat at a table playing chess, using the skulls of small birds as the pieces. A female demon with long flowing black hair played the harp while others stood conversing.

A woman sat at a throne carved of yew, flanked by two large male demons who took turns feeding her grapes from a golden bowl. Three more hounds, these the color of alabaster, sat at her feet.

"Pretty nice digs for a banished goddess," I said.

"You flatter me," the woman said. She stood, but didn't approach us. I didn't waste time with formalities. I was certain she knew who I was. Her next words confirmed it. "Why is a son of Fate in the underworld?"

"I'm Fortuna's son," I corrected. My mother had been the fourth Fate, but she wasn't anything like her sisters.

She nodded. "Which is why I allowed you to come this

far," she said. "But my curiosity does not ensure your safe passage."

Hecate was beautiful. She was tall and curvy, with a bit of a younger-Sophia-Loren thing going on. She had a Roman nose and a death stare. A fine Roman nose was a thing of beauty, but mortals with their knives and their doctors had almost obliterated the trait in the modern world.

"Where is she?" I asked.

"Why have you wandered into my domain, son of Fortuna?" Hecate asked. Her inhuman eyes glinted.

"You know why."

She made a dismissive motion and then her laser gaze focused on Naomi. "You've brought me a present."

Talbot and I both stepped in front of Naomi and our shoulders collided painfully.

Hecate snickered like a schoolgirl.

"Keep her out of it," I said. "We're here for Claire."

"Claire is here of her own volition," Hecate replied.

I snorted. "I don't believe you."

She gave me a stare that would have frightened a smarter man. "I don't care what you believe. Claire is free to leave whenever she chooses."

"I want to see her," I said.

Hecate's head whipped around and her dogs snarled, but I didn't back down. "You come here and make demands of me?"

"Please?" Naomi asked. "We just want to see her and make sure she's okay."

That wasn't what we wanted, but it would do for a start.

"One of you," Hecate finally agreed.

"I'm going," I stated.

"Not you," she replied. "The girl."

"No."

Naomi clutched my arm. "Nyx, Claire doesn't know you anyway. Let me go."

She had no idea what could happen to her. I stood my ground. "I said no, Naomi. We all go or none of us do."

"I can take care of myself," she hissed back.

"What guarantee do I have that you won't try to keep us here?" I asked Hecate. She was stuck in the underworld, but I didn't fool myself that meant she was powerless.

She grinned at me, which was more chilling than her worst glare. "I do like my pets."

"I see you have a matched set," I said. I gestured to her two blond boy toys, who looked like brothers and, judging by their enormous size, came from a long line of mutants. They also generally matched the description of the guy Claire had been seen with—tall, blond, and good-looking, but Starling had neglected to mention the demon part. She was a mortal, though. Maybe she hadn't known.

"Hroth, where are your manners?" Hecate said. "You haven't offered our guests any wine."

He brought us the wine in crystal goblets. He handed the first glass to Naomi. Before I could warn her, she brought it to her lips and drank.

Talbot took it from her before she could take more than a sip. I gave her a worried glance, but she didn't seem to be suffering from any ill effects. Talbot and I both declined the beverage anyway.

I said, "I prefer beer."

"Ain't that the truth," Talbot muttered.

One of the tall blond demons had no sense of personal space, at least not when it came to Naomi. I didn't like the way pretty boy was looking at my cousin. Then he bumped up against her and grinned lasciviously.

I shoved him hard. "If you even glance at her again, I'll carve out those blue eyes of yours."

His smile promised me pain. His fist bunched, but Hecate's stopped him midstrike. "Hroth, please remember these are our guests."

She wanted something from me or she wouldn't be telling Hroth to play nice, but what? I'd never met her before, but she was acting more like a Southern belle than an avenging goddess. I wasn't fooled.

"Speaking of pets," she said, "how are my little harpies?"

I had a feeling she already knew the answer, but I said it anyway, just to piss her off. "Not so great, last time I saw them."

I wanted to go down swinging if I was going to go down. Hecate didn't bite, though. Apparently, she wasn't ready to pick a fight.

"You ask a favor of me, son of Fortuna, and I expect one in return," she said. "I miss my harpies."

The harpies were half-woman, half-bird, and all kinds of trouble. My aunts had used them to torture me and kill those I loved, back before I realized it wasn't safe to get close to anyone. I'd killed Swift Wing, but I hadn't seen Shadow or Fleet Foot lately.

"You want me to steal from my aunts?"

"Aren't you already? Stealing a life that should have ended long ago?"

"Can we see her or not?"

"Hroth, show our guests to Lady Claire," she said.

"Not him," I insisted. "Bernie can do it."

Bernie had been trying to hide in the background, behind a

demon who looked and smelled like a trash truck, but I'd spotted her right away.

Hecate raised an eyebrow. "Bernie? Oh, you must be speaking of Bernadette. I'm afraid she has other duties." There was undisguised contempt in her tone.

Bernie flinched at the name.

Hecate snapped her finger at Hroth's twin. "Gar, show the little Fate the way."

"Show us *all* the way," I corrected.

"One or none," Hecate pronounced.

"It seems like we have no other choice," I reluctantly agreed. Naomi was pretending that she wasn't scared, but when she thought no one was looking, terror washed over her face.

Talbot leaned over and whispered something in her ear and she giggled and kissed him lingeringly. I shot him a grateful look. A scared Fate was a dangerous one, and Naomi was inexperienced. I didn't want her to do something stupid and get us all killed. Besides, stupidity was *my* specialty.

Hroth snorted in annoyance, which made me smile.

I pulled Naomi aside. "Be careful," I said. "And make it quick." I wasn't sure how long Hecate's good mood would last.

Turns out, not long. It wasn't really my fault. My nerves were shot. I felt claustrophobic underground and the smells weren't helping my mood.

Naomi had barely left the room when Hroth decided to start a pissing contest. He sidled up next to me and, careful to make sure that Hecate was out of earshot, started whispering all the nasty things he would do to my little cousin. His brother grinned evilly.

I ignored him, but unfortunately, Talbot did not. He hit

Hroth hard on the jaw, but the demon only grinned before he jumped Talbot and had him flat on the ground. Hroth was on top of Talbot's chest. Hroth's fangs came out, which did nothing for his looks, but also told me Talbot was in danger of losing a body part. I had to pull Hroth off him before the demon chewed off an ear.

The demon snapped and snarled, straining still to reach Talbot. The muscles in my arm pulled tight as I struggled to restrain Hroth.

The rest of the demon party didn't even look up, but then Hecate said something in a language I didn't understand and Hroth subsided.

I helped Talbot to his feet. "Don't ever try that again," I scolded him in a low voice. "That demon could tear off your head and not even break a sweat."

"And I will," Hroth murmured.

"Big words when your boss is out of earshot," I said.

Hecate's gaze returned to us, but before she could say anything, Gar and Naomi returned.

Naomi's long red braid was askew and her eyes held the look of someone who'd seen something that would haunt her for a long time.

"Did you see her?" I asked.

"I want to stay," she said.

"What happened?" Talbot asked.

"I'll tell you later," she replied. "I want to stay. Please let me stay!"

Talbot and I exchanged a glance. *Something in the wine*, I mouthed. He nodded to let me know he understood.

"Thank you for letting Claire see her," I said to Hecate. "We'll be back."

She smiled. "You will be most welcome," she said. "If you bring me one little present."

"Which would be?"

"My harpies."

"That's not possible," I said.

"Then I'm afraid it won't be possible for you to visit with your cousin again."

Naomi gripped my arm tightly. "Nyx," she whispered urgently, but I ignored her.

"I'll see what I can do."

My answer seemed to satisfy Hecate, at least temporarily. A crossroads bargain had been struck, which never ended well for anybody but Hecate.

Talbot picked Naomi up and sprinted for the door. It took a few seconds before the demons realized what was happening and headed after him. They tackled him and pulled on his arms and legs to try to drag him to the floor. I waded into the melee and threw a couple of demons off them. Naomi screeched and squirmed in protest, but Talbot held on to her.

The harp player tugged at Naomi to pull her from Talbot's arms. I threw my athame at the demon. The knife hit her in the neck.

"Enough!" Hecate said. "Let them go."

Talbot didn't wait for her to change her mind. He took off in a sprint. I could hear Naomi screaming as he headed back to the gate. I was seconds behind him.

I stopped to retrieve my athame and the harp player tried to bite me. I stepped on her hand and the bones crunched, which made her recede her fangs immediately.

None of the other demons were stupid enough to disobey

Hecate. My path was clear. I looked back at her as I left. She was smiling, which made me shudder with dread.

We were about five hundred yards from the gate when we heard the sound of baying hounds.

I turned and looked. Bernie was on the path, dragging something large and bloody behind her.

She looked up and saw me, then made a shooing motion. "Go, son of Fortuna. This will keep them occupied, but not for long."

Why was she helping us? I didn't wait for an explanation. We ran. We returned the way we had come, stumbling over shards of bone. Naomi's voice had grown hoarse. Finally, she went limp in his arms.

"What's wrong with her?" Talbot asked, panicked. "It was the wine, wasn't it?"

"When we're topside," I said. "Hurry." I wasn't entirely convinced Hecate wouldn't change her mind and send the demons after us. We still had the hounds to contend with, but when we reached the gate, there was no sign of them.

"What now?" Talbot asked when we finally emerged and stood blinking in the sun.

"Now we find a remedy for Naomi, ask the aunties for the harpies, and go back for Claire."

But like everything in my life, it wasn't as easy as all that.

Chapter Fourteen

The Caddy was parked a block from Hell's Belles. Talbot sat in the backseat with Naomi, who'd sunk into a stupor. He'd draped his coat over her, but she still shivered.

I broke a few speed limits as I headed back to my apartment above Eternity Road. Talbot carried Naomi up the stairs to my bedroom. He placed her on the bed and then took off her boots. "Do you have any more blankets? She's freezing."

I grabbed some blankets from the closet and put them over her.

"This is my fault," Talbot said. "It's all my fault."

"It was my idea to go to the underworld," I said.

"What are we going to do?" he asked. "She's obviously been bewitched by Hecate."

"Find that guy, the one who helped Elizabeth," I told Talbot. "I'll stay here with her."

"Do you know what to do to help her?" he asked.

"Do you?" I replied. He winced and I softened. "Look, just the sight of me makes that guy skittish for some reason. It's better if you go look for him."

He nodded. "Should we try to reverse the spell before I leave?"

"Not without researching it first," I told him. "Otherwise, we could make things worse."

He kissed Naomi on the forehead and murmured something in her ear. I looked away, unbearably sad at the sight of so much love.

"I'll be back as soon as I can. Keep her safe."

I nodded.

Ten minutes after he left, Naomi's lips turned blue and she convulsed. Her body shook so hard that the headboard nearly banged a hole in the wall.

I had to help Naomi. I didn't want to leave her, but the book I needed was in the other room.

I grabbed the book and did the healing spell quickly. I found my jacket and ripped open the lining to get to the healing amulets I'd concealed there.

Naomi stopped thrashing and for one moment, I thought it had worked. I put a hand to her forehead. She was hot—too hot.

"Damn it!" Why had I let her come with us?

A new shipment of magical items had just arrived last week. I was certain I'd seen a lodestone in there somewhere.

I ran downstairs to Eternity Road. I disabled the wards and then smashed a pane of glass to unlock the door. My knuckles were bleeding, so I grabbed a fat seventies-style tie and wrapped it around my hand.

Ambrose kept the really good stuff in a locked display case, but the key was taped underneath it. I unlocked the case. My stomach cramped when I couldn't find the lodestone, but I finally found it on the bottom shelf.

I grabbed the lodestone and a book on ancient spells and ran back to my apartment.

"Naomi, I'm back," I called out, even though I knew my cousin was beyond hearing me. I put the lodestone in her palm and folded her hand closed. "*Actus me invito factus non est meus actus,*" I said.

Her body went stiff and then she started to seize. I repeated the spell over and over.

Finally, a thin trickle of what looked like grape Kool-Aid dripped from her mouth and she stopped thrashing. I grabbed a washcloth and sponged away the vomit.

She grew so still that I put my ear to her mouth to make sure she was breathing. I was relieved when her chest rose and fell. Her skin was cold and clammy to the touch, so I piled the blankets back on her.

Two hours later, I heard my front door open. Talbot came into the bedroom.

"I found him," Talbot said. "How is she doing?"

"I don't know," I said. "Better, I think, but she's still not awake."

The scarred man came in behind Talbot, looking like he would bolt any second. He inhaled sharply and then picked up Naomi's hand.

He turned to me. "What did you do?" he asked brusquely.

"I used a lodestone. I had to break a store window to get it," I told Talbot apologetically.

"Like I care about that. You saved her."

"What else?" the scarred man interrupted.

I told him and then added, "I didn't know what else to do."

"You may have saved her life," he said. "With the wasting

sickness, it's not just that the victim doesn't eat or drink, it's that he or she can go mad within hours."

"So she's cured?" Talbot asked.

"I'm afraid not," he replied. "Nyx managed to slow the damage, but without a cure, she'll die."

"I'm not going to let that happen," I said. I would protect my cousin, no matter what the cost.

I headed for Parsi Enterprises to give Morta the good news. "We found Claire," I said. I didn't mention the bad news, which was that Naomi was going to die if I didn't do something.

Right or wrong, they'd blame me. Or worse, Talbot. I shuddered to think what they'd do to him if they knew we'd brought Naomi into harm's way.

She gazed at me with cold eyes. "Yet I do not see my daughter before me."

"She's in the underworld," I said. "With Hecate."

I thought I detected a tiny flinch at the mention of her archenemy, but it could have been the usual twitch she got from talking with me. She was probably restraining herself from trying to tear out my heart.

"And?" Morta finally said. She was showing about as much emotion as a robot.

"And Hecate wants the harpies."

"She'll free my daughter if she gets her pets back?" Morta didn't sound as if she believed it.

"That's what she said."

Morta nodded. "Very good."

"So you'll let me have the harpies?" Or at least the surviving ones. I wasn't sure that Swift Wing made it out alive after our last encounter. In fact, I was pretty sure I'd killed her.

"We don't have the harpies," she said. "We gave them to Gaston, and after his death, they did not return."

"Do you have any idea where they are?"

I doubted she would tell me, even if it would help me find her daughter, but she surprised me.

"Perhaps that human masquerading as a witch has them."

"Jenny?" Elizabeth's former roommate had a touch of magic in her and terrible taste in boyfriends, but she was the last person I expected to be harboring harpies.

Morta nodded. "Is that a problem?"

"No problem."

Jenny had made it clear the last time I saw her that she'd love to see me dead. I wasn't relishing having a chat with her.

"I'll get the harpies and trade them for Claire," I said.

"Do not fail me, son of Fortuna, or you will live to regret it," Morta said as I left.

I already did, but I made my way to the magic shop anyway.

Chapter Fifteen

Zora's was downtown, just off Nicolett. The yellow crescent moon sign above the door seemed to glow red when I looked at it, but I told myself it was just a figment of my imagination.

I wasn't expecting a welcoming committee. Elizabeth's roommate Jenny worked there most days.

I'd found my mother's ebony cat at the store, so I scanned the shelves for the missing charms. It was all stuff for the tourists: fake crystals, fringed moon-and-stars scarves, and statues made in China on an assembly line. Not anything of real magic.

They kept a few ingredients for real spells in the stockroom, but I doubted any true magician would shop there.

Jenny was helping a customer, a wild-haired girl wearing a pentagram necklace. When she noticed me, Jenny swore, reached behind the register, and drew out a wicked-looking knife. The customer made a swift exit, but Jenny didn't seem to care.

"Get out of my store before I gut you like the pig you are," she said. Jenny was openly hostile now that Elizabeth wasn't around to act as a buffer.

"Is this about Elizabeth?"

"Wherever you go, trouble follows. And you killed my boyfriend, remember?"

"Why are you mourning him?" I asked softly. "He didn't love you. He didn't love anybody." Gaston had been a waste of a heartbeat, but his girlfriend hadn't realized that.

"He loved me," she said, but there was a note of uncertainty in her voice.

"He was using you. The only thing he loved was power," I said. I didn't have time to soften the blow, so the words came out harsher than intended.

"Why should I believe you?" she replied. "You hated him."

"I did," I said. "But that doesn't mean I'm not telling you the truth."

She spat in my face.

I calmly grabbed one of her bargain bin scarves, wiped the spit off my face, and then handed it to her. "Don't do that again."

"Get out of my store!" she said.

"What do you want with the harpies?" I peered over her shoulder, but she moved to block my line of vision.

"What makes you think I have the harpies?"

"Because Gaston had them before he died," I said.

"You mean before you killed him." She still hadn't put the knife down.

"Do you have them or not?" I asked. "It's life or death."

"Yours? Then no."

"So you do know something."

She grinned, clearly delighted by what she was about to tell me. "Not about the harpies."

She was lying, but I decided to play along. "Just tell me, Jenny."

"Someone wants you dead."

This was becoming a theme. "I know," I said. "But who and why?"

She ignored my questions. "I hope he manages to do the job and kills you. Nothing would make me happier."

"Others have tried and failed," I replied. "Like Gaston." Reminding her I'd killed her ex was dicey, but maybe if I pissed her off, she'd let something slip.

"What do you want?" she spit out.

"Can't you tell me anything about a necromancer? Please?" I hated to beg, but time was running out.

She smiled. "I heard about a necromancer who doesn't like you too much."

But no matter how hard I pleaded with her, she wouldn't tell me anything else.

Jenny was enjoying toying with me, but it was a waste of time. Even if she knew anything, she wouldn't tell me. I started to leave, but then came a sound I'd heard in my nightmares many times. A harpy's song.

I pushed past Jenny into the backroom. She followed at my heels, squawking almost as loudly as the harpies.

In one corner of the back room, black draping covered something large. I was sure it was their cage, so I pulled the covering off.

"Hello, Shadow, Fleet Foot," I said. "We're going on a little trip."

They hissed something in their garbled tongue. I'm sure it was something highly complimentary, since I'd killed their sister, Swift Wing.

"You can't take them," Jenny said.

"Watch me," I said.

"I've already sold them to someone else," she admitted.

"I'll double whatever they're paying," I offered.

She was hesitant, but I could see the greed in her eyes. "Triple," I said.

"Done," she said. She held out her hand. "Where's my money?"

I paid her in the gold doubloons I'd won off a treasure hunter in tarot poker. My already stellar game-playing ability had gotten even better since I'd arrived in Minneapolis. You know what they say, though. Lucky in cards, unlucky in love.

"How am I going to manage to get them home?"

"Not my problem," Jenny snapped. "Just get them out of here before Mr.—" She started to say his name, but clearly thought better of it.

"Why would anybody want a pair of harpies?" I wondered. "They're killers."

There was no way their cage would fit in the Caddy. Besides, I'd never get the stench of harpies out of the upholstery. I ran next door to the giant hardware store and rented a pickup. I loaded the harpies into the back and headed for my apartment.

I'd only gone a few blocks when I heard a voice in my head.

"You know what you have to do," Sawyer said.

I swerved violently and nearly hit a telephone pole. "Stop doing that," I said. "You nearly killed me."

"You can talk to the dead, Nyx," he replied. "Get used to it. It's not always convenient."

"What do you want?"

"You have to resurrect Swift Wing," he repeated.

"I can't," I said. "Besides, I don't even know where the body's buried."

"Pull over here," he directed.

I pulled the truck into the parking lot of some financial group. It was late and most of the worker bees had already gone home.

I put my head on the steering wheel. Why was my dead uncle still in my head?

"Now call to her," he said.

I felt like a fool, but did as he ordered. "Here, harpy, harpy. C'mon, girl."

"Not like that," he said. "You know what to do, Nyx. Quit fighting it."

I tried again. "Swift Wing, *mortui resurgunt*!"

My stomach cramped as I said the words. I doubled over from the pain. I waited, gut clenching, as I repeated the words. The words of a necromancer.

I got out of the truck and pulled the tarp off the cage. Still no sign of Swift Wing.

"How am I supposed to get her into the cage?"

"You summoned her," Sawyer said. "She will do as you command if..."

"If what? Sawyer?" But he'd faded away.

I smelled her before I saw her. A fetid wind blew, fouling the late-spring night. Then I spotted a harpy swooping in for the kill. I ducked in the nick of time, but her hot breath fanned my face.

Harpy claws could shred through steel like it was paper, but the cage was made of bespelled silver and would contain them long enough to deliver them to Hecate.

At least I hoped it would.

Swift Wing had spent hundreds of years hunting me, carrying out the Fates' torture as they decreed. Plus, I'd killed her, which should be enough to piss anybody off.

She dive-bombed me repeatedly, but I ducked every time. Her claws caught purchase in my hair and she dug into my scalp. I threw a spell her way, which shocked her like a joy buzzer and she released her grip.

She was slightly worse for wear, missing the eye I'd stabbed, and reeking of a foul odor even more noxious than usual. But the gleam in her one good eye let me know that her desire to rip out my heart was alive and well.

I tried to think of a spell, but I was too busy trying to protect my eyes from being gouged out.

Hecate had asked me to bring her all three of the harpies. She didn't mention what condition the last one had to be in. I knew a loophole when I saw one.

I needed some bait to capture her. Harpies were garbage eaters. They'd eat anything they could get their claws into, but they loved the taste of rotting flesh more than anything. In a pinch, fresh blood would do.

I grasped my athame and slid the blade across my forearm. "Lunchtime," I shouted. Then it occurred to me. I had one of the ingredients to cook up a batch of dark magic: blood. I needed the words and quickly. Swift Wing was in a dive, heading straight for my blood splattering on the ground. She was almost on me and I didn't think her appetite would be satiated by a few drops of blood.

Her claws came out. I ducked, but not before they raked across my arm, opening the wound so she could get more blood. Greedy thing.

"I command thee, Swift Wing, to do my bidding."

She looked at the blood longingly, but bowed her head in submission.

"Get in the cage," I ordered. Shadow and Fleet Foot were so happy to see their sister that they didn't even try to escape, but as soon as Swift Wing saw the cage close around her, her razor-sharp claws extended and she kicked the side of the cage over and over.

I covered them with the tarp and then leaned against the cab, woozy from loss of blood. I managed a quick healing spell, which stopped the bleeding, but I'd need the amulets sewn in my jacket to mend the gash in my arm from Swift Wing.

I made it back to my apartment without incident. I parked the rental in the alley behind the store and put a very nasty ward on it.

Talbot was sitting by Naomi's bedside, reading to her.

"Any change?" I asked him.

He shook his head. "Did you get them?"

"Yes," I said. I had the harpies, but I would need help if I wanted to get out of the underworld alive. I trusted Talbot to have my back, but he had Naomi to worry about.

"That's good news," he said. But we both knew it wasn't, not really. Hecate was going to double-cross us. I might not make it out of the underworld.

"I need to take them back to Hecate tonight."

"I'm in," he said.

"You can't leave Naomi," I said.

"I'll stay with her," the scarred man offered. I hadn't even noticed he was sitting in a folding chair just beyond the reading lamp's glow.

"Excuse us a moment," I said. Talbot and I stepped into the other room.

"We can't leave her alone with him, Talbot," I said. "I'll have to go alone."

"How are you going to get the harpies through the tunnels on your own?" he said. "We don't have a choice. We have to trust him."

"Do you even know his name?"

The scarred man appeared in the doorway. "Everyone calls me Doc."

I decided to be straight with him. "We're not sure we can trust you alone with Naomi, but we don't have many options. But if you even think about hurting her, I'll take great pleasure in taking you apart piece by piece. And if I can't manage it, the Fates will."

"I swear to you I would never harm your cousin," he said. He met my eyes. There was some emotion in there that I couldn't define, but it was enough that I believed him.

"We'll be back as soon as we can," I said. "And thank you."

I thought he said, "It's the least I can do," but he said it so softly that I wasn't sure I'd heard right.

Chapter Sixteen

In the alley behind the store, I made sure the cheap tarp concealing the harpies was still securely fastened and then started the truck.

"God, they stink," Talbot said as he got in on the passenger side.

"I can't wait to be rid of them. Shadow tries to take a bite out of me every chance she gets."

"We have a problem," Talbot said. "The harpies won't fit down the tunnels in the cage, and there's no way we can control them otherwise."

"We're not taking them through the tunnels," I said. "We're using the altar and Bernie's going to help us, whether she wants to or not."

I planned to check in with Bernie anyway. She'd saved our asses in the underworld, but she was one of Hecate's acolytes. She had some explaining to do.

Hell's Belles was packed with a bunch of late-night partiers, including drunk House of Zeus mages who downed omelets and strong coffee. They were clearly on the tail end of a bachelor party and wore gaudy T-shirts with WIZARDS DO IT WITH BIGGER WANDS emblazoned on the front. I recognized Sean Danvers and Baxter and gave them a short nod.

"Wonder who is getting married," Talbot said.

"I'm wondering what House of Zeus mages are doing hanging out with someone from the House of Hades."

He looked over at the partiers. "I recognize some of those guys. They'd go to a hanging if they thought there was free booze involved."

"What about Baxter?"

"Baxter? I've never seen him at any social event."

"Maybe he's the groom," I commented.

"Who'd marry him?"

"Good question."

We found seats at the counter. I looked for Bernie's stocky form, but I didn't spot her.

Finally, a server came to take our order. I waved the menus away.

"Where's Bernie?" I asked.

"Downstairs," he replied shortly.

"Get her for me," I ordered.

"I'm not going down there," he replied. That's when I realized he meant she was in the underworld.

"Why would she be stupid enough to go back? Hecate's pissed," I muttered, but the server overheard.

He scowled. "Same reason she was stupid enough to help you."

"What do you mean?"

He studied us and then seemed to make up his mind about something. "Bernie works for your aunts," he said in a hushed tone. "They own this building. Hell, they own Bernie, or at least that's what it seems like to me. She does whatever they tell her to do."

If Bernie was the Fates' spy, why hadn't she told them where Claire was? Another thought struck me. What if Bernie had told them and the Fates had known where Claire was the entire time?

"Then you won't mind if we use the altar," I said. "Fates business."

He shrugged, which was close enough to permission for me.

We carried the cage through the back, ignoring the surprised comments from the graveyard shift. One of the cooks looked like he might stop us, but Talbot's eyes went silverlight and the guy returned his attention to the grill.

The basement altar was deserted.

"Set it down," I said. The corner of the cage landed on my finger and I swore.

I tried to repeat what Bernie had chanted, but the entrance remained stubbornly closed. "Open up, damn it!" I kicked the altar and the goblet full of demon blood shifted precariously.

"Blood. I forgot about the blood." I made a swift cut across my arm and blood dripped into the bowl.

The altar disappeared and we were at the gate. "That's handy," Talbot said.

"Why take the long way when you can take the hell express?"

I took the key from around my neck and unlocked the padlock. There was no sign of Hecate's dogs.

We dragged the harpies' cage along the same path as before, but it had narrowed since our last visit. The black and twisted trees pressed close to us and the wind whipped through the branches, sounding like someone howling in pain. We were in the underworld, so it was possible it wasn't just a trick of my imagination.

I set the cage down with a thud, breathing hard. "Let's take five."

I spotted a patch of wolfsbane a few feet from the path. I cut a piece off of the tarp and wrapped it around my hand. Wolfsbane was easily absorbed into the skin. One touch of the stuff and I'd be praying for death.

I grabbed a handful and wrapped it in the cloth before putting it in my jacket pocket. My fingers brushed against a piece of paper. Alex's thank-you note. I'd completely forgotten about it. I'd read it once I was safely out of the underworld.

"What's that for?" Talbot asked.

"Might come in handy."

A thick branch flew off and nearly hit me on the head.

Fleet Foot gave a screech of delight.

"Let's get going. I get the feeling Hecate's in a bad mood," I commented.

Talbot said, "You're always on somebody's shit list."

"Soon there won't be a House left that doesn't want to kill me," I admitted cheerfully. "Too bad they can't."

"Don't joke about it."

"C'mon, Talbot, you know I can't be killed," I said. "Even if I want to be." I had spent the last fifty years yearning for death, but things changed when I came to Minneapolis.

He tugged on the chain we were using to drag the harpies' cage along the uneven ground. Shadow started to chirp as soon as she caught sight of Hecate's castle.

"Someone's happy to be home," Talbot commented.

"She just smells rotting flesh," I said. "Hecate has an endless supply."

"So it's just cupboard love," he replied. "I'm disappointed."

"These harpies are heavy," I commented.

"So?"

"They're well fed. I wonder who has been supplying Jenny with their food?" Rotting human flesh wasn't impossible to get, but it wasn't easy, either. Harpies would eat other mammals in the food chain, but it took a hunk of man to keep them happy.

We finally made it to Hecate's castle, out of breath and sweaty. The cage scraped the polished marble floors as we went, but I didn't really care.

Hecate was alone in her banquet hall, except for the gargantuan Hroth. Or maybe it was Gar.

Time was different in the underworld, but from the looks of it, we'd interrupted her breakfast. I didn't want to examine the contents of her coffee mug too closely. I highly doubted that it contained coffee. It was thick and black, but it smelled more like boiled demon's blood than a cuppa joe.

"I'm surprised you dared to show your face here, son of Fortuna," she said. "You took something of mine."

"Naomi is a person, not a thing," Talbot objected. "If she belongs to anyone, it's the House of Fates, not to you."

"You're not helping," I hissed. I motioned at him to shut up and fortunately, he did.

"I thought we were pals," I said to Hecate. "Look, I even brought you a present."

"That is why you and your friend are still breathing," she said. "Or, more accurately, since you can't die, why you aren't screaming already."

"But I did bring you the harpies," I said. I threw off the tarp to reveal three beaming harpies. Their smiles scared me more than their snarls ever had.

"And?"

"And I need a favor."

"You are in no position to ask a boon." She tried the lock, but it didn't give.

She raised her eyebrow.

"I'm not stupid enough to let those things loose when I'm in the room," I said. "They've been hunting me since childhood." I'd spelled the lock. She'd figure it out eventually, but I hoped to be long gone by then.

Talbot rubbed his cheek, touching the scar he'd received from Swift Wing right before I killed her.

She smiled. "Of course."

"I kept my part of the bargain." I didn't know why I was so surprised she was screwing me over, but surprise didn't mean I was completely ill prepared. I'd done some research since the last time I'd been to the underworld.

"And I am allowing you to continue to live," she said. "You may be a little worse for the wear when Hroth is done with you. Consider it a warning not to enter my domain again."

Hroth smiled at me, clearly pleased with the idea of beating me to a bloody pulp.

I smiled back. I was going to enjoy wiping the floor with his smile. Before I could react, he hit Talbot, hard, on the jaw and Talbot crumbled to the floor. "She didn't say anything about your friend's survival." He jumped on Talbot and began methodically pounding his face until it was bloody. He wasn't going to stop until I made him.

"You're going to regret that." I took out my athame, which I'd concealed with a spell in the inside pocket of my jacket.

Hroth snorted, but he stopped wailing on Talbot. "C'mon, pretty boy."

Hecate had already lost interest and had walked away. Her back was to us when I made my move.

"The sight of blood usually makes me queasy," I said conversationally. "But this time, I need yours." With a quick motion, I slit his throat and grabbed one of Hecate's breakfast dishes to hold the blood. Demon blood was black and thick like used motor oil, and chunky. I fought the bile that rose in my throat. I needed to finish the spell before Hecate realized what was happening or we wouldn't make it out of the underworld alive.

Hecate raised her hand to strike, but I blew the wolfsbane into her face. The surprise on her face told me she hadn't thought anyone would dare use her own poisons against her.

But the poison alone wasn't enough to stop Hecate for long, which is why I needed Hroth's blood donation.

"*Da Deus fortunae*," I said. I wasn't completely sure the spell had taken, but I was out of time.

I hauled Talbot to his feet. "Wake up, damn it."

A few seconds later, he stirred and put a hand to his head. "What happened?"

He looked around and saw Hroth dead at our feet, Hecate still as a statue. "You've been busy," he said wryly.

"Yeah, well, I didn't have much choice. You didn't warn me that you had a glass jaw," I said. "Besides, I needed a little demon blood, and his was as good as any."

He looked at my hands, which were still stained black with demon blood. "What for?"

"A spell," I said. "I don't have time to explain. We've got to get Claire and get out of here."

I took a few precious seconds to sprinkle salt on the doorway. Hecate couldn't follow us topside, but I didn't want her minions chasing us, either. It wouldn't last, but it would buy us some time.

"What else you got in that jacket?" Talbot asked.

I grinned at him, but it faded with his next words.

"What about an antidote for Naomi?"

"We'll grab a carafe of the wine," I said. "Maybe that will work." It was our only shot. We were out of time.

He swayed but managed to stay on his feet.

"Need me to carry you?"

"I can walk on my own," he said.

"Good," I said. "But can you run?"

I grabbed the wine and took off. He followed me down the hall. There were demons frozen in place all along our path.

Naomi had given me fairly accurate directions to Claire's chamber.

At first glance, Claire looked nothing like the sunny blonde in her picture. The golden streaks in her hair had faded without the daylight. It was longer, but a dull beige. Her face was drawn and thin. She wore an acolyte robe that looked like it was almost too heavy for her to wear.

Claire wasn't alone. There was another girl in the room. She was a few years older than Naomi, but I could see the resemblance. Her hair was brown with red highlights. Her eyes were cat-shaped like Hecate's, but were golden brown, like amber honey.

Claire looked up calmly. "Wren, get the guards," she said to the other girl. The name suited her. Her gaze was quick and curious, like a bird's.

"You're coming with us," I said. "Your mommy misses you."

"I'm not going with you. And Morta doesn't miss anyone."

"You can deal with your mommy issues later. She's going to do something very nasty to someone I care about if I don't deliver you, so you're coming whether you want to or not. Besides, I had to kill someone to get you out of here. Don't make me do it again."

Talbot hoisted Claire over his shoulder and she started to scream.

I wheeled around and clapped a hand over Wren's mouth.

"Talbot, can you manage a silencing spell for Claire?"

He looked offended. "I looked it up after the last time with Naomi." Seconds later, Claire's muffled noises of outrage had ceased, silenced by Talbot's magic.

Wren mumbled something through my hand. "Don't scream," I said. I took my hand away from her mouth. "What is it?"

"Take me with you," she begged.

"No way," I said. "Your mother would raise all sorts of hell."

"I can help her," she said. "My sister is going to die unless you take me with you. She has been given the wasting sickness. Or would you rather bring her back to the underworld?"

"You knew Naomi was your sister?"

"The second I laid eyes on her," Wren said. She held out her hand. There were two wrinkly grapes resting in her palm. "This is the only thing that will help Claire and Naomi."

"The wine won't work?"

She shook her head.

"There are only two grapes," I said. "What about you?"

"I won't need it," she said.

"We don't have much time," Talbot warned, but I still hesitated.

"I don't need it," she said. "I convinced Mother I was allergic." I wanted to know more, but Talbot was right. We were out of time.

"We have to take her," Talbot said. "Naomi's life is in danger. If you won't do it, I will."

"Don't be an idiot," I told him. "Of course we have to bring her along."

Even when our lives were in danger, I couldn't help but notice that Naomi's sister was gorgeous. "Wren, don't lose those raisins."

"I will guard them zealously," she promised.

I set down the wine. I wanted to throw it against the wall but resisted the temptation. I needed both hands free to protect Wren, who had suddenly become precious to me, since she held the lives of my cousins in her hands.

We were almost at the gate when I heard Hecate's shriek of outrage, and then a stream of extremely specific and violent orders.

Claire cocked her head to listen, a tiny smile on her lips. "She's going to kill you."

My cousin was a bitch.

"That spell didn't last long," Talbot said. He sounded vexed.

"It did the trick," I assured him. I twisted the key in the lock, but it wouldn't give.

"Let me try," Talbot said. He set Claire down and I grabbed hold of her wrist.

"Naomi said you were shy," I said to Claire. "You have her fooled, don't you?"

"Naomi?" I'd finally surprised her.

"She actually seems to miss you," I replied. "Can't think why."

"A loser like you wouldn't know anything about family, would you?" She sneered.

She'd taken an immediate dislike to me and the feeling was mutual. She didn't know who I was, though, so I didn't point out I'd learned all I needed when the Fates killed my mother, their own sister. So much for family.

"We have about five seconds before a whole herd of demons are going to catch up to us," I said. "So haul your ass, Talbot."

The gate finally opened and we staggered out into the dawn. It had seemed like we'd been in the underworld only minutes, but it had been dark when we'd gone down.

Claire and Wren held up hands to shield their eyes and I cursed myself for not remembering to bring along some extra shades.

"Get them to the truck," I said to Talbot. I tossed him the keys to the rental and then got out my athame. "If I'm not there in five minutes, go without me."

Hecate couldn't go topside, but her demons could. A demon had managed to catch up with us. It was the harp player and she was holding a grudge, along with a very large cudgel.

I didn't have time to play around, especially with a cudgel headed my way. I ducked under her swinging arm and then slit her throat in one quick motion. I was already running for the truck by the time she dropped to the ground.

Talbot had the truck running. "Everything okay?"

I joined them in the cab. It was a tight fit with all four of us in the front. "Drive," I said.

He peeled out and Wren slid into me as we rounded a corner. I felt a jolt of lust as her hip touched mine. She looked at me and then looked away. She held up her hand to shield her eyes from the light. "It's so bright."

Claire was on the other side of Wren, but my cousin had fallen into the same stupor as Naomi. She'd stopped struggling and had lapsed into a sweaty silence, even though the silencing spell had worn off.

Morta would flay me alive if something happened to her daughter, but Talbot would never forgive me if something happened to Naomi. I wouldn't forgive myself.

"Are you sure those shriveled grapes are going to work?" I asked.

Wren put a hand on my arm. "I know you're worried," she said. "But it'll work. Trust me."

"It had better," I said under my breath.

Talbot parked the truck, but nobody made a move to get out for a second. "Do you think we were followed?" he finally asked.

"No," I said. "Let's get that remedy to Naomi."

Talbot escorted Claire, while I took Wren's hand to guide her. The pale sunlight was nearly blinding them.

"Wait a second," I said. I went around to the front passenger seat, fished a pair of sunglasses out of the glove compartment, and slid them onto her face. "These will help."

Upstairs, Doc paced. "What took you so long?" he asked.

"Hauling three nasty harpies took longer than expected," I explained. "And then Hecate screwed me over."

"Predictable," he muttered. "What are we going to do now?"

"Fortunately, Hecate wasn't our only option."

Wren held up the grapes for his inspection. He nodded. "Good. Very good."

He held out his hand and after a small hesitation, Wren gave him the shriveled grapes.

He strode into the bedroom, and Talbot and I trailed behind.

Naomi's face was covered in green blotches. Talbot propped her up on the pillows and opened Naomi's jaw with gentle fingers, but Naomi resisted and slid back down. "She has to swallow it."

Naomi resisted until Talbot took over. "Let me," he said. He helped her back into a sitting position and murmured something in her ear. He put the grape on her tongue and coaxed her into swallowing.

"Now what?" I asked.

"Now we wait," Doc replied. "Where is the other patient?"

I'd nearly forgotten her, but she was in the living room with Wren. Claire was lying on the couch, covered in sweat.

"The remedy should be quicker for her, right?" I asked. "Since she hasn't been topside as long?"

"Not necessarily," Doc replied. "She was in the underworld much longer and may have drunk a lot more of the wine. Naomi had only a sip."

I hoped the cure worked quickly. He forced the grape into Claire's mouth, but she fought him. Wren said something in another language and Claire swallowed it obediently.

I went back to my bedroom to check on Naomi.

"How's she doing?"

"Better," Talbot said. "The spots are nearly gone."

"We need to get her back home as soon as possible," I said. It was a miracle that my aunts hadn't already come looking for Naomi.

To my surprise, Talbot blushed. "We have a little time," he said. He cleared his throat. "Naomi has been…sleeping over a lot. Her mom probably thinks she's with me."

"Has there been any sleeping involved?" I asked. "No, wait, don't answer that. I don't want to know. As far as I'm concerned, you guys have good old-fashioned slumber parties, in separate sleeping bags."

"Why are you two discussing my sex life?" Naomi asked sleepily. She opened her eyes all the way and added, "And why am I in Nyx's bed?"

"Don't you remember?" Talbot asked.

"I remember following you guys to the diner," she said. "And that's it."

"You drank something in the underworld and we had to drag you out of there. Then we went back for the cure."

Her mouth fell open. "You're kidding me." She looked me up and down but didn't comment on my bloodstained hands. "What about Claire?"

"She's in the other room," I said.

"I want to see her," she said. She started to get out of bed, but Talbot put a hand on her shoulder.

"Wait a few minutes, babe," he said. "She's…recuperating."

"What aren't you telling me?"

"We don't know if the remedy will work for Claire," Talbot said. "She was in the underworld a lot longer."

"And she may have chugged a gallon of the stuff," I said. "You only had a sip."

There was a shriek from the other room and then a thump as something or someone hit the floor.

Chapter Seventeen

"Stay here!" I told Talbot. I raced into the living room. Claire was lying on the floor, Doc beside her. Wren stood over them, staring down at Claire as she thrashed.

"She's fine," Wren said. "She's fine. It's only the antidote taking effect."

Claire's thrashing stopped. She lay there on my floor, limp and white.

Doc felt her pulse. "Her pulse is steady and her breathing is normal, but she just had a seizure."

"From the wine or the cure?" I asked.

"Could be either, or both. Or something else entirely." He grabbed a pillow from the couch and put it under her head. "I don't want to move her yet."

I couldn't look away, couldn't move. Naomi's fate was riding on the success of Wren's antidote.

"Help me up," Claire finally said weakly.

"You're awake," Wren said. She gave her a hand and pulled her to her feet. She steadied Claire as she whispered something in her ear.

"Claire, it's really you!" Naomi said. She stood in the doorway, supported by Talbot.

"I thought I told you two to stay in the bedroom," I said.

"You try telling a Fate what to do," Talbot said.

Naomi flew over and hugged her cousin. "Everyone was so worried about you," she said. "Especially your mom."

"I'm taking you home," I said. The sooner Claire was reunited with the Fates, the sooner Elizabeth would be free. I didn't kid myself that the aunts weren't trying their damnedest to find where my ex-girlfriend was hiding. But maybe Claire's return would make them lose interest.

"Doc, thanks for everything," Talbot said. "I don't know what we'd have done without you."

Doc shifted uneasily on his feet. "I almost forgot," he said. He fished in his voluminous trench coat and brought out a book. "I believe you were reading this?"

He handed it to me. It was the loosely veiled story of my family, the one Ambrose and another man had written. It had disappeared from my apartment before I'd finished reading it.

"Did you take this from my apartment?"

He nodded.

"Why?"

"I wasn't ready for you to read it," he said. "But now I am."

"You were the other man," I said. "Did you get that in the duel?" I gestured toward his face.

"The duel never happened," he said. "Your mother stopped it. It's in the book."

"Can I ask you something?"

"You can ask," he said. "Doesn't mean I'll answer."

"What happened to your face?"

He studied my face for a long moment. "I dallied with two

women. I loved only one of them. The other one did this." He tapped the ruined side of his face.

"Your taste in women is as good as mine," I said dryly.

For some reason, the comment seemed to agitate him. "I've got to go."

I had many more questions for him, but he looked ready to bolt any second. Maybe in time, I could get him to trust me.

I gave him all the cash I had. He didn't want to take it, but I insisted. "Get a hot meal, maybe a hotel room for the week," I said.

He finally took the money. "Take care of yourself, my boy," he said.

"I wonder what his story is," Talbot said, after Doc left. "Dad won't say."

I was curious about the scarred man, too, but my first priority was Claire's safe return to the chilly bosom of her family.

I started the Caddy and broke a few speed limits to get to the Polydoros house.

I rang the doorbell. I was relieved that nobody answered. "Why are you ringing the doorbell?" Naomi asked. She gave me a little shove. "I have a key, you know."

I was checking to see if Nona was home. "Your mom's not here."

"She's probably at the office," Naomi replied.

"Good," I said. "Let's help Claire out of the car."

She ran to the Caddy and peered into the backseat. "Ready to go home? I'll fix you all something to eat. You look like you could use a good meal. And you can borrow some of my clothes. Mom would freak if she saw you in that robe."

Claire seemed overwhelmed at Naomi's volley of conversation. She held up her hand to shield her eyes as Naomi helped her out of the car. "You can borrow a pair of my sunglasses, too," Naomi chirped.

Claire wore a red robe similar to Wren's, but Claire's was embroidered with the symbols of the Tria Prima instead of silver keys.

"I'll leave you to it, then," I said. I needed to get Wren stashed somewhere before Aunt Nona came home.

"No, Nyx, you come, too," Naomi said. "And Talbot and your friend."

We followed her into the kitchen. "Naomi, I don't have a lot of time." I needed to get Wren out of there before Nona came home.

"Nonsense," she said. "It's time you get to know your cousin."

"Cousin?" Claire asked. "You mean he's..."

"The son of Fortuna," Naomi finished for her. "Yes."

"The Fates know this and he's still alive?" Claire was trying to hide her contempt for me, but she wasn't succeeding.

I grinned at her. "I even work at Parsi Enterprises." It was an overstatement. I showed up occasionally.

"The aunts have gotten soft during my absence," she said.

"Yeah, about that," I said. "Why did you go down under in the first place?"

That shut her up.

"Nyx, quit grilling Claire," Naomi said. "She just got home."

Naomi bustled around the kitchen. She was practically skipping with glee, which almost made it worth it.

It wasn't over, not when I had Hecate's daughter. Claire seemed to read my mind.

"I can't believe you two geniuses took Wren," she said.

"She wanted to get out of there," I said.

"What are you going to do with her?"

"You can't tell your mom," I said. "Or the other aunties."

"I'm not stupid," Claire replied. "One look at her and they'd know."

"Know what?" Naomi asked. She didn't seem to notice how much Wren resembled her.

Claire and I exchanged a look. "That she's Hecate's daughter," Claire answered. The real problem was that even a casual observer would assume they were sisters.

"Wren will have to stay with you," Talbot told me.

"What am I supposed to do with her?" But my traitorous libido supplied me with a few ideas, which I quickly squelched.

Talbot gave me a stern look. "Whatever you do, Nyx, don't touch her," he warned. "But she can't stay here."

"You act like I don't have any control," I said. He gave me another look.

"All right, all right. I'll take her to my place, but we've got to figure something else out long-term," I said. I'd have to try an occulo spell on my own. I'd used one to hide my identity when I first arrived in Minneapolis. I'd purchased it, but I might be able to replicate one for Wren. She looked too much like Sawyer.

I couldn't be sure what Nona would do if faced with her dead husband's child, the one he conceived with her mortal enemy. Nona had always seemed like the most reasonable of the three Fates, but finding out about a secret love child would be enough to set anyone off.

Chapter Eighteen

Back at my apartment, I collapsed on the couch. Wren watched me from a chair. I felt drained, but as I lay there, some of the tension I'd carried since the fire disappeared. I'd kept my side of the bargain and now Elizabeth was safe.

"Give me a minute," I said. I intended to close my eyes for a second. Hours later, I woke up with a growling stomach and an aching feeling I'd forgotten something.

"Wren?" I'd left her to her own devices in a strange place. Not the best host.

She was curled up in the chair, sound asleep, but woke immediately when I said her name.

I fixed Wren something to eat, which I carried from my tiny kitchen into the living room.

"It's just PB&J," I said. I watched her as she examined the sandwich. I missed having someone to take care of.

"PB&J?"

"Peanut-butter-and-jelly sandwich," I explained. "You've never had one?"

She shook her head. "Sounds…delicious."

She'd never had a peanut-butter-and-jelly sandwich, an American staple. It brought home that although we were both from magical Houses, her upbringing in the underworld had been very different from mine.

"Want a beer?" I asked.

She wrinkled her nose. "No, thank you," she said politely.

"I don't have any wine," I said, trying to make a joke.

"Trying to keep me here?" she tried to joke back, but the exchange was an awkward one. Wren and I stared at the walls and then each other. I wondered what it was like for her to be topside, out in the bright sunlight for the first time. She had helped us escape with Claire, but I wasn't sure why.

She sat next to me on the sofa, even though a comfy chair was an option. Her thigh touched mine and I scooted away.

"So can I ask you something?"

She nodded.

"Why are the symbols on your robe different from Claire's?"

She hesitated. "I stole that robe from the wash days before we left. The key is worn by the lowliest acolyte."

"What about the Tria Prima symbols?"

"Only Hecate's inner circle may wear the Tria Prima robes," she said.

"Claire was part of your mother's inner circle?" The information surprised me. The Fates and Hecate were mortal enemies. I hadn't considered that Claire might have been in the underworld willingly.

"Claire and I are very close," she said. "She's like a sister to me."

Her word choice made me squirm. If Nona found out I had Hecate's daughter, she'd rip Wren to shreds. I'd been desperate to save Naomi, but now that she was cured, I had a whole new set of problems. How was I going to keep Wren away from the Fates and her own mother?

Wren reached for the sandwich and I jumped. She gave me an amused look before she took a bite of the sandwich I'd prepared.

"How is it?" I asked.

"Delicious," she lied. She chewed gingerly for a moment and then put the sandwich down. "I guess I'm not very hungry."

"I'll go grocery shopping in the morning," I said.

"Maybe I'll have some beer," she said.

I started to get up.

"No, stay," she said. "I'll just have a sip of yours." I watched her mouth as it touched the place where mine had been only moments before and blood left my brain and headed straight to another part of my body.

Getting a stiffy from watching her lips meant it had been way too long since I'd had sex.

I realized alone time with Wren was a very bad idea. "I'm going to take a shower." I needed to think, and besides, I was covered in dried demon blood.

"Want company?"

I didn't know how to answer. My throat went dry as images of Wren and me wrapped in a steamy embrace entered my head. I shook my head and then changed the subject.

"Why did you want to leave the underworld? Leave your mother?" Granted, it was a strange world, but it had been the only one she'd ever known.

"Before, it was because I wanted to meet my father," she said. "I was topside one other time, just for a day or two. I saw him then."

"You didn't talk to Sawyer?"

She shook her head. "Naomi must have been around fourteen. She was with him. I realized he already had a daughter."

"He would have welcomed another one," I said.

"Maybe," she said. "But one of Mother's demons found me before I had the chance to find out. What was he like?" she asked.

"He was a nice guy," I said. "Even though he was a necromancer."

"The two aren't mutually exclusive," she replied.

I raised a skeptical eyebrow. "Dark magic and nice don't usually mix."

She yawned. I watched her mouth move and thought about all the ways I would like to kiss her.

"You can have the bedroom," I told her.

"Where will you sleep?"

"The couch is pretty comfortable." I lied.

"Good night, then."

"Night."

But she still stood there like she wanted to say something.

"Wren, do you need something?"

She bit her lip. "I've lived among mortals before," she finally said.

I was missing something. "And?"

"It went badly."

"How badly?"

"I am the daughter of a goddess," she said, as if I needed to be reminded. "I am not always able to control my powers."

I nodded to let her know I understood, but my mind reeled as I thought about the implication of her statement. The daughter of a goddess and a necromancer, who didn't know how to use her own gifts? That spelled danger of epic proportions.

"We'll work on it," I said. "I'm sure Ambrose has a book somewhere."

"Ambrose?"

"Talbot's dad," I explained. "He owns Eternity Road, the shop below us."

After she went to bed, I took off my shirt, which made my charms clack together.

I usually slept in the nude, but it wasn't a good idea. Not with a gorgeous woman in the other room. I didn't trust her, but I had a very bad feeling that I couldn't resist her. At least not for long.

I downed five beers before the couch was anywhere near comfy enough to sleep on.

Wren's bloodcurdling scream woke me from a dreamless sleep. I bolted to the bedroom, athame in hand, but there was no one in the room except Wren. She was sitting up, rigid with fear, still screaming.

"Wren, are you okay?"

Her eyes were wide open, but she wasn't responding. I touched her shoulder gently. "It was just a dream."

Her eyes gradually came into focus. "Not a dream," she said. "A wraith. Here in the room." The mention of a wraith sent my scabby scar throbbing in remembrance.

"There's nothing here," I soothed. "You were dreaming." She clung to me. She was cold with dread.

"I wasn't dreaming," she insisted. "I woke up thirsty, so I reached over to get a drink of water. I felt it. It was in the room with me."

"It's not here now," I said. It was possible that a wraith had been there, but if so, where had it gone? Why hadn't it attacked?

"Stay with me," she said. "I won't be able to sleep otherwise."

I slid under the covers and tried to make sure I kept a safe distance between us. She finally fell asleep, but I couldn't close my eyes.

It wasn't easy to call up a wraith, but a skilled necromancer could do it. Who in Minneapolis hated me? That list was a long one, with my aunts at the top, but if I factored in the ability to command a wraith, it became a very short list.

Wren let out a little snore, which I thought was unbearably cute. I watched her until my eyes finally drifted closed.

She was still sleeping when I woke up the next morning. Our bodies had managed to tangle together somehow during the night. Her head was snuggled into my shoulder and I had my arms around her.

Her curly hair fanned out on my pillow. She'd kicked off the covers, and the nightgown she'd borrowed from Naomi had ridden up to reveal a smooth expanse of leg.

I tried to ease away quietly, but she yawned and stretched. "Nyx?"

"Sorry, I didn't mean to wake you," I said. I noticed her eyes on my bare chest. She put a tentative finger out. I steeled myself to resist, but she only hooked a finger under the silver chain I always wore and sent the charms tinkling.

"Where did you get these?" she asked. This time, her hand wandered down my chest. Her touch sizzled my skin and I had an immediate reaction.

Her cheeks flushed and she moved infinitesimally closer to me.

I cleared my throat. "Are you hungry?" I set her away from me gently and crossed to the dresser, which I hoped would give me time to control my raging libido. She wanted me. Elizabeth didn't. Even though Wren's ardency was suspect, it was a balm to my wounded ego.

I grabbed a tee and put it on. "I'm going to check on things." If there were wraiths waiting for us in the kitchen, I didn't want Wren to see.

"It was time for me to get out of bed anyway," she replied. She stretched and the nightgown rode higher. I looked away.

"I thought I'd run to the diner and get us breakfast," I said. "There's not much food in my fridge right now."

"Can I come with you?"

"I don't think that's a good idea."

"So I've merely exchanged prisons?"

I hated the thought of being anything like her mother. "It's not that," I said. "You don't have any clothes."

"I have to go out eventually," she said.

I gave in. "We can buy something for you to wear at Eternity Road."

She'd been wearing the red robes of a Hecate acolyte when I'd snatched her. Parading Wren around in that outfit would just be rubbing Hecate's nose in it, and she was already pissed enough.

She nodded. "Then I'd love some breakfast. And coffee," she said. "It's been a long time since I've had a decent cup of coffee."

"Before we leave, I need to try a spell on you," I said. I explained the basics of the occulo spell and she agreed.

I managed to duplicate the occulo spell. It wasn't as good as the one I'd purchased or as strong, but it would mask Wren's resemblance to Naomi, at least for a few weeks. We'd have to figure out a more permanent solution eventually.

The store was already open and Ambrose barely raised an eyebrow when we came in. "Ambrose, this is Wren. Ambrose Bardoff is the owner of Eternity Road."

"Wren?" he repeated. "Where have I heard that name before?"

I tried to look innocent. "She needs something a little less noticeable." I gestured to the red robe she wore, which was embroidered with silver keys. Any sorcerer worth his salt would know she was Hecate's.

"I see." There was a long pause from Ambrose. Then he added, "We got some vintage stuff in yesterday. It might fit her."

I pointed Wren in the right direction and then went back to fill Ambrose in.

Even tacky seventies polyester couldn't hide Wren's hotness. She posed next to a vase filled with feathers.

She plucked an ancient peacock feather from its resting place and brushed it against my cheek, then held it there. "Peacock blue," she said. "That's the exact color of your eyes."

The touch of the feather sent me somewhere else, under a hot India sun. I heard the screech of the peacocks and felt the sun blazing on my face. My head spun. I reached out a hand to steady myself and felt something smooth beneath my hand. I gripped it, looking for something, anything to stop the spinning. The pebble pulsed in my hand and everything stopped. I was in a void, somewhere with neither heat nor light.

From very far away, I heard Talbot's voice saying, "What the hell did you do to him?"

Then I snapped back. I was lying on the floor at Eternity Road, gazing at Wren's bare feet.

My throat was dry, like I'd swallowed half a desert. "How did you do that?" I rasped out.

"I didn't mean to," she said.

Ambrose took the peacock feather from her. "I'll take that," he said.

I realized there was something clenched in my fist and I uncurled it. There was a crimson bead in the palm of my hand.

The bright color attracted Wren's attention. "What is that? It's so pretty."

"It came back with me." I thought about giving it to her, but changed my mind and pocketed the bead instead.

She pouted adorably, but I held firm. I wanted to hold on to it until I figured out what it was and why I'd ended up with it.

I coughed several times before I finally said, "Wren, why don't you see if you can find a pair of jeans?"

"Jeans?" she asked.

"Where's my girlfriend when I need her? She loves to shop," Talbot said. "I'll help you find something."

He and Wren went to the other side of the store where we kept a few pairs of old Levi's. Ambrose would buy anything he thought he could sell to the mortals, but he made most of his profits by selling large-ticket magical items.

"What happened to you when you were out?" Ambrose asked.

"I was in another time and place," I said. I held up the bead. "Ever see this before?"

He shook his head. "Maybe it's a bead of power," he said. "But I've never seen one like that. It looks like something you could buy at any tourist trap. There's no energy emanating from it."

"I'll hold on to it anyway," I said. There were ways to hide magic in plain sight. "Have you ever heard of anyone being able to do that? Transport someone with one touch?"

"Not anyone from the House of Zeus," he said. "But she is the daughter of a goddess and a necromancer, so there's no telling what she can do."

"Do you think she did it on purpose?" I asked. "She seemed as surprised as I was."

"Or maybe she's just a good actress," Ambrose said.

The word *actress* reminded me of Elizabeth, which reminded me how easily I'd been betrayed. I wasn't going to be that gullible again. If Wren was out to scam me, what was in it for her? Besides freedom from her mother?

"That reminds me," I replied. "Do you have any books I can borrow about Hecate? Specifically, about how my aunts managed to trap her in the underworld?"

"There are many books about Hecate," he said. "But nothing about how your aunts trapped her. I'll keep a lookout, though."

"Thanks, Ambrose," I said. "The aunts won't tell me anything. I've even tried to get a glimpse of the Book of Fates."

"Be careful. And I'm not just talking about Wren's powers, Nyx. Any scorned woman is powerful, but it's another thing when you add magic to the mix."

"I'm not going to hurt her," I said. I wasn't sure of the reverse, though.

He gave me a stern look. "You mean you don't *want* to hurt her," he said. "There's a difference."

"I don't know what else to do," I said. "She can't stay at Claire's or Naomi's."

"Just tread cautiously," he said.

"I'll try." Caution wasn't one of my finer traits.

Wren came back wearing a pair of jeans that fit her like a second skin and a Victorian lace top. Her feet were bare. The sight of her made me want to carry her upstairs and stay there until we'd had enough of each other.

"She'll need shoes," Talbot said, interrupting some very vivid fantasies.

"We'll get her some flip-flops at the convenience store."

After Wren was properly shod, we headed for Hell's Belles. Bernie was working the counter and nearly scalded some poor House of Poseidon merman with his herbal tea.

"Hey, Bernie," I said. "Can we get two blue-plate specials and a couple of cups of coffee?"

"Are you out of your mind, bringing her here?" she shouted. Conversation around us ceased. She lowered her voice. "Her mother is tearing apart the underworld right now."

"Thank you for—" I didn't get to finish thanking her for saving us in the underworld.

"Shut your gob, Nyx Fortuna," she hissed.

Bernie was scared, but of who? I glanced around the diner, but didn't see any other demons. A group of businessmen sat in a booth in the far corner, clearly in the middle of a meeting. I didn't see anything to worry about, but Bernie's gaze drifted over there.

Sean Danvers was one of the businessmen, and I realized Bernie didn't want to talk in front of him.

"Can you get a message to Hecate?" I said softly. "Let her know that Wren is unharmed."

"She's not going to believe that her daughter is safe in the hands of someone from the House of Fates."

"I'm not from the House of Fates," I said sharply.

"She won't see it that way," Bernie replied. "You'll have a legion of demons at your door before you know it."

"She wouldn't dare," I said.

Bernie frowned. "Maybe. Maybe not. Now what can I get you?"

After we ordered, Wren stared at Bernie's retreating back. "She's right, you know. My mother will try to kill you."

"Haven't you heard? I can't be killed."

"Do not joke about death," she said. "My mother will find a way."

The dark pronouncement didn't faze me. Hecate wasn't the first one to try and she probably wouldn't be the last.

The rest of the day was uneventful. I waited until Wren was in the shower to hide the bead. I taped it to the back of a framed picture of Elizabeth and then put it in my closet. Anyone snooping would assume it was nothing more than a painful reminder of a failed relationship. For good measure, I grabbed the only photo I had of the two of us and stacked it on top of the first photo.

We'd gone to bed when they came for her.

She shook me from sleep. "Nyx, wake up," she whispered. "There's someone here."

"At the door?" I yawned.

"Inside," she said.

Wide-awake now, I grabbed my athame. "Wraiths?"

"No, demons," she said.

"Stay here," I said. "No matter what you hear."

"I'm coming with you," she said.

There wasn't any more time to argue. I stopped and listened. I could hear someone breathing. There was a demon in my living room.

I flicked on the light, hoping it would take her by surprise, but she only smirked at me. She was tall and slim, with shiny black hair.

"You took something that doesn't belong to you," she said. "The goddess wants it back."

"Wren doesn't belong to anybody," I said.

"I'm not going with you, Antara," Wren said.

"You know her?" I asked.

"She's one of Hecate's personal bodyguards. Martial arts expert," Wren warned.

Antara's skills soon became evident. She punched me so hard that my ears rang. I feinted and slashed out with my athame, but she kicked it out of my hand effortlessly.

She hit me hard and I skidded and fell. She was on top of me within seconds. She grabbed a handful of my hair and bashed my head against the kitchen floor tile.

"Hey, I want to get my deposit back when I leave," I said as my blood splattered all over the white tiles.

"I wouldn't worry about it if I were you," Antara grunted.

That was the last thing she said, because Wren grabbed Antara by her hair, exposing her neck, and sliced clean through it with the kitchen knife I'd used to chop the salad I'd made for dinner.

Drops of demon blood fell on my bare chest and scalded it. I shoved the demon's dead body off me, careful to avoid as much of her blood as I could.

"Now your mom's going to be really pissed," I said.

Wren looked at me. Her brown eyes had turned amber and her gaze was unfocused, like she was somewhere far away.

"Are you okay?"

"I've never killed anyone before," she said. "I find it quite..." But I never found out how she found it, because she pitched forward in a dead faint.

I carried her to the couch and then went to the sink to wet a cloth. I dabbed her face and wrists. Her eyelids fluttered open, and she sat up. "What happened?"

"You fainted," I said.

She was all big eyes and trembling lips. Her gaze went to Antara's body, which I'd left lying on the floor. I cursed myself for being an idiot.

"Why don't you go back to bed," I said. "While I clean up."

She nodded and then stood, swaying slightly. I picked her up and carried her to the bed. "I'm going to go out for a bit," I said. "I won't be long. Will you be okay by yourself?"

She'd just killed a trained fighter. She could obviously take care of herself. I didn't know why I was reluctant to leave her, but I was.

"I'll be fine," she said. "But where are you going?"

"I'm going to return Hecate's bodyguard to where she came from," I said.

I used a concealing spell, dragged Antara's body to the gate leading to the underworld, and dumped it there. Hecate would get the message.

Chapter Nineteen

I was on edge all week, but Hecate's demons didn't make an appearance. Sometimes, late at night, I heard the sound of a baying hound.

I managed to keep my hands off Wren, despite her best efforts. She had insisted she was too scared to sleep alone, which meant temptation was within easy reach. I'd tried everything short of bringing someone else home to keep her at a distance, but Wren was determined.

I woke in the middle of the night to absolute quiet.

"Wren?" I called out, but there was no answer. She was gone.

I searched the apartment. The front door was unlocked, but there was no sign of a break-in. The wards were in place. Nothing was out of place or broken. It seemed as though Wren had left on her own.

I reached for the absinthe bottle I kept in my fridge and chugged it back. I watched the clock as the hands moved slowly toward dawn.

Had she gone back to the underworld? The thought disturbed me, which agitated me even more. Did I have feelings for Wren? Was I jealous? Getting involved with Hecate's daughter was possibly the dumbest thing I'd ever done in my long history of stupid actions.

Sickly yellow light streamed through my kitchen window. It was almost morning and she still wasn't home.

I was putting on my Docs to go look for her when she returned. She wore her acolyte robe and her feet were bare. The robe was heavy with dew.

"Where have you been?" I knew my aunt had been messing with my head, but I couldn't seem to shake Deci's proclamation that I'd be betrayed again. There was a good chance Wren was playing me, but she was hard to resist.

"I couldn't sleep," she said. "So I went for a walk." She yawned.

"In the middle of the night? In this neighborhood?"

"I know how to take care of myself," she said. "I thought you said I wasn't a prisoner here."

"You're not," I replied. "I was worried about you." My words were slurred. I'd drunk more of the green fairy than I'd intended. "Why are you wearing that robe?"

"It's the warmest thing I own," she snapped. She studied my face for a moment. "Did you really think I'd take a stroll down below for a visit with dear old Mom?"

"I don't know what to think," I said. But I did. She was trying to play me, but to what end?

"I'm going to bed," she said. She didn't wait to see if I followed, but I did.

My stomach roiled at the thought of another betrayal.

Her back was to me when she dropped the robe. "Are you

coming to bed?" The invitation was obvious, but I was transfixed by something besides her naked body.

One shoulder was marked with an angry scar, faded, but the ridges were stark against her milky-white skin. My own scars started to itch at the sight of hers.

"Can I see?" I asked.

She nodded and pulled her hair back to reveal that the scar went up her neck and disappeared into her hairline.

I stepped closer. She shivered when my hot breath touched her neck and I felt a surge of lust. It was replaced by anger when I realized that her skin had been sliced.

"How did that happen?" I asked. "What did they use?"

"A demon claw."

"Who did it?"

"Let's just say I wasn't sorry you killed Hroth," she said.

I wished I hadn't, so I could do it again, only more slowly.

"What did your mother do to him when she found out?"

"She's the one who ordered him to do it," Wren said bitterly.

"Why?" I couldn't imagine having such a vengeful mother.

"I went topside without her permission," she said. "She can't come up, you know. Not ever. No matter how badly she wants to leave the underworld, she can't, because of your aunts."

I couldn't resist her any longer. I pressed a gentle kiss to the scar. She was hot, sweating like she'd just run a marathon. I licked a drop of moisture from her skin.

"You saved me, you know," she said.

I wanted Wren. Acting on those feelings would make my fucked-up situation even worse, but I'd never let that stop me before.

I trailed kisses down her neck, following the path of the scar. She moved away from me. At first, I thought she was rejecting me, but she was only facing me to kiss my lips.

"When I was topside before, before Hroth found me and dragged me back, I seduced a mortal," she said. "It wasn't magical. In fact, it was a considerable disappointment."

"That's unfortunate," I said.

"Would it be magical with you?"

If she didn't stop looking at me like that, it was going to be blink-and-you-might-miss-it quick. Hardly magical.

"Wren, I can't sleep with you," I said.

She slid a hand where it didn't belong—not if I wanted to stick to my resolution to keep things uncomplicated. "Feels like you can to me."

"You know what I mean," I replied. "We shouldn't sleep together."

"But I want you," she said. "And I think you want me."

"I'm involved with someone else." I moved her hand away from the danger zone.

The statement might keep me out of trouble, but it wasn't strictly true. Elizabeth was gone and Willow wasn't interested in anything more than a fling.

"And you have made promises to her?" she asked. "Are you together now?"

"No, but—" The hand was back before I could get the words out.

"Then what's the problem?" she asked. She kissed me and the answer to her question disappeared from my brain, dissolved by the feeling of her tongue stroking mine.

Sleeping with Hecate's daughter was dangerous, but I was sick of depriving myself. It had taken every bit of my admittedly little self-control not to take her up on it the first time she'd offered. Wren had made it clear she wanted me, but so had Elizabeth. What was Wren's motivation: lust or something more sinister?

The thought dissolved when she yanked off my jeans.

"We all have scars, Nyx," she said. "Show me yours. Please?"

I was never going to get a happily ever after, but I could have a taste of what others took for granted. I reached for her.

Chapter Twenty

I spent the next day in bed with Wren, but eventually, reality intruded. Hecate's demons would come for Wren and we needed a plan. Nothing occurred to me, but proximity to Wren wasn't helping, either. I needed to think of something besides sex, like surviving my latest predicament.

I resumed my early morning swims. The quiet helped me think. I missed the exercise, but even more, I missed starting my day seeing Naomi.

When I arrived at the Y, she was already in the pool, but she wasn't alone, judging from the raised voices echoing over the water.

"You have to tell him," Naomi said.

"Why?" Claire replied, the bitterness in her voice clear. "He's just like all the others: fooled by a pretty face."

I stopped in my tracks. Were they talking about me?

"And whose fault is that?" Naomi snapped. "He wouldn't have even met her if it weren't for you."

Me and Wren, then. I cleared my throat and stepped out of

the shadows. "Sorry, am I interrupting something? I can come back."

"Nyx," Naomi cried. "I haven't seen you here in ages. I was starting to think you'd given up swimming altogether."

I jumped into the water next to her, splashing her in the process. I came up for air and then grinned at her as I treaded water. "I've been a little busy lately."

Claire snorted and then hauled herself out of the water. "I'll leave you to it, then."

I watched her stomp off. "She doesn't like me very much."

"Don't take it personally," Naomi replied. "She doesn't like anyone very much right now."

"Even you?"

"Especially me," Naomi said somberly and then changed the subject. "Race you!" She shoved off against the side, getting a crucial three-second head start. I trailed behind her but touched the side a beat later.

She surfaced and smiled at me as she shook the water from her swim cap. "You're out of shape."

"Rematch in a few days?" I suggested as she jumped out of the pool.

"Of course," she said. "You'll need to practice, though." I could hear her laughter as she went into the changing room.

I was back a couple of days later. I'd decided to wait until I was sure my cousins had finished their swim before I ventured into the pool. I watched from the Caddy as Naomi exited the building, arm in arm with Claire.

Sawyer's voice made me jump. "She's so grown-up," he said.

"Stop doing that," I said. "You scared the shit out of me."

"You *should* be scared, Nyx," he said. He was probably right, but I wanted a few answers.

"Sawyer, tell me about Hecate. How did the two of you get together?"

"I was young and stupid," he said. "I thought I was a badass necromancer. She was beautiful and deadly. She got what she wanted and then tossed me aside."

"Did you know about Wren?"

"Not until after I was married to Nona," he said. "I couldn't tell her."

"I have to tell Naomi she has a sister," I said.

"I know." His voice held regret. "Tell her I'm sorry."

"I will," I said. "Why do you talk to me? Do you know anything about the naiad deaths?"

"Naiads? Trouble ahead," was his vague response.

"Sawyer, quit being all mysterious and just spit it out," I said.

But he didn't reply. He'd gone as abruptly as he'd appeared.

"Why do the dead have to be so ambiguous?" I asked no one and then got my stuff and headed for the gym.

The smell of blood mingled with the usual scent of chlorine. The lifeguard was slumped over in his chair. A steady stream of blood ran from the back of his head, but he was breathing.

The water in the pool was tinged pink with blood. A body, or at least pieces of it, floated to the surface. I took a closer look and gagged. It was a woman, torn to pieces, just like the others. The deep blue tinge to the skin made me think the victim was a naiad. I fished my cell out of my gym bag and dialed.

"Ambrose, get to the Y on Ninth Street, fast. There's been another murder."

His voice had been thick with sleep, but he quickly absorbed what I told him. "We'll be right there. Ward the door and don't let anyone in."

I did as he suggested and warded the door to the pool. I didn't want to chance a mortal stumbling upon the crime scene and trying to pin it on me.

I checked on the lifeguard. His breathing was shallow but steady. I had one tiny healing amulet in my gym bag—hardly enough to help, but I used it on the lifeguard anyway.

The seconds ticked by. It couldn't be a coincidence that the murder had occurred in the same pool where I swam every day.

It seemed personal, but I couldn't think of anyone who hated me, at least not more than usual, except Hecate, and the naiad killings had begun before I'd ever entered the underworld.

Ambrose arrived in the company of an older man whose erect bearing hinted at former military. His sun-bleached hair held traces of gray among the blond and around his eyes were wrinkles from repeated squinting into the sun.

"Nyx, this is Trey Marin, from the House of Poseidon," Ambrose said. "He's the head of the inter-House task force investigating the naiad murders."

"I think you already know my colleague Mr. Baxter," Trey said.

Baxter grinned wickedly. "I'm in charge of cleanup."

"Mr. Baxter, it is not appropriate for you to show glee at the death of one of my people," Trey said sternly. "You will conduct yourself with respect or you will be reassigned."

"Yes, Triton, sir," Baxter said, with the proper amount of humility, but he winked at me when Trey's back was turned.

"What about the human?" Baxter asked. The guy had the appetite of a competitive eater.

"He's alive," I said. "And he needs to stay that way."

Baxter ignored me and gave Trey a hopeful look.

"Nyx is right," Trey said. "We'll question the human and then erase the memory. I must examine the body first and then allow Mr. Baxter to work."

I hoped Baxter got major indigestion or a bad case of black magic poison, but he seemed to have a cast-iron stomach.

I didn't really want to watch Baxter do his "cleanup," so I hung back while Trey and Baxter examined the body. Ambrose stayed put, too.

"Triton, huh?" I whispered to Ambrose. "As in Poseidon's son?"

He shook his head. "You're close. He's three greats removed. He's Triton the third, hence his nickname, Trey."

"So a mucky-muck then?"

He nodded. "The muckiest."

Trey revived the lifeguard. "What happened?"

"Someone hit me on the back of the head," he said.

"Obviously," Trey said. "Anything else?"

"No," the lifeguard said. "Wait, I smelled cologne."

"What kind of cologne?" I asked.

He put his hands to his head and groaned. "I have no idea, but it was strong."

Trey put a finger to the lifeguard's forehead and sent him into a healing and forgetful sleep. "As suspected, necromancy was used to kill this poor sea nymph. Very dark magic."

"We already knew that," I pointed out. "So you didn't learn anything new?"

He gave me a long measuring look. "Someone obviously dislikes you intensely. They brought her here alive and then ritualistically killed her. Seems personal."

My cousins had just left minutes before it had happened. The Fates weren't any more popular than I was. Maybe I wasn't the target of the gruesome message. Or maybe Naomi or Claire had seen something.

"Danvers is the only necromancer in Minneapolis," I pointed out. "And I saw him with Aspen before she was killed." The deaths had black magic written all over them.

There was also the cologne, but probably thousands of men wore the same fragrance.

Trey and Ambrose exchanged glances.

"Not the only one," Ambrose said, but he didn't elaborate.

Trey cleared his throat. "Danvers is on our list of possibilities, of course, but politically, he's hard to touch."

"Willow," I said. "I need to go check on Willow."

Trey grabbed me by the arm. "It's not Willow."

"I know," I said. I swallowed hard. "I noticed blonde hair in the pool." I tried not to think about what else I'd seen there.

"Willow is fine," Trey said.

"How do you know?"

He met my eyes. "I assure you I would know if anything happened to her."

I glanced at Ambrose, who gave me a reassuring smile. "You can help her by telling Trey everything you noticed."

I gave them a brief rundown, but I couldn't tell them anything they didn't already know.

"What spell would do that?" I asked. "And why would anyone kill so many naiads?"

"That, son of Fortuna, is a very good question," Trey replied. But he didn't seem that surprised about any of it. I wondered why.

Chapter Twenty-One

I'd asked Naomi to bring Claire by Parsi so I could question them about the murder at the pool. They stopped by my desk the next afternoon. I'd commandeered Alex's old office and nobody had said anything. Maybe they just hadn't noticed.

I hadn't seen much of Claire since the rescue. Her hair had been freshly cut and styled and a stylish skirt and blouse had replaced her acolyte robes. The superior expression hadn't changed, though.

"What did you want to talk to me about?" she asked.

"I wanted to talk to both of you," I replied. "Did either of you see anything strange at the Y yesterday?"

"How did you know we were at the Y?" she asked defensively.

Jesus, paranoid much? "Because I swim there, too," I reminded her patiently. "I saw you as you were leaving."

"I didn't notice anything," Naomi said. "Why?"

I hesitated. "There was a murder there, another naiad."

"Same thing as Asp—as the others?" She'd avoided Aspen's name, but we were both thinking of her.

"I smelled cologne," Claire said.

"Yeah, not much help," I said. "That's all the lifeguard remembered, too."

I might have sounded a trifle dismissive, because Claire glared at me. "I recognized the kind of cologne," she said. "I suppose you know that, too."

"What was it?"

"Blood Moon cologne," she replied. "I dated this magician in college who used to bathe in the stuff."

"Thanks," I said. Blood Moon was expensive and had a heavy wet-dog undertone that only men with more money than sense of smell would choose.

Naomi nudged Claire when she thought I wasn't paying attention.

"I'm having a dinner party and you and Wren are invited," Claire said.

"Why?"

She gave Naomi a startled look, but Naomi just smiled. "I wanted to thank you for rescuing me."

"No thanks necessary," I replied.

Claire's brow furrowed, so I clarified. "Didn't the aunties tell you? They harassed the girl I loved until I found you," I said. "It's not like I really had a choice."

Her glance sharpened. "What girl? Does Wren know about her?"

"None of your business," I said.

Claire gave a short, exasperated laugh. "Are you coming or not?"

"He's coming," Naomi replied for me. She gave me a stare that reminded me she was a Fate-in-training. At that moment, I didn't like my favorite cousin very much.

"Quit being so bossy," I told her.

"Then quit being a dick," she said. "Claire is trying, which is more than I can say for you."

She'd admonished me like I was a naughty schoolboy. Maybe I was acting about as maturely as one, but I trusted Claire almost less than the aunties. She'd been evasive about how she'd ended up in the underworld and was even more tight-lipped about why she'd stayed there.

"Thank you for the invitation, Claire," I said. "Wren and I will be there."

She gave me the first real smile I'd seen from her. "Great."

"The aunts won't be there, will they?"

"I guess you'll have to wait until tonight to find out," she said, then laughed at my expression. "No, they won't be there. It's just me, Talbot, and Naomi, and you and Wren. Here's the address. And don't be late."

She left the room, and Naomi started to follow, but then ran back to plant a swift kiss on my cheek. "Thank you," she said before exiting.

Claire lived in a luxury condo in Elliot Park. I'd been there before, during the early stages of my search for her.

"Nice place," Talbot commented as the four of us entered the elevator. Naomi hit the button for the penthouse and I snickered.

"Probably paid with money from the Fates' ill-gotten gains," I said.

"Nyx, you promised you'd behave tonight," Wren said woefully.

I gave her hand a squeeze. "I will."

The smell of stir-fry came through the door as it opened. "Come in," Claire said. "Dinner's ready."

Her place had signs of a decorator's touch, adorned in a riot of primary colors. There were lit scented candles everywhere, permeating the condo with a heavy fragrance of ambergris, rose attar, and sandalwood.

We followed our host into the dining room, where dinner was already set out in covered dishes. There was a framed photo of Claire hanging above the dining room buffet. There were no other photos, not of her mother or her aunts or even her cousin Naomi. I don't know why, but it made her seem lonely.

"You cut your hair," Wren commented.

Claire put a hand to her head and, for the first time since I'd met her, looked self-conscious. "The long hair seemed too much to deal with once I was topside."

"But all of Hecate's acolytes keep their hair long," Wren said.

"I'm not an acolyte anymore," Claire said. "And neither are you."

Wren tensed, clearly uncomfortable with the conversation. "She's still my mother."

"And a Fate is mine," Claire replied. "Doesn't mean we have to act like them."

Now it was Wren's turn to look self-conscious. "Maybe I should cut my hair and buy some different clothes."

"I like the way you look," I said. I was only trying to make her feel better. She was sexy with long hair or short. I didn't care. But Claire took it the wrong way.

"Do you always tell your women how to dress?" she snapped.

I took a bite of stir-fry and chewed slowly in an attempt to hold on to my temper. It hadn't worked by the time I swallowed.

"First of all, Wren's not my woman," I said. "She's her own woman. And I don't give a fuck if she's bald. She'd still be sexy as hell." I glared at Claire and she backed down, but not before she muttered, "And you're too stupid to see beyond that."

"What did you say?"

Naomi intervened before the situation could deteriorate any further. "This stir-fry is delicious," she said brightly. "It's a wonderful thank-you dinner for Nyx."

Claire caught the note in her voice and said, "Sorry, Nyx, I have a bit of a chip on my shoulder about controlling men."

I opened my mouth to ask her more, but Naomi gave a tiny shake of her head. There was no sense in upsetting my favorite cousin, so I kept quiet.

Claire poured generous servings of sake with dinner, which took the edge off enough that we made it through the rest of the meal without quarreling.

"It's good to be home." Claire leaned back with a satisfied sigh. "I missed my place so much. And you, too, of course," she added to Naomi.

"Then why did you stay with Hecate? Didn't you realize the wine was enchanted?" I asked. Naomi glared at me, but I ignored her and tossed back another shot of sake.

"I stayed because I didn't have a choice," she said. "I drank the wine. I didn't have anyone to help me."

"We didn't know where you were," Naomi said softly.

"How did you end up in the underworld in the first place?" I persisted.

Naomi kicked me under the table. "All that matters is she's back," she said.

She refused to believe there was anything suspicious about Claire's time in the underworld, but I was sure that Claire had been drinking the Hecate Kool-Aid willingly. Which meant she couldn't be trusted.

"I need some air," I said.

"There's a balcony through those doors," Naomi said, pointing to a glass slider. "I love looking at the city at night."

"I'll join you," Talbot said. I grabbed the bottle of sake and headed outside.

Talbot stood there shivering while I polished off the bottle. "So what's your beef with your cousin? Claire, I mean."

"I don't trust her," I said.

"Why? Because she's a Fate? So is Naomi and you trust her."

"Not because she's a Fate," I said. "Because when we found her, she was mighty cozy with Hecate."

"Stockholm syndrome," he said. "And the grapes."

"Maybe," I said. "Or maybe she's up to something."

"Or maybe someone else is," Talbot said flatly. "You're doing it again."

"Doing what?"

"Getting involved with someone you don't know anything about because you're lonely."

Lonely? It was an understatement. I'd put my emotions in cold storage, having been taught by my murderous aunts not to get attached.

"I know Wren saved Claire," I said. "Saved Naomi."

"And I'll always be grateful," he replied. "But that doesn't mean I trust her."

"Who says I trust her?"

He blinked. "I assumed..."

"You assumed that Elizabeth hadn't taught me anything? I'm lonely, not stupid." I had been stupid—stupid to trust Elizabeth, stupid to hope for a scrap of love—but that was all over.

He watched Naomi through the clear glass. "Look at Naomi. She's thrilled to have Claire home."

I watched Claire through the glass door. She and Wren were smiling at Naomi, who had her arm slung affectionately across her cousin's shoulder.

"I was hunted for two hundred years," I reminded him. "I have reason enough to be suspicious."

"But things are better now with your aunts, right?"

"I'm not sure," I admitted. "The deal was I'd find Claire and they'd leave Elizabeth alone, not that they'd leave me alone."

"Naomi would never let them hurt you," he said.

"She's one little Fate-in-training," I said. "They are three very powerful witches."

"She'd do anything for you."

"And I'd do anything for her," I said.

"Then cut Claire some slack," Talbot said. "Please."

"I'll try," I replied. We rejoined the party just in time. Morta and Deci stood in the entryway.

"Mom, Aunt Deci," Claire said. "What a surprise. Where's Aunt Nona?"

Morta gave Claire a peck on the cheek. "She's not feeling well."

More likely, Nona was passed out drunk. She hadn't handled Sawyer's death well.

"Oh, you have company," Deci said. Something about the

way she said it made me nervous. Wren? Where was Wren? If my aunts figured out who she was, all hell was going to break loose.

"Who is your friend?" Deci asked, looking at Wren, who sat frozen on the sofa.

"She's my date," I snapped. I sat next to Wren and grabbed her hand.

Morta inspected Wren. I watched as Morta's face changed. She put a finger to her cheek and tapped it, theatrically. "Now, where have I seen your face before?"

"She's a friend, Mom," Claire said, casting Naomi a desperate glance.

Morta said, "Can someone tell me why the son of Fortuna is dallying with the daughter of our worst enemy?"

It was cold comfort that she hadn't recognized Wren's paternity. My attention had been focused on Morta, but then a movement caught my eye. Deci stood practically on top of us.

She held up one of Claire's candles, seemingly oblivious to the tension in the room. "Claire, this is quite lovely," she said. "And it smells divine."

Then she dropped the candle in Wren's lap. The hem of her dress ignited instantaneously. The flames burning greener than any naturally occurring flame. Magic.

Wren shrieked as the fire grew. It licked at her hair, which she'd worn down. Deci was transfixed by the burning girl.

"*Exstinguo*," I said, but nothing happened. "Out! Extinguish!"

The fire went out, but I felt as if all oxygen had been removed from the room.

"Are you okay?" I asked Wren. I grabbed her and hauled her to the feet. "Let me look at you."

"I'm fine," she said. "I'll probably need a trim, though." She held up a handful of hair, which was singed at the ends. There didn't seem to be any damage to Wren, but the strong smell of singed hair permeated the room.

Deci breathed it in like she was sniffing a bouquet of roses. "Wasn't it pretty?" Someone had a mad crush on Hephaestus, the god of fire.

"Deci?" Morta said sharply. "Deci, what was pretty?"

Deci's eyes regained their focus. "The candle, of course," she finally replied. "I am so sorry. It just slipped out of my hand."

"So clumsy of you," I said.

"It was an accident," Naomi said. "Accidents happen."

"Seem to be happening a lot lately," Talbot muttered.

Naomi narrowed her eyes at him and then turned to Wren. "C'mon, Wren. I'll help you get cleaned up. I'm sure Claire has something you can borrow."

"Go ahead and take her to my bedroom," Claire said. "I need to talk to my mom a minute."

While Morta and Claire conducted a low-voiced conversation in the kitchen, Deci and I had a staring contest in the living room.

Whatever Claire said to her mother convinced her to leave without causing a scene or trying to kill the dinner guests.

Chapter Twenty-Two

I was on high alert for the next few days, but there was no response from Hecate or the Fates. When Claire proposed a night out with Wren and Naomi, no guys allowed, I went along with it.

Talbot and I decided to hit the Red Dragon after work. We ordered a pitcher of beer and snagged the last available booth.

"What do you think the girls are up to tonight?" I asked.

He gave me an amused look. "Are you worried?"

"You mean about Hecate? Not after I saw Wren kill a demon in my kitchen." I took a sip of my beer. "What is this stuff?" I asked.

"Red Dragon's going upscale," he said. "It's from a microbrewery."

"You couldn't just order PBR, like usual?"

He laughed.

I changed the subject. "Do you think Naomi knows that Wren's her sister?"

He raised an eyebrow. "I can't picture Naomi keeping it a secret if she did know."

"We have to tell her eventually, you know," I replied.

"I know," he said. "I think we can use a couple of shots before taking on that Herculean task."

When he got up to go to the bar, I glanced over at the entrance, out of habit more than any fear I was about to be ambushed.

Willow walked into the Red Dragon in the middle of happy hour. I'd never seen a naiad in a dive bar before. Something must be wrong.

She wore what could loosely be called a dress, with her favorite necklace of river rock. She was barefoot and her hair was still damp and curled about her face. It made her look impossibly young and innocent.

I felt a twinge of guilt, but then I noticed her dress was hanging on with difficulty. I wasn't the only one who noticed.

Some guy walked up to her and said something and she laughed, which sent the bodice of her dress sliding even lower, until it clung precariously to her breasts.

I felt another twinge, this time in my balls, as desire replaced guilt.

She scanned the bar until she found me. Every male in the place watched her walk over to me.

"Nyx," she said. "I've been looking all over for you."

Was it possible that I had feelings for Willow? That was a complication I didn't need. Besides, I was sleeping with Wren. And I still loved Elizabeth, despite the fact that she'd made it clear she never wanted to see me again.

Maybe Talbot was right. Maybe drinking was part of my

self-destructive behavior, but my complicated love life wasn't getting any less complicated.

I waved the cocktail server over. "Another."

When she brought it over, I tossed it back. "Let's get out of here," I said.

"What?" Willow asked.

"I assume that you didn't bother with the mortal disguise because you were looking for a quickie. We'll talk about it on the way back to your place."

I paid our tab, which was more than expected, and said good-bye to Talbot, who frowned but kept his mouth shut.

Willow kept her eyes on her feet. Whatever she wanted to tell me, she didn't think I was going to be happy about it.

"I am going to be wed," she said when we were a few blocks from the lake.

It was the last thing I'd expected to hear. Naiad marriage rituals were peculiar. A thought struck me. Was I the intended bridegroom? The thought made me shudder, which, unfortunately, she noticed.

"Don't flatter yourself," she said. "You don't know him."

"Who is he?"

"He's a businessman," she said.

"Why are you getting married?" I asked. "What about…?" My voice trailed off. I couldn't ask her about us, not when I was involved with Wren.

"Nyx, you are my friend," she said. "And besides, I thought there was someone new in your life."

"Wren and I are— We aren't…" I sputtered, but she waved away my half-assed explanation.

"Is he a decent guy? Will he treat you right?" I was conflicted by her news.

She shrugged. "I have no idea."

I stopped. "Then why are you marrying him?"

"It was arranged," she said vaguely.

I was getting over my initial shock. Maybe her marriage would uncomplicate things for me, but Willow didn't seem particularly joyous about the engagement, which, in my limited experience, was a little odd.

"Is he from the House of Poseidon?"

"No," she said.

"Mortal?" The thought astounded me. Naiads were happy to dally with mortals, but when it came to commitment, they stuck to their own.

"No," she said again." Then, "Let's talk about something else."

"Is that what you came to tell me?"

"Yes," she said. "And now I have."

"Anything else you want to tell me?"

She hesitated. "Please be careful, son of Fortuna."

"Of what?"

"Your heart," she said. "Tell me about this Wren. Does she love you?"

"No," I said. I didn't trust Wren, but I lusted after her.

"Do you love her?"

It felt awkward to talk about my relationship with Wren to Willow, so I just shook my head.

"I am sorry to have to tell you that we can no longer consort," she said. "My fiancé is aware of our relationship and expects sexual fidelity."

"Who is this guy?" Willow was talking like it was a business deal, not a love match. I didn't expect a happily ever after for everybody, but I'd more at ease if there was even a trace of affection in her voice.

She hesitated. "Sean Danvers," she said.

Despite the fact that I'd spotted him at a bachelor party the other night, his was the last name I had expected to hear.

Chapter Twenty-Three

I brooded about Willow's engagement all week, but I still had other things on my plate.

I stopped by the morgue to check in with Baxter.

"Any more naiads come through here?" I asked him.

"It's been quiet," he said.

"You didn't answer my question," I pointed out.

He grinned at me. "You're learning, son of Fortuna," he said. "No naiads or any other magical creature."

I studied him for a moment. "How was the bachelor party the other night?"

For some reason, the subject made him uneasy. "Fine."

"Fine? A night of debauchery was *fine*?" There was definitely something he wasn't telling me.

"Yeah, fine," he said. "Anything else?"

"What happened?"

"Nothin'."

"Baxter, just spit it out and save me the trouble of knocking the answers out of you."

He stared at me. "The groom roughed up one of the strippers, is all."

"Sean Danvers hits women?"

"Not my cup of tea, but the groom seemed to get off on it," Baxter replied.

"That guy's a real asshole," I said.

"We finally agree on something," Baxter replied.

"Call me if you see any more naiads come through," I said.

"I don't think there will be," he said.

"What makes you say that?"

"Word is that Trey was able to broker a deal," he replied. "His niece's hand in marriage if the killings ended."

"And the groom was able to make that promise?"

Baxter met my eyes. "Exactly."

I left the morgue, but couldn't stop thinking about what Baxter had told me. Was what he had told me true? Would the naiad killings stop? More importantly, could I stop the wedding? I'd be the charms around my neck that Danvers was the murderer.

Wren came to work with me on Saturday. Daylight still hurt her eyes, so I made sure she had a pair of sunglasses before we left.

"About time you showed up," Talbot said. He and Naomi were sitting on a silk-covered chaise lounge. I was pretty sure they'd been making out until the bell above the door had warned them someone was coming.

I looked around Eternity Road, which was noticeably lacking in customers. "Sorry to leave you to handle the rush by yourself."

"How is Claire?" Wren asked Naomi.

"She's adjusting," she replied. "She'll be starting back at Parsi next week."

"Nice to be related to the boss," I commented.

"That's how you got your job," Naomi said.

"No." I corrected her. "I lied my way into the job. Being related is how I keep it. And that's just because the Fates want to keep an eye on me."

Naomi snorted. "Do you blame them?"

I didn't want to fight with her, so I changed the subject.

"Where's your dad?" I asked Talbot. Maybe Ambrose would have some advice.

"He's out of town for a few days, buying inventory," he replied. He snapped his fingers. "That reminds me, this came for you yesterday." He rummaged through a pile of mail on the counter and then held up a creamy white envelope, edged in black ribbon.

I opened it gingerly and scanned the paper. "It's a wedding invitation. To Willow's wedding to Sean Danvers." I tossed it aside. "I'll have to send my regrets." There wasn't going to be a wedding, not if I could stop it.

"I've never been to a wedding before," Wren said wistfully. "Can we go? Please, Nyx," she coaxed.

"You want me to take you to Willow's wedding?"

"Yes, I want to go," she replied. "You said yourself that you and Willow are just friends," she said.

"With benefits," Naomi replied. There was a definite tone in her voice.

"Just friends, period," I said. "She's getting married."

I didn't know how else to describe it. I'd put my feelings for Willow into storage when I'd found out she was going to be Danvers's blushing bride, but I couldn't stand by and let her marry a monster.

"But you don't have feelings for her?" she challenged. Why was Naomi pursuing this? And in front of Wren?

"Of course I do," I admitted. "She's my friend. I like her and I owe her a debt of gratitude. Besides, I bet you've never been to a necromancer's wedding." I hadn't been to one, either.

"What about the aunts?"

"I don't think they're invited," I replied.

She raised an eyebrow. "Of course they're attending. I mean Wren. What if they recognize Wren?"

"Deci and Morta met her the other night at Claire's," I reminded her. Contrarily, I wanted to go to the wedding now. "Having Claire back will keep them off my back, at least temporarily."

"What should I wear?" Wren asked.

"We'll go shopping," Naomi said.

"It's an evening wedding, so I'd go with formal attire."

"Where's it going to be?" Naomi asked. "Some moldy old graveyard at midnight?"

"No," Talbot said. "It's at the Saint Paul Hotel."

I whistled. "Fancy. How do you know that?"

"We got an invite as well," he explained. "A few years ago, Dad sold Sean Danvers a rare athame, one of two owned by famous necromancer twins. Danvers stops in the store every once in a while to see if the matching knife has shown up."

"Been studying up on necromancers, have we?"

He gave me a meaningful look. "I thought the knowledge might be useful."

Wren and Naomi had their heads together.

"I'm taking Wren shopping," Naomi announced.

"I'll come with you," I said.

Naomi and Wren both gave me amused looks. "No way,"

Naomi said. "We'll be fine. I've wanted to get to know Wren better anyway, and a shopping trip is the perfect opportunity."

Talbot and I exchanged worried glances, but there was no stopping my cousin.

"I don't have any money," Wren said.

"I can take care of that," I said. I dug through my jeans pockets and came up with five hundred dollars.

"That's a start," Naomi said. "Nyx, having a girlfriend is expensive."

"She's not my girlfriend," I muttered.

I said good-bye to Wren reluctantly, but she couldn't follow me around forever. "Be careful," I called out after them, but they were already out the door.

"You two have been spending a lot of time together," Talbot said.

I glared at him. "Are you forgetting that I just broke up with Elizabeth?"

"You're practically acting like an old married couple."

"We spend twenty-four seven together," I said. "What did you expect?"

"Do you like her?" he asked.

"What's not to like?"

"You know what I'm talking about," he said.

There was a surprising rush, and it was almost four o'clock before there was a break.

"We didn't even have time for lunch," I complained, but it was halfhearted. I had actually enjoyed the rush, even though it was a short-lived one.

Talbot stared at me. "There's something different about you."

I pushed the memory of the night I'd spent with Wren to

the back of my mind. "Quit fucking with me and get back to work," I said.

"No, really," he replied. "You look... older."

"Older? Not possible," I said. "I'm stuck, remember?" I'd been twenty-three ever since my mother had died, over two hundred years ago. I'd stay that way until I found my thread of fate.

"Well, something unstuck you," he said. "You look older." I shrugged it off, but Talbot's comment bothered me the rest of my shift. "We need to talk to Dad when he comes back."

Wren and Naomi came back hours later. Naomi didn't look like she'd enjoyed their little excursion, though. Her face looked like she'd swallowed a tornado.

"When were you going to tell me?" Naomi asked.

"Tell you what?" Talbot asked, but we both knew what she was talking about. The message was clear on her face.

I glanced at Wren to see if she'd spilled the sibling beans, but she shook her head.

"That Wren is my sister," Naomi continued. "Or, more accurately, *half* sister, since her mother is Hecate."

"I'm sorry, Naomi," Wren said. "I wanted to tell you, but..."

"But Nyx convinced you not to," Naomi replied. "It's not your fault, Wren."

My cousin was angrier than I'd ever seen her. Her face was red, her eyes were squinty from the effort of holding back tears, and she was sweating. But underneath the anger, there was pain and disappointment.

There was no sense in denying it. "How did you find out?"

"I noticed when we were in the underworld," Naomi said coldly. "But I thought it was just a coincidence until Nyx did that tricky little occulo spell to conceal what Wren looked like."

"We had to," I said. "She looks so much like—"

"Like Sawyer," Naomi finished coldly. "And me."

"He's still your dad," I said.

"*Was* my dad," she said. "He's dead, remember?"

"Naomi, he loved you, you know that."

"He neglected to tell me I had a sister," she said. "You don't do that to someone you love. So everyone knew? Everyone but me?"

"Your mom doesn't know," I said. "And I think we should keep it that way."

She folded her arms across her chest. "You want me to lie to my own mother?"

"Don't you think Nona's been through enough lately?" I asked. "Do you think telling her that her deceased husband had a child with her mortal enemy is going to make her feel any better?"

"Sometimes truth is more important than anything else," Naomi said stubbornly.

"More important than your sister's safety?" Talbot interjected. "What do you think the Fates will do if they find out that Wren is Sawyer's daughter?"

The discussion ended without a resolution to the question he posed, but it haunted my dreams. What would the Fates do to Wren? And how could I protect her if they came after her?

Chapter Twenty-Four

Although Naomi still wasn't talking to me, she'd embraced her sister wholeheartedly. The evening of Willow's wedding came and they were getting ready for the event at Claire's; she had also been invited. That information should have set off warning bells somewhere in my brain, but I was distracted. I hated the thought of Willow marrying the necromancer, but I didn't see how I could stop it.

When I picked Wren up at Claire's, I was in a pissy mood. Even seeing Wren in a low-cut dress that fit her like a second skin didn't cheer me up. Well, not much, anyway.

I chanced a kiss on her cheek. "You look beautiful."

"We'd better leave or we'll be late," she said.

"Are you sure you want to go?" I asked. There was something in her voice that made me think she'd changed her mind.

She squared her chin like she was preparing for a fight. "I'm sure."

On the surface, it looked almost like a high-dollar mortal wedding. The bridegroom had rented out the ballroom and spared no expense decorating it.

It was all wrong for Willow, though. She was a naiad. She should be married under the stars next to the lake where she was born, standing next to a vigorous young man. Not in a crowded ballroom to an evil man smelling of mummy dust and cruelty.

The room was full of people proudly wearing the House of Hades insignia. The House symbol had been a bident, which looked like a modern-day pitchfork, but it was too similar to Poseidon's trident. They'd then adopted the pomegranate to honor Hades's unwilling bride Persephone.

Danvers, as the bridegroom, looked handsome in his tux and tails, until you got close enough to get a whiff of his soul. He'd at least had the decency to host an open bar before the ceremony.

Or maybe he figured that his guests needed some liquid encouragement to let him get his hands on Willow.

The entire room was gorgeous. Centerpieces were precisely placed on the tables and enormous bouquets of purple calla lilies were suspended from the ceiling. More calla lilies stood in vases with belladonna and white dittany. The effect was stunning, but every time I looked up, I got an oppressive feeling in my chest, like the ceiling was pressing down on me.

"Nyx, so lovely to see you here."

We both recognized the voice. Wren flinched while I repressed a swear word. It was Nona, my least repulsive aunt. She was Naomi's mother, which counted for a lot, and Sawyer Polydoro's widow. If she was here, it was likely the rest of the family was somewhere in the crowded ballroom.

"I didn't know you knew Danvers," she continued. She swayed slightly. My aunt was drunk but was attempting to hide it.

"I don't," I said. "I know—I mean, I know the bride."

"I see," she said. I had a horrible sinking sensation that she did see exactly what my relationship with Willow had been.

"How do you know the groom?" I asked Nona.

"He knew Sawyer," she said. She'd managed to say his name without breaking down, although tears welled in her eyes. She took a long sip of her drink.

Wren flinched at the mention of her father and I rubbed her back to soothe her.

"And who is this?" Nona asked, but there only curiosity in her eyes, instead of homicidal rage, which meant the spell had held. I wondered why her sisters hadn't told her that I was involved with Hecate's daughter.

"This is Wren," I said. "Wren, this is my aunt, Nona Polydoros."

"Naomi's mother," Wren said, with every appearance of delight, but her hand trembled when she held it out to shake Nona's.

The gleaming white chandeliers were made of bone. I hoped it wasn't human, but I wasn't betting on it.

I spotted Trey at the bar. As I watched him, the wedding planner, who looked like he was more used to arranging faces than flowers, tapped him on the shoulder. They had a short conversation and Trey's lips tightened. He shook his head several times, but the wedding planner handed him a note.

Trey walked over to an older sea nymph. He whispered something in her ear and she began to screech. He hustled her away, but not before the entire room had turned their way.

"What's going on?" I asked Nona, but before she could answer, we were joined by Deci and Morta. I was surprised to find that the sight of them made me feel better, which said a lot about the tension in the room.

I had a suspicion my aunts had meddled in this somehow. Or maybe I didn't want to admit that Willow might be going through with it willingly.

Whatever Trey had learned rippled through the room like a cold breeze. A couple of older women wearing House of Poseidon jewelry stalked out of the room.

"The groom has requested a *Pignus Sanguinus*," Morta explained.

"What is that?" I asked. "Why is everyone so riled up?" For a second, I'd had the irrational hope that Willow had refused to go through with the marriage.

"He's called for a blood oath," Naomi said. I hadn't seen her and Talbot arrive. I gave her a hug.

"How old-school," Nona said, her nose wrinkling.

"What's a blood oath?" I asked, though it was probably what it sounded like.

Nona didn't meet my eyes. "If the bride is ever disloyal, she dies."

"You mean he has the right to kill her?"

"No," Nona replied. "The spell kills her. The groom might not even know."

"That's barbaric."

"What about for him?" Wren asked.

"The bride's family did not make the same request," Nona replied.

Willow would probably be happy if he did cheat. Why was she tying herself to such a loathsome creature as Sean Danvers?

"I'll be right back," I said.

There was no sign of Willow. I wandered around until I spotted a giggling pack of naiads.

"Where's the happy bride?" I asked.

The youngest one giggled. I smiled at her, but her sisters scolded her. She looked at her feet until they'd lost interest. Then she gave me a beaming grin and pointed upward and held up six fingers, before skipping away.

The sixth floor.

I knocked on a few of the wrong doors, which got me nothing but cursing and, in one case, an invitation to join them. I declined politely.

I finally found the right door. Willow was surrounded by chattering naiads, but they all fell silent when they saw me.

Willow was in her wedding gown, which consisted of so many layers of tulle that it looked like they were smothering her. Her dark hair had been severely straightened. She sat at a vanity, staring into its shiny glass surface. I doubt she even saw her own reflection, though.

"Willow?" I said softly. "I've brought you a present."

Her pale blue skin had been covered with a heavy white powder. She smelled of misery and dark magic. She didn't seem to hear me, so I touched her shoulder. She finally looked up, but her eyes were faraway. They finally regained their focus. "Nyx, what are you doing here?"

"I'm worried about you," I said. "Why are you marrying that asshole?"

"It is none of your concern," she said. She looked at her staring bridesmaids and snapped, "Leave us."

They filed out of the room, but Willow still didn't say anything.

"Don't do it," I said.

"You are a child," she hissed at me. "Wanting only what you cannot have."

"That is probably true," I said. Her words hurt me more than I expected. "But that's not why I'm here. I'm your friend."

She didn't answer me, just kept staring into the mirror. Finally, she said, "I have to marry him."

"You don't have to," I said.

"You don't understand," she replied. "I am marrying him today and that's final. He's even put in a specially made pool at his house on Magician's Row."

"Since when do you care about a pool?"

"Since I need water to live," she reminded me. "Danvers expects us to live together. Always." The gloomy tone in her voice made me want to scoop her up and carry her out of there, but she'd just go back.

I took a small wrapped box out of my pocket. "A wedding gift."

"Thank you, Nyx," she said, but she didn't pick it up.

"Open it," I said. "Please."

She unwrapped it carefully. The moonstone gleamed up at her. "I thought it could be your something blue," I said.

"What?"

"Something borrowed, something blue," I said. "It's a mortal wedding custom."

"Oh," she said. Willow's expression didn't change, but I noticed a slight tremor in her hand. "It's beautiful. Thank you."

I undid the clasp and put the chain around her neck, tucking the moonstone under her layers of tulle, where her groom wouldn't see it. At least not right away.

I shut my mind against the thought of her wedding night.

"It's for protection," I said.

"Protection from what?" she asked, but the answer was in her eyes. Her future husband was a woman-hating fanatic. Her life with him would be a living hell. What I couldn't figure out was why she was chaining herself to such a monster.

"From whatever," I said. I kissed her forehead. "Willow, promise me that if you ever need help, you will come to me. No matter what."

She nodded. "I promise. Now you must leave me."

I cradled her cheek in my palm, reluctant to leave her. We stayed that for a long time, but then Willow stirred. "I must finish my preparations now."

I returned to the ballroom, not relieved at all. "Where were you?" Wren asked. "You've been gone for half an hour."

"I needed to talk to Willow," I said in a low voice. I didn't want to advertise the fact that I'd been trying to talk the bride out of going through with it.

Unfortunately, our little talk didn't seem to have done any good.

I caught Deci staring at us. What did she want? "I'm going to get us some drinks," I said.

It was an open bar, after all. I ordered a glass of wine for Naomi, and a shot of Jack for Talbot and me.

When I turned around, Deci was there. "You brought the hell spawn to the wedding?"

"Nice to see you, too," I said. "You're looking better than the last time I saw you." I wasn't expecting a thank-you and none was forthcoming, but she looked like she'd made a miraculous recovery from Gaston's poisoning.

She curled her lip at me. "You are blind, son of Fortuna, like all men," she said.

Before I could ask what she was babbling about, the wedding planner tapped on the microphone for the band. "Please be seated," he said. "The ceremony is about to begin."

"It's starting," Deci said. "We have seats in the front, of course."

"Nyx, you and your date should join us," Morta said. It was a command cloaked in an invitation.

I took Wren's hand and we followed my aunts to the folded chairs in the front row. Naomi led Talbot to chairs behind us. I turned around and mouthed, *Traitor*. She gave me a cheeky grin.

"Your aunts seem nice," Wren said.

I snorted with laughter. "Morta makes Lady Macbeth look like a pussycat," I replied. "And Deci is the most bitter person I've ever met."

"What's Nona like?" she asked.

Before I could reply, the groom and his best man took their places at the front. Danvers had a smug smile on his face and I wanted to wipe it away with my fist. I hated the sight of him, and it wasn't because he was marrying Willow. Okay, it wasn't *only* because of that.

There was something off-putting about the way his head was too large for his body, his slicked-back hair, and his chiseled jawline. He was a hair too tall, too rich, and too sure of himself.

The traditional wedding march began to play. It played all the way through, but the bridal party did not appear. The wedding planner got a panicky look on his face. The music died and the room was completely silent.

I looked at the groom. His smile was fixed firmly in place, his body language relaxed, but his fingers were curled into fists. He jerked his head at the wedding planner, who tried to discreetly slip out of the room, despite the fact that everyone was watching with avid gazes. He was obviously going in search of the bride.

Finally, the music started up again and the bridal party made their way to the front at a sedate pace, as if they hadn't kept everyone waiting for almost half an hour.

Then Willow made her grand entrance, beautifully pale but composed, on Trey's arm.

"She looks as though she's going to her own execution," Wren whispered. "Couldn't you talk her out of it?"

I shook my head, unwilling to reveal to her how much Willow's nuptials upset me.

Morta turned and stared right at me as Willow passed by. Why were they here? Just how friendly were they with that slime Danvers?

The first part of the wedding ceremony was fairly traditional, but right before the part where the minister usually said something about pronouncing you man and wife, there was a deviation. The blood oath spell was conducted with great pomp and circumstance, but many guests looked at their feet, as if ashamed of what they were witnessing.

I looked at a point above Willow's head and prayed that she'd stop the wedding, but she said her vows in a carrying voice that reached all the way to the back row.

I almost lost it during the first dance. The guy had his hands all over Willow. I don't know what was more repulsive, the way he touched her or the way she let him.

I managed to control myself until after they'd cut the cake.

"Are you ready to go?" I asked Wren abruptly.

"I want to stay," she said. "Please? I've never been to a wedding before."

I smiled at her. "Another hour."

The only good thing about the entire wedding was the open bar. I made my way there. "Give me a couple of whiskeys. Straight."

I watched Danvers and Willow circulate among their guests as I threw back a couple of more drinks, courtesy of the groom.

Finally, Talbot came up to me. "You're not going to cause a scene, are you?" His eyes gleamed silverlight, which only happened when he was doing magic or was upset about something.

I chugged the last of my drink. I'd lost count how many I'd had. "Why do you ask?"

"You've been staring at them all night," he said. "You haven't been paying any attention to your date."

"Wren?"

"Yeah, Wren. Do you even know where she is?"

I pretended not to feel guilty. "I'm sure you're going to tell me."

"Some guy has been chatting her up all night," Talbot said. "And you didn't even notice. You were too busy glowering at the bride and groom."

"Wren is fine," I said. "I'm worried about Willow because she's my friend, nothing more."

"You look like a jealous ex-boyfriend to me," he replied.

"Jesus, Talbot, give me a break. I just broke up with Elizabeth. Willow is my friend and Wren is a distraction. She knows it's nothing serious."

He stalked off, but his words did sink in. After he went back to Naomi, I looked around for Wren, blurry-eyed. I finally found her on the dance floor, in Danvers's arms.

I stalked toward them, but Trey grabbed me by the arm. "Nyx, that would not be a good idea. Danvers is much more dangerous than you think. Your girlfriend is fine. He has been completely circumspect with her."

"She's not my girlfriend," I said.

I stood where I was and watched them as I waited for the song to end. As far as I knew, Wren and Danvers had never met, but they were laughing with easy intimacy. Had the whiskey I'd been pouring down my throat dulled my powers of observation or honed them?

Chapter Twenty-Five

That week, I slept poorly every night, awakened periodically by the baying of hounds.

I reported to my Saturday shift at Eternity Road, sleep-deprived and hungover. Even copious amounts of alcohol hadn't drowned the sound of Hecate's hounds. Even trapped in the underworld, she still managed to send me a message.

I hadn't seen much of Talbot since the wedding. He'd been pissed at me.

"About time you showed up," he said. Judging from his snotty tone, guess he still was.

I glanced around the store and understood his irritation. There were at least twenty people in the store, a curious combo of hipsters and senior citizens.

"What gives?"

"There was a write-up in yesterday's paper," he explained. "Apparently, Eternity Road is one of the Twin Cities' hidden gems."

"And your dad's still out of town," I said. "Sorry, Talbot. I assumed..."

He waved me away. "I know, I know. You assumed the store would be empty, like it almost always is. Now go man the cash register while I show this very patient woman to a dressing room."

The woman, who had an armful of vintage dresses, glared at me before she followed Talbot.

The unexpected rush died down about three and a welcome silence fell over the store.

Talbot seemed to have gotten over his snit. "How did Willow know the murders would stop if she married Danvers?" he asked.

"The obvious answer is that she knows he's the killer," I replied.

"But how is marriage going to stop a serial killer?"

"It's not," I said. "Unless..."

"Unless what?"

"Unless he's not a serial killer," I told him. There was a theory working its way through the sodden recesses of my brain.

Talbot's eyebrows scrunched together. "I thought you just said Danvers is the killer."

"Maybe he's not *trying* to kill them," I explained. "He has some other goal. The deaths are incidental."

"Then what's his real goal?" Talbot challenged.

I slumped on the stool, defeated. "I have no idea." I sat up again, galvanized. "When is your dad back? I want to ask him some questions about the Houses and Willow."

"He's due back any time," Talbot replied.

Ambrose finally showed up a few minutes after closing. Talbot and I had made ourselves comfortable on a couple of chairs shaped like eggs and had cracked a couple of beers when Ambrose strode in.

"Talbot, where are you? I need help with the load," he bellowed.

"I'll do it," I told him.

I made my way to the front of the store. "Ambrose, lead me to those boxes."

His U-Haul was stacked high. I wasn't going to make it home any time soon. I clambered up and grabbed the top boxes. "Where do you want these?"

"Those can go into storage," Ambrose directed. "Use the dolly. Do we have room for any of the furniture in the store? I found some great deals."

We made at least ten trips to the storage room in the basement before I could reach any furniture.

"Ambrose," I said, setting down a spinning wheel straight out of *Sleeping Beauty*, "why did Trey walk Willow down the aisle at her wedding?"

"That's right," he said. "I missed the event of the season. Maybe even the century."

"Why was it such a big event?"

"The two Houses don't get along," he said.

"I already knew that," I said. "So?"

"So they were this close to war a few years ago," he said. He held up his thumb and finger a sliver apart.

"Baxter said that they cut a deal to stop the killings," I said. "But what does Willow have to do with all this?"

"Willow is Trey's niece," he said. "I thought you knew."

"Why would he let her marry a monster like Danvers?" I asked, horrified.

"Willow is a direct descendent of the mortal Cleito and Poseidon," he replied. "Nobody *lets* her do anything. She's the most powerful naiad in the states, possibly the world."

"You're saying that Willow went into this marriage willingly?"

"You're asking the wrong questions, Nyx," he replied. "What is important in this equation is why Danvers wants Willow."

"Who *wouldn't* want Willow?" I said aloud.

Ambrose gave me a sharp look but didn't comment.

It wasn't just Danvers who wanted her. I wanted her, too, and not just for an occasional drunken hookup. The realization kept repeating in my head as we finished putting away Ambrose's haul.

"We need to talk to Dad," Talbot reminded me.

He dragged me into the office, where Ambrose was doing a crossword puzzle. "What's another word for *stubborn*?"

"Nyx Fortuna," Talbot said.

"It fits!" Ambrose chuckled. Was he really writing my name in the crossword squares?

"Nyx has a problem," Talbot told him.

"What can I help you with, dear boy?" Ambrose asked.

"I think it's Talbot's imagination," I said.

"It's not," Talbot said. "Dad, focus for a minute. Take a good look at Nyx and tell me if you see anything different about him."

Ambrose examined my face. "It's definitely a spell," he said. "And a particularly nasty one."

I shrugged, but inside, my stomach squirmed like I'd eaten a bellyful of eels. "I have a lot of enemies."

"Talbot, fetch the camera," Ambrose said. "The one on the top shelf in my office."

"The *nota bene* camera?" Talbot asked. "You told me not to touch that under any circumstance."

Nota bene meant "take note," loosely, in Latin. I was intrigued.

Ambrose sighed patiently. "Now I'm telling you to get it." His voice was tense.

Talbot picked up on his father's tone and made for the office. He came back with what looked like an old-fashioned Polaroid, but I knew better. It was, after all, something Ambrose kept on the top shelf.

"What does it do?"

"It reveals," Ambrose said.

"That clears things up," Talbot said dryly.

His father ignored him. "Nyx, please stand against that wall."

I did as he asked and waited while he took a series of instant photos. He shook them gently and then put on a pair of glasses. He went quiet.

"Well?" Talbot prodded, but Ambrose shushed him.

Ambrose finally said. "Nyx, I'm afraid you've been cursed."

"Is that all?" But my stomach sank. I had enough on my to-do list to last me the millennium.

"Can I see?" Talbot made a grab for one of the photos, but his dad slapped his hand away.

"I don't need to waste precious time hunting down some piddly-ass curse," I said.

"You need to make the time," Ambrose replied. "This is serious."

"How serious?"

"If we don't find a cure, you'll be old and wrinkled and gasping for air, unable to move or feed yourself, but you won't die. That sound attractive to you? Your mind will be the same, but your body will turn to mush."

I shuddered. I had thought living forever was the worst fate possible until I was staring down a worse one.

"I want to live out a life," I said. "Not accelerate to the end and then get stuck there."

"We'll figure it out," Talbot said soothingly.

"What if we don't?" I asked. "We have to find my thread of fate."

"And break the curse," Ambrose reminded me.

"How do you suggest we do that?" I asked him. Ambrose was a big magician mucky-muck in the House of Zeus.

"Let me make some inquiries," Ambrose replied. "I've seen this before, but it requires a delicate hand. We mustn't rush into this or we could do more damage."

"Like what?"

"Exactly how old are you, anyway?" Talbot asked me.

"Two twenty, give or take a few years."

Ambrose answered my question. "If we're not careful, you could wake up one day looking every one of those years."

I'd thought, or at least pretended, that I didn't care about my looks, but I found that I did. I couldn't picture Wren dating me if I looked like someone's great-grandfather. I suppressed the image of growing old with Elizabeth. That wasn't going to happen, not ever. I wasn't going to grow old with anybody.

"I'll sit tight until you find out more," I promised.

"The good news is that this is a relatively slow-acting spell," Ambrose said. "Perhaps the sorcerer hoped you wouldn't notice until it was too late."

"I probably wouldn't have," I admitted. "Talbot's the one who noticed."

"Very good, "Ambrose told his son. "You have the makings of a very good magician."

"Could the curse have been implanted in the wraith bite somehow?"

"It's possible," Ambrose said. "I'll do some research, make some calls, but in the meantime, Nyx, try to take it easy."

"I'd like nothing more than to relax," I said. "But my plate's kind of full."

"True," Ambrose said. "Try not to get bitten by another wraith."

"Or stabbed," Talbot added.

Underneath their forced jocularity, Talbot and his dad were clearly worried. And so was I.

I remembered the lighter and took it out of my jeans pocket, where I'd stashed it. It was blackened and twisted and still smelled of smoke. "Have you ever seen a lighter like this?"

Ambrose had owned the pawnshop a long time, and I didn't have any other leads. It was a casual question, but he paled when he saw it. "Where did you get this?"

"I found it at the theater fire," I said.

He stared at it. "Your father gave them out as gifts one Christmas," he said. He reached into his pocket and pulled out a matching silver lighter. "He gave one to me, one to your mother, and one to another woman." I recognized the lighter. It was engraved with a peacock feather.

"What other woman? You make it sound like my father had been cheating on my mother."

His silence told me all I needed to know. "Do you know who she was?"

He shook his head. "He wouldn't tell me."

"Please tell me who my father is," I begged.

"That is not my story to tell, Nyx," he said. No matter how much I persisted, Ambrose refused to tell me anything else.

* * *

On Sunday, Wren and I met Talbot and Naomi for breakfast. I sat in the booth with a beer and a shitty attitude. I was daring Bernie to say something, but she took our order without commenting.

"That was some wedding, wasn't it?" Naomi commented but shut up when she saw my face.

I was angry, but I didn't know why. Or maybe I knew why, but I didn't want to admit it. My brain kept returning to the image of Willow in Danvers's arms. I'd done everything I could to convince her not to, but she was now his wife.

I was itching for a fight.

"I'm going back to talk to your mother," I told Wren.

"That's a very bad idea, Nyx," she said.

"What other choice do we have? She won't stop until she gets you back. And that's not going to happen. I have to do something."

Talbot interrupted me. "You must still be drunk. You're not thinking this through."

I put the beer bottle down with more force than necessary. "It's the only way she'll leave us alone. Plus, it'll piss off the Fates."

"Do you ever think about anything else besides that Greek tragedy thing you got going on with them?" Talbot bellowed. "When you're not killing your liver or chasing women, that is."

"Talbot, I..."

"You don't have anything to say, do you? For once in your life, think of us before you recklessly charge in," he said. He stalked off and left the restaurant. I could see him through the window, pacing angrily.

I started to follow him, but Naomi put a hand on my shoulder. "I'll talk to him," she said. She slid out of the both and joined Talbot outside.

Even Talbot's anger couldn't sway me. Wren didn't say anything until I got up to pay the check.

"Your friend is worried about you," Bernie said as she took my money. "He should be."

"Why do you say that?"

She started to say something else, but then her face closed. "Never mind."

A second later, Wren's hand was on my shoulder. "Ready to go?"

After breakfast, I changed into warm clothes, grabbed my jacket, and headed down.

This time, I went alone. Hecate would want to rip me apart and I didn't want any innocent bystanders getting injured.

The trip down was cold and miserable without Talbot for company.

When I entered the underworld, Hecate was a few hundred yards from the gate, waiting for me, her three enormous dogs lying at her feet. Her dark hair, which had been bound up last time we'd met, was down and blowing in the wind.

"You have a lot of nerve, son of Fortuna," she said. But she didn't sic the dogs on me, which seemed promising.

"Where is my daughter?" Hecate asked. "I want her back. I was sure even someone as thick-skulled as you would have gotten the message by now."

I glared back. "Message received," I said. "But that doesn't mean I'm going to do what you want."

She smiled. "I think you will. I have what you're looking for," she said. "A very special charm of your mother's. One I understand you have been searching for your whole *life*." She placed special emphasis on the last word.

"You're lying." She couldn't have the charm containing my thread of fate.

She raised one eyebrow. "Am I?" The confidence in her voice convinced me. Hecate had one of my mother's charms and was prepared to trade for it. I had a feeling I wasn't going to like the trade, though.

"What do you want in return?" I already knew the answer.

"My daughter," she replied. "You took her from me."

"Wren doesn't want to come back."

"Now who's lying?" she replied. "My daughter loves me."

It hadn't been love in Wren's eyes when she'd spoken of her mother. It had been fear.

"I'm not giving her to you."

"You're hesitating," she replied. "How chivalrous. I assure you no harm will come to my daughter."

"Wren wants to stay topside. She's your daughter. Don't you want her to be happy?"

"Happiness is overrated."

"What isn't?"

"I'll tell you what's not overrated," she replied. "Revenge."

"I'm not stupid enough to do a trade in the underworld, anyway," I said. "You'd never let me leave."

"You're not ready to bargain? Pity."

"A crossroads bargain? I don't think so, Hecate."

"I'd give you the same deal I gave Robert Johnson," she said.

"Didn't turn out so well for him, now did it?" Legend was the blues guitarist Robert Johnson had traded his soul for success. Fame and fortune alluded him, but I'd seen him play once, and he had a magical touch with a guitar.

She smiled grimly. "If you don't give me back my daughter, I will slaughter anyone you've ever loved. Including the mortal, who thinks she's hidden herself away from the affairs of the Houses."

I tried to suppress the rage I felt when she threatened Elizabeth, but she chuckled when she saw how it lit my eyes.

"Wren is happy where she is," I said. "Why can't you understand that?"

"She does not belong in the mortal realm," Hecate said. "She belongs with me."

"No dice," I said.

Her catlike eyes gleamed.

"What do you want? Besides Wren?"

"I want you to bring me the bead," she said.

"I don't know what you're talking about."

"Now who's lying?" she replied.

The back-and-forth was growing old. "I'll see what I can do about getting you the bead, but Wren stays with me."

"How can you keep us apart?" Hecate said. "My daughter loves me."

"I'm not giving her to you." The fear in Wren's eyes hadn't convinced me, but the scars on her body had.

"I will get my daughter back, with or without you," she replied. "You don't want me as an enemy."

"You'd never honor your side of the bargain and you'd never let Wren leave ever again. She'd be a prisoner." Why did Hecate have one of my mother's charms in the first place? Had Wren's escape been planned?

"Is that your final word?"

"It is." Before she could react, I wheeled and started running back for my side of the gate. Over my shoulder, I chanted the spell Talbot had used on the dogs previously, but it didn't work. They were gaining on me. I reached the gate and rammed the key into the lock, but the dogs were already upon me.

The largest of the dog bit into my leg and then shook me like I was a chew toy. Pain ripped through me. Before I passed out from the loss of blood and sheer agony, I used a concealment spell.

The dog, startled, yelped and released the grip on my leg. I yanked open the gate, trailing blood. The dogs realized their prey was still within reach and snapped at my hand as I pulled the gate shut in their faces.

I ran through the tunnels, expecting the vicious beasts to catch up to me, but I made it topside without being turned into kibble. Once I'd made it out, I stopped to look at my leg and then wished I hadn't. I hated the smell and sight of blood. I could barely stand to look at it, especially when it was my own fluid exiting my body all too rapidly.

The dog had bitten through the jeans I wore, shredding them and several layers of my skin in the process. The leg looked remarkably like ground sausage, and I fought back the nausea rising in my throat.

Fortunately, the tunnels leading to the underworld were cold, and I'd worn my leather jacket, which had several healing amulets sewn into it. I got my hands on one and attempted a spell but had to stop to bend over and throw up. Shivering from loss of blood, I was woozy and couldn't remember where I'd left the Caddy.

Finally, I located it, but even with the healing charms, I was getting weaker. I dropped my keys and swore. When I bent down to retrieve them, I fell down and couldn't get back up. That's where Talbot found me.

"Hell and Hades, Nyx," he said. "Why didn't you tell me you were going back down there?" He scooped up my keys while I lay there. I heard the sound of the Caddy door opening and then Talbot returned. He lifted and half dragged me, half carried me to the passenger seat, then slid in behind the wheel and headed for home.

Chapter Twenty-Six

I recuperated at home for a few days. I was a bad patient, even with amulets speeding up the healing process. I spent my time brooding on the couch, with my leg propped up on a pile of pillows.

"It's going to leave a nasty scar," Wren said.

"If you haven't noticed, I already have plenty of those," I said.

She handed me a fresh glass of absinthe. Unlike everyone else around me, Wren didn't seem to mind when I drank.

She sat next to me and then slid her hand inside my shirt and found the ridged scar near my heart. "How did this one happen?"

I removed her hand as the memory of the day I'd met Elizabeth surfaced. "Someone tried to kill me. He missed."

"I thought you said you couldn't be killed," Wren replied.

"I can't," I said. "But he didn't know that."

"Why can't you be killed?" she asked.

It wasn't exactly a secret, so I told her the truth.

"And you think it was a coincidence that you found the charms after you came to Minneapolis?"

"You think it isn't?" I replied. "It's not like I found all of them."

"Is it true your aunts love intrigue?"

"More than they love breathing." I couldn't get my head around the possibility that I hadn't found my mother's charms on my own. Had the Fates had a hand in it after all? I put a hand to the silver chain I always wore and rattled the charms there.

"Do you have all the charms?" Wren asked casually.

"No," I replied. "I'm still looking for a miniature book, an ivory wheel of fortune, and a horseshoe made of moonstones."

She coiled a finger around the silver chain around my neck. "Maybe you were just lucky to stumble across them after all that time."

I was the son of Lady Fortuna, but I was starting to doubt that even I was that lucky.

She lifted my tee and placed a soft kiss on the scar, which led to longer, more intimate kisses.

It was a little awkward, making love on the couch with my leg propped up, but we managed. Later, she curled next to me.

"Do you still want to die?"

I laughed and wrapped my arms around her. "Not after that."

She leaned away and stared at me with her golden eyes. "I'm serious."

"Sometimes," I admitted. "Sometimes, I still want to die. But not all the time. Not anymore."

I wanted to stay like that for the rest of the afternoon, but Wren had other ideas. "I'm going to do a load of laundry."

She wriggled out of my arms and went into the bedroom. I eased back into my sweats, which were the only clothing I could tolerate near my leg wound, and then dozed off.

When I woke up, Wren stood in the middle of the room holding the lighter. "What is this?" she asked. "It reeks of smoke."

It was the lighter I'd taken from the fire during Elizabeth's performance. "Let me see that."

She handed it to me. I used my T-shirt to try to clean the blackened silver lighter, but nothing came off. I finally tried a spell. *Aperio!* It revealed the lighter was engraved with the inscription, *"To D. Passion is a flame—H."* H? My father had more pseudonyms than I did. In the book Doc had returned, he had been Dr. A. M. Green.

I was holding the lighter of the person who'd set the fire in the theater, the person who had scarred Elizabeth's face. I had suspected Deci since her little pyromania incident at Claire's apartment, but I'd had the proof all along.

I hobbled around trying to find my keys.

"Nyx, you should rest."

"I'm going to talk to my aunts," I said.

"I'll get Talbot," she said and ran next door.

Talbot reluctantly chauffeured me and parked the Caddy at Parsi Enterprises. "Wait here," I said.

Talbot protested, "Nyx, whatever you're planning, I think you should wait until you cool down."

"Not gonna happen," I said. The uneasy détente with my aunts was over.

I limped into the building, not bothering to see if he'd follow.

The security guard in the lobby took one look at me and

picked up the phone. I muttered an *encanto,* and it flew out of his hand.

I found all three of my aunts in the conference room. I'd interrupted a business meeting. Trevor had been pouring sodas into little paper cups for some sort of a taste test. He scurried out the door as soon as he saw me.

"You evil hags," I roared. "Deci, I wish I'd let Gaston murder you in your sleep. Why did you do it?"

Morta and Nona seemed to be honestly surprised to see me, but it took Deci a second to conceal a smirk.

"Sharpening your scissors, Morta?" I asked. "Instead of worrying about me, you should worry about your own sister."

"I don't know what you're talking about," she said calmly. "Why don't you stop shouting and have a seat?"

"Ask Deci, she knows."

"Nyx, you're upset, but the fire was an unfortunate accident, nothing more," Deci said.

I gave her a cold look. "I never said anything about the fire."

"I assumed that would be upsetting to you, especially since your girlfriend left town shortly thereafter."

"You're lying," I said. "You threatened me and then my ex-girlfriend ended up in the hospital. I don't think that's a coincidence. I knew you'd murder without a second thought, but I didn't think you'd put your own niece at risk."

"Naomi?" Nona said at the same time that Morta said, "Claire?"

"Naomi was there when the fire started," I said. "You'd know that if you ever took your face out of the bottle."

"You're one to talk," Morta snarled.

Nona turned a sickly green and I quickly added, "It could

have been Naomi in that hospital bed, thanks to your pyromaniac of a sister."

I advanced toward Deci, but Morta stepped in front of her. "Careful, son of Fortuna."

Nobody said anything for a minute.

I took a step back. "You'd protect her, after all that?"

"Why do you think Deci is responsible?" Morta asked.

"I don't think she did it," I said. "I *know* she did."

"How?" Nona asked. "She can barely walk."

"She forgot something," I said. "Her lighter."

"Deci?" Nona turned to her sister with a stricken expression. "What is he talking about?"

"Right here." I tossed the lighter on the conference table and it skittered across its smooth surface and landed in Nona's lap. "Look familiar? I'm told there are only three of them. One that belonged to my mother, one belonged to my father, whoever he is, and the other one is Deci's. I found it at the theater fire but didn't realize what I had: proof that Deci set the fire."

"He stole it," Deci accused.

I snorted. I'd bet that even her two sisters would have a hard time with that one, and I was right.

The second Deci realized she'd fucked up, it showed on her face. "Shut up, son of Fortuna, or I'll..."

"You'll what? Hurt someone I love?" I said. "You really need to find a new way to threaten me."

Nona flicked open the lighter and started the flame. Deci's eyes were drawn to the flame. She couldn't look away.

"See something you like, Deci?" I asked.

She finally looked away to glare at me. "You're soft," she hissed. "Like she was."

I took a step toward her. "She was a better person than you could ever be."

"You didn't know her as well as you think you did," Deci replied. "That makes you soft *and* stupid."

I lunged for her, but the sound of Nona's voice stopped me.

"Nyx, leave us," Nona said. "We have things to discuss."

"You're going to let her get away with lying to you both? Putting Naomi in danger?"

"It is not your concern, Nyx," Morta said. It was the first time she'd called me by my chosen name. "Leave now."

"I'm leaving," I said. "But think about this. What else has she done behind your back? How many other fires did she start?"

Morta remained stony-faced, but Nona's face twitched. Something about my last statement got to her. I could tell they knew Deci was a bit of a pyromaniac. The question was: Who else had my aunt tried to burn alive?

Chapter Twenty-Seven

It was barely dawn when my cell phone rang.

I held it to my ear groggily. "Nyx, you need to get down here," a voice ordered.

"Who is this?"

"Baxter, you wonk. Get to the morgue."

"There's been another murder?" I asked in a hushed tone. In her sleep, Wren snuggled closer to me.

"You could say that," he said. "I'm up to my tits in exploded nymphs. Get your ass down here." I realized he'd hung up and put the phone down.

Wren stirred beside me. "What's wrong?"

"Nothing," I lied. "I've got to go out for a while. I'll be back as soon as I can."

She nodded sleepily before sinking back into dreamland.

"Where are they?" I asked Baxter when I finally made it to his basement.

He gestured to a couple of commercial-grade buckets in the corner. "Right there." There was blood up to his elbows.

"Jesus, Baxter," I said. "How can you eat at a time like this?"

He looked offended. "I didn't touch them. They came in like that. The blood is from the autopsy."

I gulped. The smell of blood mingled with the heavy odor of dark magic, dank and coppery. "How many?"

He shrugged. "Three. Maybe four. It's hard to tell. A mortal beat cop found them before anyone from the Houses could take care of them."

"Exactly how long have the Houses been taking care of stuff like this?"

"As long as I can remember," he said. "And that's a very long time. They don't want the mortals to realize we're living among them."

"Some mortals know," I said, thinking of Elizabeth and Alex.

"Some," he agreed. "But not many. And it's not like the Houses want to advertise that there's a magical killer loose."

"But he's not killing mortals," I said. "You said you've lived a long time. You've never seen anything like it?"

"Once," he said. "Only once." His eyes lost their focus and a shudder went over him. "When Hecate was still free."

"What was it like then?"

"It rained blood," he said. "Your aunts did us all a favor when they trapped her. I hope she rots in hell."

"How did they do it? Trap her?" I asked.

"It wasn't in the company newsletter," he snarked. I glared at him, and he added, "They took away her power somehow. She's been trying to get topside again ever since."

"What will happen if she does?"

"She'll make the Dark Ages look like a picnic in the park," he replied.

How could Sawyer have slept with someone like that?

Danvers was waiting for me outside my apartment door when I got home. I had a giddy feeling in my chest. I was certain I knew why he was there. Willow had taken my advice and made a run for it. The idea made me smile.

"Aren't you supposed to be on your honeymoon?" I asked. Maybe I had a bit of a smirk on my face, but it was just a tiny one. Hardly noticeable.

His bodyguard didn't wait for his boss to answer. Conversation ceased entirely when his big, meaty paw wrapped around my throat and squeezed the smile from my face.

"Where is she?" Danvers asked, like he was asking me the time of day.

Lurch stopped squeezing long enough for me to suck in a breath and wheeze out an "I don't know."

It was true, but I wouldn't tell him even if I did.

The apartment door opposite us opened and Ambrose stuck his head out. "Is there a problem?"

Danvers bowed to him and Lurch let go of me. I dropped to the floor and gasped, trying to get air back into my tortured lungs again.

Ambrose was not a man most people messed with, and the necromancer apparently realized that even with his great hulk of a bodyguard, he was outgunned.

"Mr. Danvers, I really must protest," Ambrose continued, all affability. "I cannot allow you to mishandle my employee in such a way."

Danvers's eyes narrowed. "Your employee?"

"Yes," Ambrose replied blandly. "Nyx works for me. And as such, under the protection of the House of Zeus. He is also a member of the House of Fate and under his aunts' protection."

It hurt too much to raise an eyebrow at the last part, but I thought about it.

Danvers bowed. "I understand," he said. "But I was told he might have something of mine."

"I don't have anything of yours," I said.

He gave me a thin smile. "I hope you are telling me the truth. Or you will regret it."

He jerked his head at the bodyguard and then they took the stairs without looking back.

"The curse. It was you," I called out.

He turned leisurely and faced me with an oily smile. "It scared you, didn't it? It made you realize you didn't want to die after all."

It was true, but I wasn't going to give him any satisfaction by admitting it. He was practically admitting he'd sent the wraiths to my apartment, but there'd been a brief flicker of some emotion in his eyes. Was it surprise or satisfaction?

"But you are quite ingenious," he continued. "That's when I knew you were my son."

"There's no way in hell I'm related to you."

"I could be your daddy," he said. "I bet they didn't tell you that part, did they? I'm one of the oldest necromancers around. I knew your mother intimately." He smacked his lips.

"You're lying." The thought of the sick old letch touching my mother made the bile rise in my throat.

He seemed delighted with my repulsion. What a dick.

"It's been real," I said. "But it's time for you to go."

The truth was my father could have been anybody. My mother never talked about him, wouldn't tell me his name even when I'd asked.

He seemed to be composing himself before he took another step and then disappeared around the corner.

It was pretty obvious that Willow's husband had it out for me. But why would he have wanted to kill me even before he'd married her? Before he'd even met me?

I had some questions for my aunts. I wasn't sure they would answer them, but it was worth a shot. They'd always danced around my father's identity before, but I had a feeling they knew more than they were telling me. It could wait, though.

Ambrose shoved me into his apartment and then closed the door and locked it. "Nyx, what have you gotten yourself into this time?"

I avoided his gaze. "I have no idea."

"Guess," Ambrose replied through gritted teeth.

"Runaway bride. Pissed-off necromancer would be my guess."

I sat at the kitchen counter while he poured me a glass of something strong. "Drink this."

"It smells vile," I said.

"It's a curse cure," he said. "Remember that little curse thing?"

"I have had a few other things on my plate," I said. My throat was swelling from Lurch's roughhousing, but I chugged the concoction anyway. It tasted as nasty as it smelled.

"Something more than that is going on," he said. "But I haven't been able to figure out what."

"You mean besides Willow marrying that creep to prevent more naiads from dying?" Baxter had told me Trey's niece was the sacrificial lamb, but Ambrose's expression confirmed it.

I got up. "Thanks for the drink."

"Where are you going?"

"I've got to find Willow before Danvers does," I said.

I figured she'd head for home, so I pointed the Caddy to the lake where we'd first met.

Willow's lake. She needed me and I needed to know she was safe.

The bench felt hard and cold, despite the spring weather. Pristine blue water was unmoving and silent. Even the tadpoles were hiding.

"Damn it, Willow! Where are you?" I said. The sound of my voice carried over the water, but there was no response. I waited, but all was still. I finally gave up and stood. A ladybug landed on my shoulder.

I extended a finger to set the bug in flight when I saw her through the tangled moonflower vines, like a mermaid from a fairy tale, wobbly on new legs, waiting for her prince. But it was no fairy tale and there was no prince.

"Willow?" When I got closer, I could see the blood trickling out of the corner of her mouth, her eye already turning black.

A pattern of bruises marred her upper arms, chest, and legs. She couldn't stop shivering. Her wedding night hadn't been a pleasant one.

"I'll kill him," I said. I took off my jacket and wrapped it around her.

She whimpered. "You can't." Then, more strongly, "You won't."

I was upsetting her. She didn't have to know what I had planned for that bastard. "You're cold," I said. "Let me warm you up."

There was a vicious-looking bite mark on her neck. "Your moonstone," I said. "It's gone."

She shook her head and slowly unclenched her fist. Her fingers unfurled and then I saw her fingernails were grimy with dried blood. The gemstone was imbedded into the palm of her hand. She'd fought back, then.

"Did he..." I started and then stopped, not sure how to say it.

She finally met my eyes. "The marriage was not consummated."

"We need to get out of here," I said.

"He's already been here looking for me," Willow said. "I hid."

"Good." I picked her up and carried her to the Caddy. I placed her gently in the front passenger seat and then went to the trunk for the blanket I kept there. I'd learned quickly to be prepared for Minnesota weather. It was spring, but my idea of spring was slightly different from a Minnesota native's.

I wrapped the blanket around her and started the car, turning the heater on full blast to warm her up. "Where to?" I asked. "One of the other lakes?"

She shook her head. "It's not safe," she said. "The other naiads will just send me back." She didn't sound bitter that her own colony wouldn't protect her.

"What about someone in the House of Poseidon?"

"There's no one," she said. "No one but you."

"He's been to my apartment, too," I said. "But I know a place no one will find us."

I'd take her to the Dead House. I'd killed a troll there. In fact, he was still there, his stone image guarding the entrance.

The place hadn't changed a bit. A boarded-up window hung loosely, and I put her down gently.

"I'll be right back," I said. I slithered through the window and then went around and opened the back door. I carried her in and put the blanket on top of the bedroll that had been there before.

The décor was early graffiti and beer bottles, but nobody would look for us there. "Home sweet home," I muttered.

I ripped the last of the healing amulets out of my jacket and used them to try to heal her, but it wasn't enough.

"You need a doctor," I said. She was drifting in and out of consciousness, but she heard that.

"No, please," she said. "He'll find me."

"I know someone who can help," I said. "You can trust him." That is, if I could find him.

She was sweating and blood was still oozing from her injuries, but the spell had sent her into a healing sleep.

"I won't be gone long," I said to her sleeping form. I kissed her hair gently before I left.

I looked everywhere, but I couldn't find Doc. I called Talbot, who gave me the address of the shelter where Doc sometimes stayed, but the doors were closed for the night.

I didn't want to leave Willow alone for too long, so I finally gave up the search. I stopped by a drugstore and bought some first-aid supplies before I headed back to the Dead House.

When I crawled through the window, Willow was gasping and her blue skin had turned an unhealthy purplish color, but she was awake.

"How long since you've been in the water?" I asked her. I'd found her in the shallows, but a naiad needed water like we needed air.

She shook her head. "I don't know."

There was an old trough standing in the middle of what used to be an autopsy chamber. I didn't want to think about what used to be in it. I scared away the spiders and then chanted a spell to get it to fill with water. I placed Willow in it gently.

She seemed a little better, but not enough. She was fading in and out again. I was starting to panic, but then I remembered we were in Minneapolis. There had to be a lake or river within spitting distance. I gathered up her wet, slippery form and ran, then told myself to calm down.

I did a locater spell and then followed the trail of light until we came to a lake. I unceremoniously dumped her into the water and then she slowly sank out of sight.

I waited for a long time. Was I too late? Was Willow at the bottom of the lake? Finally, there was a splash and her head broke the surface. She swam to the edge and treaded water as she watched me.

"Thank you, son of Fortuna," she said gravely. "You saved my life."

"I should have thought of it sooner," I said angrily. "I almost killed you."

She splashed me and then giggled at the surprise on my face. "You saved me," she repeated. "I'd almost forgotten I was a naiad. I'd become a puppet."

Interesting choice of words. "We should get out of here," I said. "He'll probably have people looking for you at the lakes and rivers."

We spent another day and night at the Dead House. I didn't think about Wren, who was probably waiting for me at my apartment. I didn't think about Elizabeth. I didn't think about anyone except Willow.

Chapter Twenty-Eight

Sometime during our second night at the Dead House, Willow stole away while I slept. I waited for her for hours, but she never returned. Maybe she was somewhere in the Driftless, the watery world where I'd found Elizabeth's brother Alex. Or maybe she'd decided to leave Minneapolis altogether. Wherever she was, I hoped she was far away from her husband. Not knowing where she was or if she was safe was taking its toll on me.

I stopped by the Red Dragon, looking for information. It was early, so there were only a few regulars at the bar, but I was hoping I'd hear something, anything. I was nursing a glass of beer when Ambrose came in and took a seat beside me.

"Have you heard?" he said. "There have been two more murders, both naiads."

I swiveled around to face him. "Why are you telling me?"

"I thought it might stir you out of your personal pity party long enough for you to try to help those poor unfortunates," he said. "Apparently, I was wrong."

"What do you want me to do?"

"Get off your ass," he said.

"I've got a few things on my plate," I replied.

He sighed. "Nyx, for an intelligent man, you are somewhat oblivious."

"Are you insulting me?" I took a long sip of my beer.

"You are ignoring something that is right in front of you," he said. "And people are dying. I am asking you for your help."

I felt like an ass. Ambrose had gone out of his way to be kind to me. "I'll do what I can," I said. "Anything I should know?"

He hesitated. "I do not want to point fingers, but it has been said that Mr. Danvers is taking out his recent disappointment upon his runaway bride's colony."

The stein shattered in my hand. "What? That's insane."

"I'm afraid that describes the man rather perfectly." He handed me a clean napkin. "You're bleeding."

"I'm fine, but Danvers isn't going to be." I used the napkin to wipe away the blood.

"Be careful, Nyx," Ambrose warned. "The man is dangerous."

"Then why hasn't the House of Poseidon taken care of him?" I asked. "Or the House of Hades?"

"He's too powerful," Ambrose said. "And he has powerful friends."

"You're telling me that Hades is okay with this?"

"The old gods no longer exist," Ambrose replied. "Or if they do, they've lost interest in the mortal world."

"Naiads are magical, not mortal," I pointed out unnecessarily. "Isn't there some sort of law about this sort of thing?"

Now it was his turn to shrug. "As with mortal law, our laws are sometimes broken."

"Do you know where he lives?"

He nodded. "One of the old houses on Summit."

"That surprises me," I said. "He seemed like such a suburban douche bag. Not old magic."

"He's not," Ambrose said. "He bought it after the previous owner died under mysterious circumstances."

"It seems a little excessive, doesn't it? Killing his wife's cousins to get her to come back to him? And some of the naiad killings happened before Willow left him."

"Maybe he's just a psychopath. Or maybe it's how he forced her into marrying him."

"What do you know about his background? How long has he lived in Minneapolis?"

Ambrose told me all he knew about Danvers, which wasn't much, and then left, but not without a parting shot. "You are your mother's son, Nyx. It's time you started acting like it."

When I finally gave up waiting for Willow and headed home, Wren wasn't at the apartment.

I called Naomi. "Is she with you?"

"Who?" But her careful tone told me that Wren was there, probably listening.

"Look, I was helping a friend," I said. "I don't know why I'm explaining this."

"Maybe because you think you have something to explain."

"Danvers was looking for Willow," I said.

"I see."

"No, you don't fucking see," I said. "She's my friend. She needed my help."

There was a long pause and then Wren came on the line. "Nyx?"

"I'm sorry, Wren."

"I was worried about you."

"Willow is my friend and she was in trouble."

"You could have called me," she said.

"I know," I said. "I'm sorry." I said it again.

Long pause. "I think I'm going to stay at Claire's for a few days."

"If that's what you want."

"It is," she replied. "At least until you figure out what you want."

She wanted me to say I wanted her, and part of me did. But the other part was focused on Willow.

After Wren hung up, I stared at the walls of my apartment until I couldn't stand it any longer.

I drove by Danvers's house, which was a limestone three-story mansion in the Park Avenue area. The street was known to the magical in Minneapolis as Magicians' Row because the Houses' upper echelon had homes there.

His house looked like a castle or a fortress, depending on how you looked at it. I knew which way Willow saw it.

There were a couple of kids playing on the sidewalk, but they weren't paying any attention to me.

I didn't spot Danvers or Willow, but I did notice my aunt Deci walking into a lime-and-pink Victorian a few houses down.

I watched her go in and then got out of the Caddy and went up to the kids, who were full of mischief but not a lick of magic.

"Hey, who lives there?" I asked. I pointed to the Victorian.

"That's the witch's house," the boy said. He looked at his sister. "If you're not careful, she'll cook and eat you, just like in Hansel and Gretel."

At least he had his facts straight, but I had had no idea Danvers and Deci were next-door neighbors. How cozy.

He glanced at the Caddy. "Nice ride."

The purple Caddy was too conspicuous. I handed him a ten. "Thanks. Now forget you saw it."

I borrowed a car and spent another afternoon following Sean Danvers around town. I'd been hunted for years by the Fates' Tracker and I'd learned a few things.

I didn't see Willow, but he seemed to have a lot of time on his hands for a successful businessman. He played a couple rounds of golf while I watched him with binoculars from a distant spot where I thought I wouldn't be noticed. I was practically asleep from boredom by the time he decided to head to the office.

I trailed well behind him. He had an office not that far from Parsi Enterprises. I circled the block as he parked the car and entered the building.

It was a little after sunset and decided to chance it. I said a quick obscura spell and then broke into his car. I rifled through the glove box but didn't find anything suspicious, except that he had shit taste in music for a villain. I was expecting some soul-crunching-dark-lord type of music, but instead it had more of a suburban-mom-car-pool vibe.

But then I found something interesting. A long flat box decorated with a familiar-looking symbol. I expected to find his athame in the box, but instead I found a robe decorated with the same symbol. The Tria Prima.

He was a Hecate worshipper. Although technically, as the queen of necromancers, she belonged to the House of Hades, she had been booted out of the club for being naughty several thousands of years ago.

Why had he married Willow? Someone had used dark magic to kill the naiads, which pointed straight to Danvers, but why was he killing them? His treatment of Willow made it clear he was a sadistic bastard.

I had to stop Danvers from murdering any more naiads, even if I had to kill him to do it.

Chapter Twenty-Nine

The opportunity to talk to Willow finally came when I wasn't expecting it. I'd parked outside Danvers's place, in a nondescript van I'd borrowed from a poker player I knew. He'd won it off a baker with a gambling problem, and it smelled yeasty, like mutant bread dough was fermenting in the back.

Willow emerged from the house, arm in arm with Danvers. He was the picture of a loving husband, if you could forget he'd beaten her half-dead. I couldn't.

Lurch came out behind them. He opened the passenger door to a town car for the happy couple and then got in behind the wheel.

He drove to a Brazilian restaurant on Hennepin. Danvers had brutally attacked Willow and now he was taking her out to lunch? I watched them enter, Lurch in tow, but stayed where I was.

I did a quick obscura spell while I was in the van. I didn't want to risk using magic too close to Danvers. He might pick up on it.

I entered the restaurant unobserved. It was essentially a high-dollar steakhouse, and they would have probably refused service if they could actually see me in my worn jeans and tee and beat-up Doc Martens.

Two mind-numbing hours went by while they dined. Willow didn't touch her food until Danvers said something to her. Then she just pretended, putting her fork to her lips and setting it down, but it seemed to satisfy him.

Finally, Willow got up to go to the restroom. Lurch went with her. For a second I thought he was going to follow her into the bathroom, but he waited outside.

Her bodyguard-slash-jailer looked right through me, but I waited until a woman herding two young children opened it.

Willow stood at the sink, staring in the mirror like the person she saw was a stranger. Maybe she was. She didn't look anything like the Willow I knew.

It felt creepy watching her when she didn't know I was there. I waited until we were alone before I spoke. "Willow, it's me." I removed the spell so she could see me.

"Nyx? What do you want from me, son of Fortuna?"

"I just wanted to make sure you were all right," I said.

"As you see, I am well," she said.

Her eyes told a different story.

"Why did you leave without saying anything? I was worried."

"He swore that he won't hurt me again. He's sorry."

"He won't keep that promise," I told her.

"I know," she said. "But would you stand idly by and let your friends get slaughtered?"

"You're my friend," I said. "I don't want you to get hurt."

Danvers was an abusive husband. As long as Willow stayed with him, there was more than a good chance she'd end up injured or dead.

She turned and put a hand to my cheek. "I know."

I grabbed her hand and put it to my lips. We stayed there for a long moment until she stepped away, pretending to straighten her skirt.

"Willow, why is he killing the naiads?"

She remained stubbornly silent.

"It's important, Willow," I said.

"Nothing is more important than keeping my people safe."

"Please."

She glanced around. "I am afraid I cannot help you," she said. "You must go now."

"I don't want to leave you like this."

She raised her eyes to mine. "You must. I will be fine. As long as you go now! He'll be suspicious if I linger much longer."

I did as she had asked, going back into stealth mode before I left. I brushed by Lurch and gave him a nasty case of adult acne.

Back at Eternity Road, I updated Ambrose. "I talked to Willow today," I said. "I'm pretty sure the naiad murders will stop as long as she toes the line with Danvers and pretends to be his blushing bride."

"Anything else?"

"Can you help me get Wren out of town?" I asked. "Things are heating up and I don't want her caught in the crossfire."

"Are you sure you want to do that?"

"I don't see a way around it," I said. "She's a distraction I can't afford."

"You don't think Hecate's daughter can protect herself?" There was a note in his voice that I didn't like.

I frowned. "I know she's not helpless, but she's innocent. She's been her mother's prisoner for years. She helped save Claire and Naomi. I owe her."

"And you believe in always paying your debts," he said. "What about Hecate?"

"After Wren is safe."

It took some persuasion, but he agreed. "I know someone who can take her to a safe house up north. It's not a perfect solution," he warned.

The Fates knew that Wren was Hecate's daughter. I didn't want her to get caught in the middle of their battle with the goddess.

We took the Caddy to Claire's condo.

Wren answered the door. "Nyx, is something wrong?" Her hair had been cut into a sharp bob. She wore a yellow dress with a deep vee and had a sophisticated palette of makeup covered her face.

"Can you pack a bag?" I asked. "Ambrose is going to take you somewhere safe."

"What's going on?" She peered anxiously into my face.

"Did you know that Sean Danvers was one of your mother's followers?" I asked.

"Willow's husband? No, of course not," she said. "The first time I laid eyes on him was at his wedding."

"I need you out of the way until I can eliminate the Danvers problem." Without her number one guy topside, Hecate would have much more difficulty keeping tabs on her daughter, and Willow would make a beautiful widow.

"Out of the way?" she replied. "I hadn't realized I was *in* your way." Her eyes clouded.

"I didn't mean it like that," I said. "I couldn't stand it if anything happened to you."

Ambrose cleared his throat. "I'll give you two some privacy. Nyx, I'll be in the car when you're ready."

After he left, we took seats at the opposite ends of the sofa. I wanted to say something, anything, but couldn't get any words out.

"I'll go pack," Wren said. I was relieved there wasn't going to be a great debate about it.

I paced in the living room. The front door opened and then Claire walked in. "Home sweet home," she said. She threw her purse on a small table in the entryway.

She spotted me. "What are you doing here?"

"Wren's leaving," I told her.

Her face worked. "She's going back to her mother?"

"No, why would you say that?" I asked. "A friend of Ambrose's is going to take her somewhere safe."

"You think you need to protect Wren? From what? Herself?"

The bitter note in her voice surprised me. "I thought you were friends."

"I thought so, too," Claire said. "But I was wrong."

Wren came back carrying a small duffel. "I'm ready." She stopped in her tracks when she saw Claire. I thought it was an odd reaction, since it was Claire's apartment.

Claire gave her a grim smile. "Surprised to see me?"

"Of course I am," Wren said. "I thought you said you'd be at work until late." She held up the bag. "I borrowed this. I'm leaving Minneapolis."

"Sounds like a good idea," Claire replied. They didn't embrace or even say good-bye. Instead, Claire turned on her heel, went into her bedroom, and slammed the door.

"Do I have to go?" Wren asked. Her lips were trembling.

I scooted closer to embrace her. "It won't be for long."

"Nyx, can I ask you something?"

"Of course," I said. "I'm an open book."

"Do you love me?"

Love? The answer must have been on my face. There was no good way to say it, but I cleared my throat and struggled through it manfully. "I like you."

"That's what I thought," she said. "You don't love anyone, not even yourself. Especially not yourself."

"Wren, I..."

"It's okay," she assured me, but a single tear streaked her perfect makeup. "Good-bye, Nyx." She gave me a gentle kiss on the cheek and then picked up her bag.

Ambrose's friend, an attractive brunette about his age who wore earrings identifying her as House of Hades, was waiting with him by the car when we went down.

"This is Thea," Ambrose said. "She'll be escorting Wren."

I swept Wren into a long hug, but she didn't hug me back. She got into Thea's waiting car without another word.

I watched the car drive away. Then I went home, had a shot or two, and sharpened my athame.

Chapter Thirty

I couldn't concentrate. The idea that Danvers had been killing naiads just to get Willow to toe the line seemed excessive, even for a creep like him. And why kill them in such a gruesome way? Willow was a prize—beautiful, intelligent, and kind—but I couldn't shake the feeling that I was missing something.

I went downstairs to Eternity Road. I went to the top cupboard to find the bottle of absinthe I'd hidden from Talbot's prying eyes. He hadn't said anything, but I knew he was trying to keep track of how much of the green fairy I'd been drinking.

I sat on the desk and poured myself a healthy shot, but kept the bottle out.

It was a lot of responsibility, the weight of a prophecy on my shoulders. But it was more than that.

I heard a noise. I reached for my knife, but it was only Talbot.

"Jesus, Nyx, I almost brained you. I thought you were a burglar."

"And I almost gutted you with my athame," I replied. "I guess we're both on edge."

"Want some company?" he asked.

The truth was, I didn't, but he'd just pout if I told him to go away. "Want a drink?"

"I'll pass," he said.

I poured myself another shot. "Suit yourself."

"What's wrong?"

"Too many things to list," I replied. "But thanks for asking."

We sat in silence for a minute.

"What are you still doing here on a Friday night?"

Talbot tried not to look like he was moping. "Nothing else to do. Naomi has a family thing."

I wasn't surprised I hadn't been invited.

"I need your help with something," I said. "I'm looking for a book. A really rare one."

"Rarer than what we usually carry in the store?"

I nodded.

"Not sure that's possible," he said. "Did you check Dad's shelves?" Ambrose had a collection of books in his office.

"I've already been through them," I said. "I want to read up on Hecate. Not the bullshit that everyone knows."

"Let's look in the storage unit."

"It's worth a shot," I replied.

I grabbed the bottle and followed him down to the basement, where Ambrose kept extra stock. The room was crammed full of interesting bits and pieces.

"What do you know about Hecate's followers?" I finally asked.

"That's what has you sitting alone in the dark?"

"Among other things."

"They're a bad bunch," he said. "Witches, demons, and necromancers."

"Naomi's a witch," I pointed out.

"She is," he said. "She's also a Fate."

"Which is worse," I replied.

"Nyx, cut it out," he said. "I know exactly who Naomi is and I love her just the way she is."

Love? They'd gotten serious pretty quickly, but then again, who was I to talk? I'd been lonely for hundreds of years. Maybe that's why I jumped in with both feet now.

We spent an hour sorting through boxes. "Someone should really inventory this mess," I said.

"Bite your tongue," Talbot replied. "Don't even mention it or Dad will have us down here every Saturday. We'd never see the light of day again."

I returned my attention to the box in front of me. "Why do you think he keeps all this stuff?"

"Maybe because he's a born pack rat," Talbot said. "Or maybe..."

"Maybe what?"

"Some of it was my mom's," Talbot said slowly.

My head snapped up. He'd never mentioned his mother before. "What happened to her?"

"Nothing," he replied. "As far as I know, she's living in Des Moines with her new, nonmagical family."

"She couldn't cut it?"

"She didn't want to." He slammed his book closed with more force than necessary. "There are a couple of boxes in the corner. I'll look there."

He got up and went behind an enormous antique armoire, which blocked my view of him. I waited, but he didn't return.

I assumed the mention of his mother had upset him more than he'd shown.

I returned to the search but came up empty-handed.

"Nyx, come here! I found something interesting," Talbot said. I squeezed around the armoire, and he held up a tattered book. I peered at the title. THE QUEEN OF THE UNDERWORLD was stamped in ornate black lettering on its cover.

Talbot had been using his finger as a placeholder and flipped back to the page he'd been reading. "It says here that Hecate's followers dabbled with black magic."

"We already know that," I said.

"Yes, but did you know that they experimented in malicious possession?"

I leaned against the armoire and studied my friend. "You think the naiads were possessed and then someone killed them?"

"I think the naiads were possessed and that's *what* killed them," he clarified.

"Why didn't any of the other Houses recognize the signs of a possession?"

"Because death by internal explosion isn't a common sign," he replied. "Normally, a demon taking up real estate in your body would result in more typical indications."

"Meaning?"

"Meaning that I can only find one historical reference to a possession resulting in something similar to what we've seen with the naiads. There's a mention of a siren in Crete who was possessed by the goddess Apate. It says here that the possession lasted an hour or so before the siren spewed all over the place and then went off like a bomb."

"Let's find your dad," I said. "Bring the book."

* * *

Ambrose was at home, sitting on the couch with his feet up, smoking a cigar.

"Danvers is looking for a vessel," I said. I pointed to the page in the book. It was a tiny mention, but it was all we had to go on.

"A vessel? What kind of a vessel? What does he want to use it for?"

"A vessel like a young naiad," I replied. "And he wants to put Hecate's soul in it. That's why the naiads look like they exploded. He can't find anyone to contain her."

Hecate's physical form was trapped in the underworld, so she and Danvers were trying something else.

"We have to stop them," Ambrose said. "I have to let Trey know. He'll convene the Houses."

"I need to get Willow out of his house," I said.

"You can't think Danvers would use his own wife," Ambrose said, shocked.

"Would you really put it past him?"

"Let me speak to Trey first," he replied. "Then we'll rescue the naiad."

He went into the bedroom to make the call, but returned a short time later. His eyes were silverlight.

"Willow and Danvers are on their honeymoon," he said. "They've left Minneapolis for an undisclosed location."

"We have to do something," I said.

"Trey has had someone following Willow since the incident," Ambrose said.

"The incident? Oh, you mean when Danvers beat her half to death?" I replied sarcastically. I threw my glass across the room and it shattered against the wall.

Ambrose stalked toward me, and I thought he might take a swing at me, but he only laid a comforting hand on my shoulder. "Steady, Nyx," he said. "Trey will find her. The House of Poseidon won't abandon one of their own."

"What was it like before when Hecate was free?" I asked.

Talbot and I dragged a likely box of books back to my place. I cracked open a couple of beers instead of any more absinthe.

It was almost dawn by the time we finished with the last book, but we weren't able to glean any more information. My eyes had begun to blur as the words danced upon the page.

"I'm done in," I said. "Want to crash here?"

His apartment was only across the hall, but he looked wiped out. Besides, since Wren left, my place felt bigger and emptier than usual.

He nodded. "Thanks, I could use some sleep."

"Naomi keeping you out late?" I teased him.

He raised an eyebrow. "No, my best friend is an insomniac."

It was true. I hadn't been sleeping much since Elizabeth had left me. I'd close my eyes and her ruined face would appear. Not even sex with Wren could blot out the vision completely, and now Wren was gone, too.

I tossed him a blanket. "I might not see you in the morning. I'm heading to Zora's to ask Jenny a few questions about Danvers."

"Jenny?" Talbot replied. "She hates the sight of you."

"True, but maybe she'll let something slip," I said.

"Maybe," he said. "Like a knife into your gullet."

Chapter Thirty-One

When I arrived at Zora's, the door was ajar, so I stepped inside. The store was empty. Strange at this time of day. It was a warm day and the air was fetid.

"Jenny?"

I smelled the blood even before I saw her. She was lying like a discarded doll on the floor behind the cash register. Wraith bites covered her body and her head had been bashed in.

Reflexively, I bent down to touch her neck for a pulse. She was cold and my hand came away sticky. Her hands were curled into fists. I gently unfurled them. Her nails were bloody and broken. She'd fought hard and tiny silver fibers clung to her fingernails. She'd been tortured before she'd been murdered.

There was something in her mouth. I pried it open as gently as I could. It was one of the gold doubloons I'd paid her for the harpies.

I searched the rest of the store, but didn't find any other clues. I had to get out of there before the cops showed up, but something made me check the back room.

From the smell, she hadn't cleaned the place since I'd taken the harpies. It was more than just a coincidence that my coin ended up in her mouth. It was a message from Danvers not to fuck with him. Danvers had been a busy man, beating Willow, killing females, and generally being a dick.

I needed to talk to my aunts.

I made it in record time to Parsi Enterprises. I had a sweet Caddy, and I was picky about where I parked her. Luckily, Deci's parking spot was open, so I took that and then muttered a quick prayer to the parking gods that she wouldn't try to have it towed. The tow-truck driver would get a nasty surprise.

I didn't bother to mess with Trevor, just muttered, "I need to see my aunts. Now," and then went down the hall before he could say anything.

I burst into Morta's office without knocking. "Danvers killed Jenny," I said without waiting for the *We want to kill you, nephew dear* that usually started and ended our conversations. "And I think it's because she gave me the harpies."

She'd been reading a contract, with her shoes off and her feet propped up on the desk, but she put her legs down and slipped on her shoes as soon as she saw me. A pair of bifocals had been perched on her nose, but she removed them. Morta didn't like to show any sign of weakness.

"Nyx, calm down," she said. "Why do you think it was Danvers?"

"It takes a necromancer to command a wraith," I said. "And didn't you get rid of all the other necromancers in Minneapolis?"

"Most of them," she admitted. "I'm beginning to think we got rid of the wrong ones, though." She stared out her window. "A necromancer isn't the only one who can command wraiths."

"You mean Hecate," I said.

"Or Hecate's daughter," she replied. She raised an eyebrow. "Any witch worth her salt who is willing to dabble in black magic could do it."

"Wren isn't in collusion with her mother," I said. "She's one of her victims."

"You have a tender heart," she said. "It's not an attractive quality."

We had bigger problems than a petty family squabble, so I ignored her last comment.

"Danvers said he could be my father," I said.

"And that would bother you?" she replied. Only a Fate would ask if it would bother me if my father were an evil psychopath.

"Yes, it would bother me. Is it true?" I asked. I couldn't imagine my gentle mother with Sean Danvers.

She gave me a long look. "Could he be your father? I have no idea."

She hadn't exactly answered my question, so I tried again. "Is he my father?"

"Does it matter?"

"Yes," I cried. "It matters very much whether or not that slimeball is my father."

"He is not your father," she finally said.

"But you know who is?"

She didn't say anything so I pressed her. "There's a story there, I know it," I said. "He hates me."

"You did sleep with his bride," she pointed out.

"Before she even met him," I argued. "Dislike, I could understand, but the guy wants to tear out my heart and roast it on a spit."

"I understand how he feels," she murmured. "You can be most annoying."

"I get that a lot." It was the same song, different verse. Annoying, scourge of the world, yada yada. But sometimes, a rare sometimes, Morta would look at me with a glimmer of affection in those stony eyes of hers.

I took a step closer to her. "Are you going to tell me anything or not?"

"It's in the past. It hardly matters now."

"The past is the only thing that does matter," I said.

"You feel that way now," she said. "But eventually you have to let go of the past."

I snorted. "Like you have?"

She met my eyes. "I have changed."

"Nobody ever changes," I said. "They just get better at hiding who they are."

"I wouldn't put much trust in anything Danvers has to say," she continued.

"I thought you were going to go into business together," I said.

"He wanted to," she said. "I did not."

"Why not?"

"Because he is a necromancer and I am a Fate. I have standards. Besides, I find him utterly repellent."

"He wanted your secret recipe," I said. "Ambrosia would be dangerous in the hands of a necromancer." I gave her a stern glance. "Or anybody else."

She crossed her arms over her chest. "If we avoided everything in life that is dangerous, we wouldn't have anything to do."

"Maybe that would be a good thing," I said.

"You have no concept of what the world would be like without the Fates," she said, "or you wouldn't say that."

I met her eyes. "I have a pretty good idea of what life is like *with* them," I said. "And if I had my druthers..."

She gave a curt nod. "But you do not."

The room was still. Finally, I inhaled, which sounded unnaturally loud in the room. "Would you tell me who my father is if you knew?"

"No," she replied.

"Do you know who my father is?"

"Maybe," she said. "But that is a story for another time. I have a meeting in exactly two minutes, and I have given you more time than I can spare."

In other words, *Get the hell out of my office.* When I left, Trevor was loitering in the hallway.

"Lost your way to your desk again?"

He glared at me but headed to the front. The receptionist was either the nosiest guy ever and was trolling for juicy gossip or Morta had a spy in her midst, but solving commercial espionage wasn't at the top of my to-do list, so I let it slide.

Chapter Thirty-Two

After I left Parsi, I headed to Jenny's. It would have taken a steady diet to keep the harpies quiet and happy. She would have had a supplier. I'd already searched the magic shop and hadn't found anything.

Jenny had lived alone in a one-bedroom apartment with, shockingly, a bunch of cats. They started mewing the second they heard the door open, but they couldn't see me. It freaked out the oversized fluffy one, and its hair stood on end. There was an empty food dish in the tiny kitchen, so I found the cat food and fed them.

Where would she keep anything interesting? Her bedroom, which smelled strongly of cheap incense and cat. I sat on the bed to think. There was a stack of books on the nightstand. I spotted a familiar-looking book. It was a reality-based tale disguised as fiction and about my mother and father. It had disappeared from my apartment back when I was still dating Elizabeth.

Jenny had probably stolen it for Gaston. I grabbed the book and put it in my leather jacket's inside pocket.

The black cat jumped on the bed and pissed on the comforter, narrowly missing me. I reached out and grabbed her collar. "Stinkerbell." Apt.

Stinkerbell pounced on a crumpled up piece of paper lying on the floor. She batted it and meowed.

"What do you have there?" I reached out to take it, but she clawed the air and drew blood on my right hand. It hurt.

I finally managed to take it away from her and smoothed it out.

A phone number, no name. I picked up the landline and dialed. Voice mail, but at least I knew who Baxter's hot date had been. I hung up without leaving a message. Time to have a little chat with my least favorite flesh eater.

It was almost dawn. His shift would be over soon. I caught him in his office.

"Tell me everything you know about Jenny," I said.

"Everything?" he said in a smart-ass voice. "She had this one trick..."

"Stop," I said. "I don't want to hear the details of your sex life. I want to know what she planned to do with the harpies."

"Ask her yourself," he replied.

"I can't. She's dead."

His eyes lost their sparkle. "Dead? When?"

"I found her body today. Someone set wraiths on her. I know you were feeding the harpies for her. Now talk."

"I might have been doing her a favor," he said. "Saving a few scraps here and there."

"Have you been doing favors for anybody else?"

"Occasionally," he admitted. "There's a small but profitable demand for rotting flesh."

"Anybody who would have the power to harness a harpy?"

"Not that I can think of." He wasn't a good liar.

"Call me if you think of anything," I said. I wasn't going to sit by the phone. In fact, I'd sit right outside until he made his move.

I told Talbot I would check in, so I walked back to the Caddy to make the call. I gave him the update and then asked, "Do you know what kind of car Baxter drives?"

"I don't know," Talbot said. "But he did mention he has personalized license plates. MUNCHU."

Baxter was a slimeball, but I needed information.

"Where did you meet this guy, anyway?" I asked.

"Long story," he replied.

After we hung up, I cruised the parking lot looking for the plates. I finally found them on a late-model luxury car. Selling body parts was obviously lucrative.

I nabbed a spot near the exit and grabbed a nap. Talbot had also told me Baxter worked the ten p.m. to six a.m. shift, and it was still a few hours before dawn.

Sunlight streamed through the Caddy's window, which woke me. I was stretched out flat in the Caddy's comfortable backseat. Baxter's car was still there. I checked my watch. It was almost seven, past time for good little ghouls to be home tucked into bed. They could stand sunlight, but they didn't like it much.

I got out of the Caddy and went over to Baxter's car. Dark liquid pooled near the driver's side. I had a very bad feeling about what I was about to see. I bent down to take a closer look. It was blood. A lot of blood. There was no way someone would survive losing all that blood, except maybe Baxter. The ancient flesh eater might be alive, but where was he?

There was no sign of Baxter, but there was a harpy feather lying by his car. Hecate had him.

Chapter Thirty-Three

I headed for Hell's Belles to talk to Bernie. She'd been the Fates' spy in the underworld. Maybe she had information about Danvers.

Bernie hadn't come in yet. I was at my usual booth at Hell's Belles waiting for her when three of Hecate's demons came in. One of the demons looked very familiar. Hecate's favorite boy toy. It had to be Gar, because I'd already killed his brother Hroth.

Gar was accompanied by an older demon with Tria Prima symbols carved into his cheek and a curvy blond demon who wore a sweater set and pearls. She looked like she belonged at the country club, which meant she was the one I needed to be careful of.

Their timing was impeccable. I was alone and not expecting any company.

They ignored the rest of the patrons, most of whom had the sense to leave immediately. One patron, a mortal, didn't get it and stepped in front of them. He had his heart torn out for his trouble. Gar swallowed it like it was an oyster and grinned at me. He hadn't needed to kill the mortal. He was just trying to make a point.

He'd bulked up some since the last time I'd seen him. These were no ordinary demons. They were demons on steroids. The Incredible Hulk of demons.

They were on me before I could get the athame out of the strap on my calf.

His teeth grazed my fingertips and I moved before his jaws snapped them off. Mary Sue went for my groin, but I kicked her in the jaw. "Not on the first date," I chided.

Her pretty French manicure was ruined when her dainty fingers turned into claws. She swiped at me again and ripped into my bicep. The wound gushed blood, but I couldn't afford to take the time to heal it. I slammed her against the wall and finally reached my athame. I slit her throat and demon blood gurgled up, stinking up the place.

Scarface and Gar both let out howls of grief before Gar picked me up and used me as a human battering ram. The athame skidded into a corner, out of reach.

"You. Killed. My. Brother," he said, in time to my skull denting the wall of horseshoes. A hail of horseshoes crashed to the floor. A particularly tacky porcelain bisque horseshoe shattered into sharp shards. Something glinted in its ruins, but I didn't have time to satisfy my curiosity.

"Bernie's gonna be pissed," I muttered through bloody lips. I reached for one of the larger fragments and used it to stab Gar in the arm until he let go of me.

Scarface had been guarding the door. When he saw that Gar was losing, he decided to join the party and came across the room at a sprint. I had about thirty seconds, tops.

I dove for the athame. The blood streaming from my forehead and arm made it slippery, but I gained a firm grip. I felt Gar's putrid breath on the back of my neck. I wheeled and stabbed, hitting flesh. The knife came out with a wet sucking noise.

Scarface wrapped an arm around my neck and squeezed. Gar advanced. He was fueled by revenge and bloodlust. It wasn't looking good, but I still had my athame. I needed to even the odds. I made a downward stabbing motion and hoped I hit one of Scarface's vital organs. He went down with a thud. I inhaled. It hurt to breathe.

Gar was still coming. His fangs raked across my chest, searching for my heart. I was dizzy from loss of blood and lack of oxygen. If I passed out, I was a goner.

The athame was so slippery with blood that I could barely hold it. I hacked blindly, hampered by someone's blood in my eyes. Probably my own. Gar went down but was still breathing.

I remembered Wren's scar, caused by the piece of shit's brother in front of me. I grabbed him by the hair and bashed his face into the wall a couple of times.

"How do you like that?" I asked.

He grinned through a bloody mouth. "I can't wait to get up close and personal with little Wren. Hroth said she's a hellion in the sack."

I bashed his head a couple of more times. "That's for even thinking about touching her." He finally crumpled, and I dropped him.

I scanned the restaurant to make sure his buddies weren't headed our way, but Mary Sue was still dead and Scarface had vanished.

My eyes fell on a tiny glittering horseshoe in the middle of the wreckage of Bernie's prized collection.

I moved closer. I reached for the horseshoe, but a pair of clawed hands beat me to it and scooped it up. Gar dangled the charm from the dip of one bloody claw. "Looking for this?" he asked through broken fangs. He grinned at me and then swallowed it.

That's what I got for losing my temper. I should have grabbed the charm and forgotten about teaching Gar a lesson.

I wasn't going to enjoy what I had to do next. The charm would be dissolved in the demon's stomach acid within minutes.

I was going to have to either cast a spell to get him to throw it up or I was going to have to slice him from stem to stern and fish through his stomach for the charm. Both were nasty, disgusting tasks, but I chose the lesser of two evils.

"*Vomui, vomui, vomui,*" I said, but nothing happened.

Gar gave a bark of laughter. "Your puny little spells don't work on me, weakling," he said.

"Oh, hell," I said. I was going to have to kill him after all.

I didn't have time to fight fair. I conjured up the foulest spell I could think of, one that would act like a fast-moving poison.

"You'll have to do better than that," Gar said. He started to laugh but choked on his own vomit before he got out the first chuckle. His eyes rolled back into his head and he fell to the floor, convulsing and foaming at the mouth.

When his death throes ceased, I sliced Gar and black demon blood splattered out. I steeled myself against the pain and reached in and fished around for the horseshoe. It was like sticking my hand in a vat of hot oil. I gritted my teeth but I managed to snag the tiny charm.

I pulled it out and examined my hands. The skin was

bubbling and pockets of pus had already formed on my left hand.

I walked behind the counter to a sink, where I washed off as much of the demon blood as I could, then ran the horseshoe under cold water.

I was dizzy, so I dragged myself over to the barstool and slumped down, head in my hands.

My head was still ringing when Willow walked into the restaurant. Or, more accurately, someone wearing Willow like a coat.

Hecate was in the house. My theory was correct. Danvers had been using the naiads as a vessel for Hecate to possess. He'd sacrificed his own wife to his cause. I would rip out his heart with my bare hands when I got the chance.

She slid onto the stool next to me.

"Hello, lover," she said. She put her hand on my thigh. I removed it.

"I'm not your lover, Hecate," I said. "Never will be."

She smiled. "Don't you like my new look? She's so young and supple." She ran her hands down Willow's body. "Want to take her for a spin?" she purred. "Oh, that's right. You already have."

I shuddered at the thought of her having access to Willow's memories.

"Let her go," I said.

Hecate smiled at me with Willow's lips. "Make me."

"Quit being a child," I said. "This isn't going to end well."

"Not for you, anyway," she said. Willow was still in there somewhere. I could feel it.

"You don't have your full powers while you're in there," I said. "Let the naiad go."

My casual tone didn't fool her. "Let me go and I'll let her go," she said. "Want to talk to her?" Her eyes rolled back and then Willow was there.

"Don't do it, Nyx," she said. "It's not worth it."

"But it is," I said. "You are worth it. I'd tear down the world to make sure you're safe."

A trickle of blood came out of her nose, then her head snapped back and she was gone.

I didn't see a way out of it. The prophecy said I'd set Hecate free, but it didn't say anything about her staying that way. I'd figure it out later. But first I needed to rescue Willow.

I owed her, more than I could ever repay.

"What do you want me to do?"

Hecate explained succinctly. "Bring me the bead."

"There's something I want from you in return," I said.

"Bargaining at this late date? How adorable."

"Are you ready to deal or not?"

"What is it that you want from me?" she asked.

"I want you to set Wren free," I said. "No repercussions. You let her go."

"Done," she said.

That was way too easy. Doubt must have been plain on my face because she added, "I know you don't believe it, but I love my daughter. If she is happier without me, so be it."

I considered her words and then nodded. It was possible that even Hecate had a tender feeling or two.

"That's not all. I want you to give me Danvers," I said.

"He has been my loyal servant for many years," she said. "And you expect me to hand him over to you?"

She wasn't sure if Willow's body would hold her and was starting to panic. "Yes."

"I will not help you," she said. "But I will not hinder you. You must fight your own battle."

"I intend to kill him," I replied.

"Many before you have tried," she warned. "Now go. Your friend does not have much time left."

"Then the clock is ticking for you as well," I replied.

"If I go, she goes," Hecate said. "Her husband seemed willing to chance it, but are you?"

"I guess you'll have to wait and see."

My legs were unsteady as I walked out.

I didn't have much time. The destruction of the world waited.

Chapter Thirty-Four

I planned a little side trip before I ventured back into the underworld to free Hecate and destroy the world. Prophecy or not, I wasn't going to go down without a fight. She was a goddess, but she was a minor one and she had weaknesses.

The only Fate I could track down was Nona, who was staring at the walls of her comfortable suburban home when I walked in.

"Don't you have some flies to ensnare? Or some webs to spin?" I teased her.

It brought a ghost of a smile to her face. "The only spinning I do is at the gym."

"That's the spirit," I said. "There's probably a class starting up soon."

"I miss Sawyer," she said.

"What do you know about a red bead?" I asked. I'd left it safely hidden at home.

She turned dull eyes my way. A cold cup of coffee was beside her. "What?"

"Focus, Nona. It's important." I took her cup and

dumped it out. Spiked. There was a full pot in the coffeemaker and it was still warm, so I reached over and refilled her drink.

"I want the good stuff," she said.

"Drinking isn't going to solve your problems," I said.

"That's rich coming from you."

She put a hand up and pointed to a bottle of bourbon. I gave in and added a healthy shot and then handed it to her.

She took a sip and then said, "I thought you'd be happy that I was so miserable."

"Honestly, I thought I would be, too," I replied.

She barked out a laugh, but then sobered and stared at her coffee. "You're so much like her."

"Is that why you hate me so much?" Hatred between the sisters and my mother didn't surprise me. They'd killed her, after all, just for defying them and protecting me.

She shook her head. "No, that's why I love you."

The words hurt me more than I had expected. "If you loved my mother so much, why did you kill her?"

She abandoned the coffee and went straight for the bottle. "Nyx, you won't understand until you're a Fate."

"I'll never be a Fate," I said. "Besides, I thought you wanted to kill me, not join the family business."

"The two are not mutually exclusive," she replied. "We need you."

"What happened to the third Fate-in-training?" I asked. Naomi was still learning, Claire had run away, but no one even mentioned the existence of a third Fate-in-training.

There had to be one. There were always three of them—always exceptionally powerful, always female, and always from our bloodline. They were down to one Fate-in-training, which explained why they were desperate enough to offer me a job. I met two of the three criteria. The fact that I wanted to kill them didn't even make them bat a collective eyelash.

She avoided a direct answer. "We can be killed, you know. It's not easy, but it can be done. Believe it or not, the job's not all fun and games. There are people out there who don't like how we do our jobs. Like you, for example."

"I'd do a better job than you ever did," I said.

It was a challenge, but she only sighed wearily and tossed back a shot. "You probably would."

"Nona, it's really important that I know what that bead does," I said. "Can you tell me anything? Please?"

"The bead was Deci's responsibility," she replied. "When we took Hecate's items of power, we each hid one item. She'd know."

"So as Custos, she wrote everything down in the Book of Fates?"

"Yes," Nona confirmed.

"She won't let go of the book and she won't tell me anything."

Nona sighed wearily. "I'll make the call."

Not for the first time, I wanted to hug my aunt, but I repressed the emotion. She was a killer, just like her sisters.

Chapter Thirty-Five

Deci answered the door in a white summer dress more suited to a maiden than a crone.

"What do you want?" Her arms were wrapped around her chest protectively. She was playing the frail card, but there was a gleam in her eyes that told me she was gloating on the inside.

"Didn't Nona call you?" I brushed past her.

"I don't take orders from my sister," Deci snapped. Her eyes gleamed with interest. "Why do you want to know about the bead, anyway?"

"None of your business."

She ignored my snarky tone and led me into an old-fashioned parlor. "Would you like a cup of tea?"

She'd probably take a page out of Gaston's book and slip some poison into it. "No, I want some answers."

The walls were painted a dark red, which made me twitchier than I usually was when I had to talk to my aunt. The furniture was authentic to the era, which meant itchy, prissy, and covered in lace doilies.

"It looks like Queen Victoria threw up in here," I commented.

"I like it," she said. "It's like fire."

"Like the one you set at the theater?"

She smirked at me.

"We had a deal," I said. "I was supposed to find Claire and you were supposed to leave me alone."

"Deals are made to be broken," she said.

"You've been scheming with Danvers," I accused. "And your little pyromania problem is getting out of hand."

The smirk never wavered. "So?"

"There's no way Morta's going to stand for you betraying her with Danvers. He's a Hecate worshipper."

"Morta, Morta, Morta," she replied. "I'm not afraid of her."

Deci really had middle-child syndrome.

"Maybe you should be."

She snarled at me. "Maybe you should worry about your own problems."

"Why did you do it?" I asked. It was a deliberately vague question. Deci had a lot of *its*.

"My sister had it all: good fortune, beauty, and love."

"And you were jealous of her," I said.

"She took the only man I ever loved," Deci hissed, "and didn't even notice the pain it caused me. But I made him pay. I made both of them pay." Her brow contracted and her eyes gleamed crazily.

The scorched man's face flashed in my mind. "Elizabeth wasn't the first time you used fire as a weapon."

She chuckled and the sound sent a chill through me. "Nobody ever notices me. They never did. Morta and Nona are blind to my faults."

I didn't break it to her that her sisters were no longer blind, if they ever had been. Maybe the two other Fates were playing a deep game, one that I wasn't able to figure out. But I would.

"What was my father's name?" I asked. "Where's the book? Maybe if I read about the prophecy, I can stop Hecate."

She snorted with laughter. "It's too late to stop it," she said. "Especially since I've been helping things along." She was practically crowing about it.

"Why?"

"It was easy enough to do, for the *Custos*. You don't think me capable of such a thing?"

"Capable, yes, but that insane, no." I couldn't believe that even my aunt would stoop to such depths. "Why?" I repeated.

"Revenge. My sister was pregnant by the man I loved. I wanted to punish them. Nothing hurts worse than the loss of a child."

The rage and sadness in her eyes convinced me. She'd experienced a similar loss, which explained why there was no Fate-in-training for Deci.

"That enlightens me about why you wanted to kill me when my mother was still alive," I replied. "But why do you still want to kill me?"

She smiled mirthlessly. "Don't take it personally, son of Fortuna," she said. "I still have a score to settle with your father."

"He's alive?"

"And in Minneapolis," she replied.

She watched my face as I added it up.

"Doc," I finally said. "Doc is my father."

"Wake up, Nyx." Sawyer's voice came from somewhere very far away. "Look around you."

There was a strange smell in the air—dark magic and blood. I heard a creak somewhere behind me. I turned in time to see at least twenty wraiths streaming into the room.

"It was you," I said. "You sent the wraiths."

She drew out a dainty little knife from her dress pocket and ran it across her hand. Blood dripped from where she'd sliced open her palm. Deci stood in the middle of the room as the wraiths streamed past her to get to me. Her lips moved, but I couldn't hear her. The wail of the wraiths drowned out the sound.

There were too many to fight. They moved as one, obeying her command.

I took out my athame anyway. A wraith bit me in the forearm. I slashed its throat, but another took its place. Another gnawed my calf until white bone showed through the red meat.

I'd live through the attack, but if I didn't do something, there wouldn't much of me left. The flesh was being torn from my body, strip by agonizing strip.

All I wanted was for the pain to stop. I gripped the handle of my knife. It was slippery with blood and gore.

I locked eyes with my aunt. It was me or her. The triumph in her eyes didn't fade, not until my athame had hit its target and sunk into her chest.

The wraiths ceased shredding my body parts. Then I collapsed.

Where was I? The house was silent as it came back to me. I stood slowly and held my head in my hands. It helped to stop the ringing in my ears. I'd been lying in a pool of my own blood. I finally remembered a healing spell and whispered it through a tight throat.

The wraiths had returned to their graves, sleeping until they heard another call of dark magic.

Where was Deci? She was lying in a heap on her floral carpet. Blood had seeped through her clothing and stained her white dress. My athame was still embedded in her chest. It was a mortal wound, but she was still breathing.

"Let me get help," I said. "Stay still." I took a shallow breath and pulled out my knife.

She reached out a bloody hand and touched my cheek. "You can't save everyone, Nyx."

I used her house phone to dial nine-one-one. As I looked around for something to staunch the bleeding, I saw a leather-bound book about the size of a daily planner. It was unmarked on the face and spine. Could it be the Book of Fates? Next to it was a frilly cotton doily. I pocketed the book and then used the doily to press against the wound.

"The Book of Fates," she gasped. "I transfer its keeping to you, son of Fortuna." Then, "*Auribus teneo lupum.*" Holding the wolf by the ears. Meaning her choices were both dangerous ones. What was she talking about?

Morta appeared, golden scissors in hand. Her cold eyes were shiny, overlarge, like she'd forbidden her tear ducts to open.

I'd hated her all my life, but in that instant, I felt sorry for her. The scissors moved, making a sharp sound in the silence. Then Deci wheezed her last breath.

Morta's face changed when she saw my knife. The coldness that seemed to make up her very fiber was gone, engulfed in a conflagration of rage. She burned with it, incandescent where she'd been ice.

I was the cause of her sister's demise. I knew what she'd

do when she found my thread. It wouldn't be swift and it wouldn't be pretty, but she'd end my life.

I dropped the bloody cloth and ran. My aunts wouldn't believe that it had been self-defense. Two people my aunts had loved had died by my athame since I'd come to Minneapolis. They weren't going to wait to see if there would be a third.

Chapter Thirty-Six

I pounded on Talbot's door. "We need to talk," I said.

He held the door open and made a sweeping gesture for me to come in.

He and Ambrose had been playing a board game in the living room. I plunked down next to Ambrose.

Ambrose frowned when he noticed the blood on my shirt. "What happened to you?"

I didn't have time to soften the blow. "I was at Deci's house. She's dead. I'm the one who killed her," I replied.

I couldn't manage even a few false words of regret, even though she had been my mother's sister.

Ambrose said. "Nyx, what have you done?"

"I didn't mean to kill her. I went to Deci's for answers."

"What kind of answers?" Talbot asked.

"I wanted to talk to her about the fire," I hedged. "And how the Fates trapped Hecate." I relayed what had happened, but left out the part about the bead.

I laid the book I'd found at Deci's on the table. "Maybe this can tell us something."

"How did you get that?" Ambrose's voice was sharp.

"Deci gave it to me," I told him.

Ambrose said, "What did she say? Tell me the exact words she used."

I stared at him. "I don't remember," I said. "She'd called wraiths, a lot of them. They just kept coming. They would have eaten me alive, so I threw my athame at her. It was self-defense."

"It was?" Talbot asked. Our eyes locked and then he gave a little nod. "Now what?"

"Just trying to figure out my next move," I replied.

"Why don't you try to get some sleep?" Ambrose suggested. "Maybe you should stay here tonight."

"Sleep? I'm not sure I'll ever be able to sleep again."

"This might help," he told me. He slid a bottle of absinthe across the table and then got out two glasses.

"You're joining me?" I was startled. Talbot didn't like the green fairy. In fact, he usually barely managed to conceal his disapproval whenever I broke it out.

He nodded. "It's been a hell of a day."

He was right. Jenny was dead, Baxter was missing, and I'd killed one of the Fates.

He held up the bottle to the rest of the group. "Anybody else?"

Ambrose reached for a glass.

We each chugged a shot of absinthe, and then I nudged Talbot. "C'mon," I said. "Let's get started."

"Never mind that," Ambrose said. "Try to remember what Deci said."

"Something about giving me the Book of Fates," I said. I thought about what she'd said as she lay dying. "'I transfer its keeping to you.'"

"She actually said that?" Ambrose asked. "Nyx Fortuna, you are the new Custos, the keeper of the Book of Fates."

"But I don't want to be," I said. "Here, you take it." I tried to hand the book to him, but he wouldn't touch it.

"It doesn't work like that," he explained. "It's yours until you die. There's usually a big ritual when the book passes from one generation to another, but all she really needed was to say the words and to have you take the book."

The Book of Fates' cover had been encrusted with jewels, but a few had been pried out or were missing. Other than that, it looked like somebody's planner until I looked closely and realized the leather was soaked in blood and tears.

"Why would she give it to Nyx?" Talbot asked. "She hated him."

"For once, I was the lesser of two evils," I said. "What would happen if she died before the book was transferred?"

"That's never happened," Ambrose said solemnly.

"Or maybe she just wanted to saddle me with something she knew I wouldn't want," I said.

"Maybe she did it to help defeat Hecate," Talbot said. "The Fates would be weakened without a Custos."

"She was working with Danvers," Ambrose pointed out. "I doubt she had the Fates' best interest in mind."

Talbot crossed his arms. "Maybe Deci had a change of heart. Or maybe she didn't want Hecate to win, in the end."

"If the Fates couldn't kill her, I doubt we can," I said. "So we have to get her back into her underworld prison."

"How are we going to do that?" Talbot asked.

"The book holds all the secrets of the Wyrd family," Ambrose said. "The secrets of the Fates."

No wonder Deci had said something about two dangerous choices. She was right.

I didn't want to open the book that held all my family secrets. I wanted to throw it in the fire and walk away.

Instead, I opened the book and began to read. "Let's see if it will tell us any of Hecate's secrets."

Ambrose and Talbot peered over my shoulder.

"I gave her the harpies," I said. "That was one of the things she needed to reverse the spell binding her in the underworld."

Ambrose cleared his throat. "It's certainly a shame that you and your aunts couldn't have found common ground. Enough to share information, at least."

"Common ground?" I said bitterly. "The best I could do was to tolerate them long enough to keep Elizabeth safe. And even that didn't work out so well."

"Nonetheless, better communication on both ends could have prevented Hecate's escape."

"Escape? I practically handed her the key to her jail."

"What else?" Talbot asked. "The harpies are magical, but they can be killed, as Nyx proved."

"Killed but resurrected," I reminded him.

"Yes, but the Fates wouldn't rely on the just the harpies," he replied. "And they gave them to Gaston. I don't think it was the harpies."

"Then what was it?" I turned my attention back to my reading. My eyes began to blur, so I handed the book to Talbot.

There was silence for several minutes. I closed my eyes and tried to blot out the image of Deci with my knife in her chest.

Ambrose said mildly, "Keep reading. Is there anything else about Hecate's Eye?"

"It was originally found in India," I continued. "That's all it says." But something about the passage made me uneasy.

I looked up and caught Talbot and Ambrose exchanging glances. "Spit it out."

"The peacock feather," Ambrose said. "When you came back, something was clutched in your hand. What was it?"

"A bead," I said. "Just a trinket. Something you could buy anywhere."

"What did it look like?"

I said. "It was a crimson eye bead."

I knew what they were thinking. "Wren didn't know where I hid it. She wanted it because it was pretty."

I couldn't tell them the truth, that I planned to trade the bead for Willow. They'd try to stop me.

"Nyx, keep reading," Ambrose prompted.

"We know what Hecate's after now," I said. "We can stop her."

"We should tell the Fates," Talbot said. "Let the Fates decide."

"I know you're in love with my cousin," I said. "But the Fates want to kill me."

"You're a family, and family should stick together," he insisted.

"Most dysfunctional family I've ever heard of," I said.

"We need to find the items of power," Ambrose said. "Hecate has a head start."

"Because I gave her the harpies," I said.

"I don't think so," he replied. "You said there's no mention of the harpies as an object of power."

"Then why else would she want them?"

"Because they're her pets," Talbot guessed. "And because

the Fates took them away from her. The harpies are a point of pride."

"What if Hecate finds a way to free herself before we can stop her?" Talbot asked.

"She won't," Ambrose said. "She can't."

We talked late into the night, trying to map out a strategy for waging war on a goddess. Gradually, the others drifted to bed, but I continued to read.

I needed to find a way to free Willow and defeat Hecate. It was going to be a long, bloody battle. Hecate wouldn't roll over and let me lock her up a second time. But I'd lost not one but two girls, and I was itching for a fight.

Chapter Thirty-Seven

Sean Danvers was first on my list. I didn't have to look far for him because he was standing in the hallway of my building.

"I can't believe you let Hecate do that to your own wife," I said. "You're a dead man."

He sneered at me. "I will make you wish you were dead."

"Bring it on, old man," I said. "If you think you can take me."

"I will enjoy killing you," he said.

I laughed. "I've had a death wish for the last two hundred years. You think a fear of dying's going to stop me?"

"You kill one retired necromancer and you think you can take me on?" He gave me a thin smile.

"I didn't kill Sawyer," I said.

He snorted. "Figures. You don't even know enough about your own heritage to know that you're supposed to take out all your rivals."

"I'm not a necromancer," I said through gritted teeth.

"I am," he said. And with one word, he immobilized me. I'd been reading up on protective magic and managed to break free, but I was dizzy and gasping.

I tackled him and knocked him to the floor. I managed one punch before he disappeared.

"Reveal," I said.

He took advantage of my inability to fight back and punched me in the face repeatedly. I could still move my mouth and spat blood in his face.

"You need to learn a lesson, son." He got out his athame and peeled off a piece of my cheek.

"I hope to hell I'm not your son," I said.

"You're not," Hecate said calmly from the stairway. She looked at me with Willow's eyes, but spoke in her own voice. "Danvers, you've done well, but that's enough."

The knife hovered over my face. "You will drown in your own blood," he said. The blade's edge was hot against my cheek.

"Danvers," Hecate warned again, and her toady stepped away, although reluctantly. I sneered at him with a bloody mouth. "Nyx, I believe you have the item I requested? The bead I mentioned?"

"Let Willow go first," I said.

"You know I can't do that," she replied.

"Then no deal."

She met my eyes. "Then I'll take what I want and kill you."

"It's worth it," I said. "Whatever you do to me is worth it as long as Wren is so far away that you'll never find her."

Hecate gave me a chilling smile. "I know exactly where my daughter is, don't I, Wren?"

She moved farther into the hallway and then I saw Wren standing behind her mother.

"Wren?"

"She is my mother-goddess," she replied. "I obey her in all things."

Not much surprised me anymore. I knew Wren had her own agenda, but I had thought she truly wanted to get away from her mother.

"But the escape," I said. "And us. What about us?"

"A contingency plan," Hecate said. She almost sounded sorry for me, which made it worse. "In case you managed to free the Fates. Wren was my eyes and ears."

"Wren, is this true?"

She wouldn't look at me, but she nodded. "It was a necessary deception."

"We've wasted enough time," Hecate said. "Wren, fetch Hecate's Bead."

Wren went into my apartment and returned an ego-bruising few minutes later. I obviously sucked at hiding things. She held the bead in her hand. "I have it, Mother."

"Then it is time."

Wren didn't look the slightest bit shaken by what she was about to do, but judging from Hecate's expression and Danvers's look of glee, it wasn't going to be good.

Delicate fingers touched the silver chain around my neck. Wren chanted something in the language of demons and then stood. They seemed to be waiting for something, but nothing happened.

She looked at Hecate. "I'm sorry, Mother," she said. "I have failed. His thread of fate is not there."

"His knife," Danvers said. "Check his knife."

My athame? I hadn't even considered it as a potential hiding spot for my thread of fate, but I realized that it must be where my mother had concealed it.

Wren waited until her mother gave a short nod before sliding my knife out of the hidden pocket in my jacket.

She repeated the chant and the knife began to shimmer. My thread of fate appeared and I half expected Morta to show up and cut it before Hecate had the chance to carry out her plan.

"You're mortal now," Danvers gloated. "You can be killed."

"Take the knife, Wren," Hecate said.

"I'll do it," Danvers offered eagerly. I knew what was coming, but no matter how hard I struggled, I couldn't break his spell.

"No," Hecate replied. "It must be Wren."

Wren picked up the athame and grasped it tightly. "Now cut the artery," Hecate ordered. I'd known my whole life that not everyone was going to like me, but it hurt more than I expected that someone I'd trusted, someone I'd had sex with enjoyably and repeatedly, secretly hated me enough to kill me.

"Farewell, son of Fortuna." She touched my face. Then she said softly, "This will give you a few minutes." She whispered a spell before she sliced my throat in a quick, efficient motion. I couldn't move to defend myself.

I didn't have the strength to reach my healing amulets in my jacket. I'd been mortally wounded, which was a surprise. I hadn't been mortal for hundreds of years, but now I was. I wasn't enjoying the experience as much as I'd hoped. I wasn't sure what good a few more minutes of gut-wrenching agony would do, but I appreciated her gesture, as futile as it was.

Danvers's spell finally wore off and I fell to the floor, blood flowing from my neck.

"Danvers, get the blood," Hecate ordered. He pressed something cold to my neck. With the last of my strength, I gripped his hand tightly and sent a curse his way. He'd be impotent in minutes and within hours, paralyzed with scorching pain running through his extremities. If Willow lived through Hecate's possession, Danvers would never touch her again.

"Time to go," Hecate said. She bent down so her face was next to mine. "You will die knowing that she betrayed you, that I am going to destroy the Fates, and then I'm going to make your precious mortals pay. All of them."

Wren stepped over my prone body and they left the office without looking back. She'd wrapped me in darkness and I'd loved it, but just like everyone else, she'd betrayed me.

I prepared to die, struck by the irony that I'd finally gotten my wish at the worst possible time.

What was that saying? I was bleeding out, so my brain was blurry, but right before I closed my eyes, it came to me. *Be careful of what you wish for.*

Chapter Thirty-Eight

Doc's face came into focus. He had a cloth pressed against my throat, but blood was everywhere, seeping through his hands, despite his best efforts.

"They missed the artery," he said. "Just barely. Hold on."

"No use," I said. "I'm a goner."

Actual tears welled in his eyes.

It hurt to breathe, to speak.

"Someday, but not today."

I didn't know how to break it to him that there wasn't going to be a someday, at least not for me.

"I'm dying, Doc," I said. "The Fates finally get their wish." The dark descent into death was almost upon me. I'd spent many years wanting to die, so I was surprised to find that I wasn't welcoming it now that it was happening.

Morta appeared, her golden scissors gleaming. My thread of fate, the very thing I'd searched for, was in Morta's hands.

I braced myself, prepared for the consequences. I'd fulfilled the prophecy, set Hecate free, and one of the Fates had fallen. Prophecies were a bitch.

What would it be like to die? I had thought I was ready, but I found that every bit of me fought against the idea.

She'd cut my mother's thread without even blinking. Deci's, too.

All my life, Morta had wanted to cut my thread, more than a kid wanted ice cream or I wanted a beer.

It was near the end. I would finally get what I'd been seeking, just in time for me to realize I wanted to live. I let out a gurgling laugh at the irony and blood bubbled on my lips.

Morta stilled. There was no glee on her face, only resignation. I heard the snip of her golden scissors, severing the last thread of my life.

"Oh no, Nyx, I'm not going to let you go," a voice said from very far away. "You still have something to do."

A low guttural wail began as everything around me slowed. There was no bright light, no flood of warmth, just the sound of the man's wail as my heartbeat slowed and then stopped. The voice repeated, continued until it became a constant buzz.

Maybe I died for a little while, but when I came to, I was in a bed, with cool sheets and closed blinds. There was a pounding in my ears and a queasy feeling, like motion sickness, knotted my stomach.

I didn't know where I was, but I knew I was alive. It hurt, but I welcomed the pain. The sucking wound in my neck had been bandaged. It still hurt to draw breath, but I did with gratitude.

I sat up and tried to get out of bed, but a searing pain discouraged me. "Talbot? Ambrose? Doc?"

The last thing I remembered was the voice, calling me back in that strange guttural wail.

"They're here," Doc said. "We're all here."

Who had brought me back from the dead? Doc or Sawyer or someone else?

"Where's Naomi?" I asked.

"She's not coming," he said gently.

"Of course not," I said. "How stupid of me." I'd killed her aunt, someone Naomi cared about. She probably hated me now, just like the rest of the Fates.

I laid back on the cool pillows and closed my eyes.

"Get some rest," Doc said. "We'll talk later."

When I woke up again, the blinds had been raised a crack and a thin ray of sunshine cast a shadow through the blinds. My throat was swollen and dry, still hurting from where Wren had slashed it.

"I am the worst judge of women," I rasped out.

I heard a dry chuckle and I realized Talbot was in a chair opposite the bed.

"That might be an understatement," Talbot said. "But she had us all fooled, even Claire, who spent months longer with her."

"I was blinded by Wren's beauty," I admitted. "And she played me. I can't believe I was suspicious of Claire when Wren was the enemy all along,"

"You're drawn to pain and darkness," Talbot replied. "They're like catnip to you, especially if they're wrapped up in an attractive woman."

"I knew she had an agenda," I said.

"You didn't know what it was," he pointed out. "But now you do. Time to fix it."

"You mean time to stop Hecate from destroying the world? I couldn't even stop Danvers."

"You will," Talbot said confidently.

"Why are you so sure?"

"Because you're the son of Fortuna," he said. "And because we'll help you. The Fates will fight Hecate, too."

"Nona drinks more than I do, Deci's dead, and Morta knows I killed her. Do you really think the Fates are up for a battle with Hecate?"

How much of Wren's passion for me had been manufactured in order to set her mother free? I used to think that passion couldn't be faked. I'd thought the same thing about love, though, and Elizabeth had proven me wrong on that count.

"I've got to get a lot better at holding on to my athame," I said. "People keep trying to stab me with it."

"And now you've got your wish," Talbot said. "You can die. How does that feel?"

"Can I die?" I asked. "My thread of fate was cut by Morta. Doc brought me back from the dead. What does that mean?"

Talbot gave me a sober look. "I don't know. How would you feel if you were back, but you're not immortal anymore?"

"I don't know how I feel about it," I replied. "I thought I'd find the charms and I'd end it. My thread of fate was cut." It was everything I'd ever wanted and it was nothing I'd wanted.

"I can't believe your mother hid it in your athame," he said. "Why do you think she chose your father's knife?"

I shrugged, but the wound in my neck reminded me not to. "She must have loved Doc," I finally said.

"Doc?" Talbot repeated. "Doc is your father?"

I nodded. "And I killed Deci and set Hecate free," I said.

"We'll stop her," he replied.

"We'll need help," I told him. "I'll have to convince the Fates that we need to work together to stop Hecate."

"Naomi said she never wants to see you again," he told me.

"I had to kill Deci," I said. "It was self-defense."

"I know," he said softly. "You're not a killer, Nyx."

But I was.

I said, "I'll convince Naomi to forgive me, but first I need to defeat Hecate."

"And I'll help you," Talbot promised. "You're not alone, Nyx."

I was mortal and I had to fight a dark goddess to save the world. But I wasn't dead and I didn't want to be. That was something. That was everything.

Acknowledgments

Thanks to my amazing agent, Stephen Barbara. My writing buddies Emily, Shana, Sandy, LJ, Terry, Debby, Alyson, Stacia, Mary, and Melissa help more than they know. A big thanks to my husband, who makes sure everything runs smoothly while I'm in another world. Thanks to the Orbit team, Devi, Susan, Ellen, and Alex.

extras

meet the author

Marlene Perez is the author of paranormal and urban fantasy books, including the bestselling Dead Is series for teens. The first book in the series, *Dead Is the New Black*, was named an ALA Quick Pick for Reluctant Young Adult Readers as well as an ALA Popular Paperback. *Dead Is Just a Rumor* was on VOYA's 2011 Best Science Fiction, Horror, & Fantasy List. Her novels have been featured in *Girls' Life*, *Seventeen*, and *Cosmopolitan*, and Disney Television has optioned the rights to the first three books in the Dead Is series.

She grew up in Story City, Iowa, and is the youngest of twelve children. She lives in Orange County, California, with her husband and children. Visit Marlene at www.marleneperez.com or at the Welcome to Nightshade Facebook community page at:
http://www.facebook.com/pages/Welcome-to-Nightshade-DEAD-IS/128231240528721

Also by Marlene Perez

Dead Is the New Black

Dead Is a State of Mind

Dead Is So Last Year

Dead Is Just a Rumor

Dead Is Not an Option

Dead Is a Battlefield

Dead Is a Killer Tune

Dead Is a Just a Dream

The Comeback

Love in the Corner Pocket

Strange Fates

introducing

If you enjoyed
DARK DESCENT,
look out for

FORTUNE'S FAVORS

Nyx Fortuna: Book Three

by Marlene Perez

To save his cousin Claire, Nyx Fortuna has set free the goddess Hecate, who is now threatening to destroy the world, starting with anyone in the Wyrd family. Nyx and company must join forces with the Fates to defeat Hecate and return her to the underworld. During the battle, magical and mortals take sides and Nyx finally discovers the identity of his father.

Chapter 1

I will seize Fate by the throat.

—Beethoven

Mortality was overrated. I'd wanted to be able to die for over two hundred years, but when I finally did, someone had brought me back. I wanted to know who and why, but first I had to stop throwing up.

I felt like someone had beaten me with a bag full of soap bars. I was shivering, sweaty. "Where's my jacket?"

I'd strangle Wren with my bare hands if she'd taken the jacket. Or my mother's charms. My hand went to my neck, but the silver chain was still there.

I felt more like myself once Talbot helped me slip on my World War II fighter pilot jacket.

"Any word on where Hecate is?"

He shook his head. "It's been quiet. Too quiet."

It had been twenty-four hours since I'd set Hecate free and she'd double-crossed me. In my defense, I had been desperate to save Willow.

"Willow?" I managed to ask.

Before Talbot could reply, Ambrose appeared in the doorway. He looked grimmer than I'd ever seen him. "It's started. We have to go."

Ambrose, Talbot and I headed out of town in the Eternity Road van. We were an hour north of Minneapolis before Ambrose turned into a long driveway. I spotted a sign that read PAN CONFERENCE CENTER.

"We're here," he announced, but he didn't sound particularly happy about it.

"Emergency pawnshop retreat?" I joked, but it still hurt to breathe, so I avoided any more smart-ass comments.

Black flies buzzed above our heads as we walked. The cabin door was ajar, letting out the putrid odors of decaying flesh, something like rotten eggs, congealed blood, and sour milk.

There was a long table in the center of the room and a fire burned in the stone fireplace. The rotten egg smell was identifiable as the picnic lunch slowly spoiling in the summer heat. Against one wall, piled high like logs for a fire, were bodies. So many bodies.

The walls dripped with blood. I tried not to gag as I surveyed the scene. Ambrose was stoic, but Talbot's skin had a green cast. He rushed outside and then we heard the unmistakable sounds of his retching.

Tria Prima symbols were smeared onto the once-white walls. Hecate's own brand of graffiti.

"It looks like she took a bath in their blood," I commented.

"She did," Ambrose said.

"What makes you say that?"

"Bathing in the blood of her enemies was her trademark in the old days," he replied. "Hecate draws power from it."

"So she chose these people randomly?"

He shook his head. "Never randomly. She's sending us a message."

"I got the message when Wren stabbed me."

"That was just a love tap compared to what Hecate has planned," Talbot said from the doorway.

"What message, anyway?" I asked. "I don't know any of these people. Or anyone from this House."

We'd managed to determine that the victims were all forest satyrs, members of the House of Zeus.

"She's declaring war on the world," Ambrose said. "These are her first casualties."

"Yeah, but why all the fuss?" I asked.

Talbot winced and then shot me a dirty look. "Show a little respect for the dead."

"I meant, why hasn't she let loose the full force of her power?"

Ambrose stared at me. "I think this is quite bad enough without asking for trouble," he said.

"I think Hecate doesn't have all her power back," I explained.

"But she has the bead," Talbot said.

The bead of power I'd practically handed to her on a fucking platter.

"Then why hasn't she released Willow?" I didn't want to think about what Danvers would do to her once he'd recovered.

Ambrose looked at his shoes. He didn't want to tell me Willow was most likely dead.

"She's not dead," I said. "She can't be."

Ambrose put a hand on my shoulder. "Let's hope you're right."

"What should we do with the bodies?" Talbot asked.

"I'll make a call," Ambrose said. "The House will send someone to identify the victims."

"The sooner we get out of here, the better."

I agreed. It wasn't a night to linger among the dead.

"Shh!" Ambrose put a finger to his lips. "I hear something."

Silence. And then a small moan.

"Someone's alive," Talbot said. "Over there."

We ran toward the faint sound. A satyr lay on the ground, almost obscured beneath a pile of dead bodies. We pulled him out of his grisly prison. He had been blinded and blood still dripped from his mutilated eyes.

"I have a message for the son of Fortuna," he said.

The message had already been received. Hecate had just declared war.

www.ingramcontent.com/pod-product-compliance
Ingram Content Group UK Ltd.
Pitfield, Milton Keynes, MK11 3LW, UK
UKHW022258280225
455674UK00001B/73